THE
INFINITE
LIBRARY

AND OTHER STORIES

THE
INFINITE
LIBRARY

AND OTHER STORIES

Victor Fernando R. Ocampo

First published 2017 by Math Paper Press by BooksActually, Singapore
First North American edition 2021 by Gaudy Boy

Published by Gaudy Boy LLC,
an imprint of Singapore Unbound
www.singaporeunbound.org/gaudyboy
New York

For more information on ordering books, contact jkoh@singaporeunbound.org.

ISBN 978-0-9994514-5-8

Cover design by Flora Chan
Interior design by Jennifer Houle

Panopticon, 2019, by Marius Black (Marius A. Funtilar), Pen & Ink Illustration

*For my steadfast wife Patricia,
my in-house editor and co-conspirator;
and our equally brilliant and beautiful daughters,
Isabella and Sophia.*

You are my life, my loves, my muses.

CONTENTS

FOREWORD

By Jason Erik Lundberg

There is something about long-term displacement that affects you as a person. It creates an intense yearning for "home", even if that home is an invented construct in the mind. This yearning—expressed concisely as *saudade* in Portuguese, *hiraeth* in Welsh, or *galimgim* in Tagalog—alters your perception of both your country of origin and your new national residence. For some people, this longing makes it almost impossible to feel immersed in either place. For others, such as writers like Victor Fernando R. Ocampo, it leads to a critical examination of both homes and to an understanding of how you fit into them and the wider world.

Victor relocated from the Philippines to Singapore in 2001, six years before I made a similar migration from the USA. Since then, he has built up an impressive oeuvre of transnational short fiction that examines the human condition in both his natal and adopted homes, and also out amongst the stars. We are fortunate that these stories can now be found all in one place, in this remarkable collection.

I first met Victor online in March 2012, as part of the "Speculative Fiction Writers of Singapore" email group, and then in person later that year, at the Singapore Writers Festival launch of my anthology

Fish Eats Lion: New Singaporean Speculative Fiction (in which he had a story). He is a relentlessly affable man, cheerful and welcoming, with a puckish sense of humour, and one might presume his fiction to showcase a similar friendly optimism. But he is also not afraid to go to dark places in his writing, to plumb the horrors of the human psyche in order to bring back truth. There is something very "right" about a Victor Ocampo story, something familiar or recognisable, as though this is something you've always known.

I've been privileged to publish four of these pieces in various editorial projects, and I always look forward to a new work of fiction from him: "Big Enough for the Entire Universe" in *Fish Eats Lion*, "Entanglement" in the second issue of *LONTAR: The Journal of Southeast Asian Speculative Fiction*, "I m d 1 in 10" in *Best New Singaporean Short Stories: Volume Two*, and "Brother to Space, Sister to Time" in *LONTAR* #6. Especial mention must be made of the latter story in this grouping, for its ambition, scope, and imaginative (and unexpected) tribute to the science fiction of Samuel R. Delany.

Victor's keen observational eye represents the clarity of the outsider—the Filipino writing about Singapore, and about the Philippines while apart from it, and about the world and the universe as an emissary of humanity—and you can almost see his verbal abilities stretching with the languidness of a well-fed housecat. Whether through the Ellisonian stylistic gymnastics of "Dyschronometria, or the Bells are Always Screaming", or the hallucinogenic Phildickian leetspeak of "I m d 1 in 10", or the faux-academic jargon of "An Excerpt from the *Philippine Journal of Archaeology*, 4 October, 1916", he pushes the limits of form and trope, all in the service of telling us about ourselves, like a shaman guiding us through a fever dream.

Let his stories, both experimental and conventional, illuminate your way through the darkness, as only someone with a foot in two worlds can do.

Jason Erik Lundberg
December 2016

THE
INFINITE
LIBRARY

AND OTHER STORIES

MENE, THECEL, PHARE∫

Do not touch me. I have no words left.

Joseph stared at the words he'd written on the slate, but he could not remember writing them. He sat as still as the grave, watching the jaundiced afternoon sun filter through his garret's only window. In the distance, he could see the search lights from the dirigible towers coming to light. A Locomotive Aerostatique was approaching the city, floating through the sky like a giant inflated spleen. Against the dying light, the airship was a gigantic shadow, an ominous black egg hatching weary crowds of nameless, faceless people, heroes and dragon fodder alike.

Joseph hated Berlin at this dreary hour. When the Angelus came, the steam turbines discharged the day's effluence into the upper atmosphere, turning the soft pink of twilight into a muddy river of grey. But of course this was Königreich Preußen, he thought, and there was no Angelus—just the sharp burst of cannon fire at 18.00, signaling the end of the working day.

∞

"Experience teaches us no less clearly than reason, that men believe themselves free, simply because they are conscious of their

1

actions and unconscious of the causes whereby those actions are determined."

—BARUCH SPINOZA,

ETHICS, DEMONSTRATED IN GEOMETRICAL ORDER (1677)

∞

Joseph was between lives. His family had spent big money to exile him to the University of Heidelberg.

"*You need to further your studies,*" his father had ordered. "*Stop this malas writing business. I did not grow this old to bury my children.*"

A post-doctorate was certainly important and prestigious, but the two of them knew why he'd really been sent away.

In his previous existence (the one he knew was his true calling), Joseph had been a writer—a man of the word, full of dreams and reckless hope. He was from the privileged class, but his Scientific Romances, *The Social Cancer* and *The Reign of Greed*, had given Indios, rich and poor alike, a voice. His books, written under the nom de plume "Señor Laong Laan", were printed and spread in secret by partisan friends and propagandists, stoking a movement for Independence that spread swiftly across the islands like a virulent disease.

The Church and the Spanish Crown burned over his incendiary stories. Joseph's wealthy family had been in trouble before, and now they feared for his life. They knew that a garrote's noose waited if Joseph's identity was ever discovered.

One evening, in the season of spawning catfish, his father's men spirited him away. Press-ganged from a *zarzuela* performance, the young man was placed on a clipper-steamer to Europe. Sailing over troubled monsoon seas, Joseph found himself lost and suddenly alone. He had left without the benefit of a single goodbye.

When he'd reached Heidelberg, an electro-gram was waiting for him.

"You once told me that babies were born, but men must create themselves. So move on. Create. Do not look back. —Your faithful brother, Paciano"

He ripped up the missive as soon as he'd read it, refusing to accept it or process its meaning.

Two months after he arrived, Joseph quit school and fled to Berlin. In the Prussian capital, he lived on the modest funds his family had sent and tried again and again to write.

"Reino de España has now blocked all non-official communication to Las Islas Felipenas," an old friend, Ferdinand Blumenttrit, warned him. *"The word is that open rebellion has broken out. The adventures of a fictional hero, Jose Rizal, are the movement's inspiration. Thus far they have not identified their true author. Beware mein bruder, spies are everywhere."*

Cut off from his old world, Joseph had grown increasingly restless and despondent. The spirit that compelled him to put pen to paper remained stilled and silent.

∞

Feeling adrift and forlorn, he had visited every brothel and *bierbrauerie* that he could afford, trying to drown his sorrows, while keeping as low a profile as possible. There was a great emptiness in his heart, a gnawing that he did not, or perhaps would not, understand. Something in the void, in the naked darkness called out to him, but his words could give it no shape.

"I am sad to hear about your situation, but it is best that secret things remain secret," Blumenttrit had written. *"Do you remember that amusing little cryptographic trifle you made with your friend Dr. Viola? It is best that we use it when we speak."*

3

The professor warned him that the *Reino de España* had eyes everywhere. The Spanish Count of Benomar and his political agents were intercepting the electro-grams and pneumatic mail of exiles.

As a noted member of the Ethnography establishment, his old friend used his influence to secure him membership at the *Berliner Gesellschaft für Anthropologie*. There they used the Society's Babbage Brain to encrypt their correspondence with a cipher of Joseph's making.

The professor had scheduled for Joseph to collect his mail every Friday at exactly 19.00 hours, during the Babbage Brain's scheduled maintenance.

The young man looked forward to this weekly ritual as faithfully as if it were Sunday Mass. Blumenttrit had become his only lifeline to his homeland, and he depended heavily on this correspondence for advice and support.

∞

"The Babaylan priests of the ancient Indios were in a sense like Newtonian physicists. They subscribed to the philosophical position called Determinism, which posited that for everything that happened, there existed conditions that could cause no other event.

This was the only possible way that a Babaylan's predictions could come true. A person's destiny had to have already been cast at birth, molded and finished from the clay of possibility. For how else could the future be correctly predicted if men and women could affect the present to change it?"

—JOSEPH MERCADO,
THE COLLECTED BERLIN LETTERS (1946)

∞

At the sound of the twilight cannon, Joseph shook himself from his brooding. He polished off a bottle of *Vin Mariani* and left his room.

The young man rushed downstairs to catch the end of the public visiting period—the only time the Society allowed people with Class C memberships within its premises.

"*Guten abend, Signore* Mercado," his landlady greeted as he passed her along the hallway. Mrs. Francesca von Kusiemski was the Italian widow of an Austrian lawyer and the proprietor of the only boarding house that took in coloured people. "If you are going out this late, it is best you wear protection."

She held up to her face a gilded mask in the form of Caravaggio's *Medusa* and batted her long, goat-hair eyelashes. "The haze outside brings progress but, ugh! It smells of witches and burning rubber. *Uffa!* Now I must drink radium tonic for my health."

Joseph bowed and the wind-up mechanism inside his bowler tipped itself, bobbing like the head of a cattle egret. He thanked Frau von Kusiemski for the timely reminder and hurried back to his room.

The young man wondered if his landlady's eyes were on him as he walked away. He always seemed to catch her looking in his direction. His lodging mates, mulattos from *Deutsch-Ostafrika* often referred to her as "*Mrs. Hill*", after the heroine of John Cleland's novel. They whispered that she would readily trade a week's rent for certain manly services, and the more exotic the man, the better.

Joseph didn't know how he felt about this. The widow was a shade past forty and by no means beautiful, but she had always been very kind to him. His funds were not being replenished, and a part of him wondered what he would do if the rumors about her turned out to be true.

5

∞

"A gold death mask found in Oton, Iloilo, was the oldest mask ever found in the Philippines. It had been dated by archaeologists to between 1300 and 1400 of the Common Era.

Like all masks, the delicately shaped metal face hid the identity of its wearer but captured the culture of the tribe that used it. When worn while a person was alive, it created a new identity from the tribe's spirit world. In death, it served the opposite purpose. The mask prevented spirits from entering the body of the deceased—thus serving instead to protect identity.

Because all masks functioned as touchstones of cultural memory, a blank mask serves no purpose and carries no meaning."

—FRANCISCO PÖLZL,

DIE MASKE DES KAMPFES (1926)

∞

The young man returned to his quarters and retrieved the Stenhouse Lung Protector Professor Blumenttrit had sent him. After replacing the used filter, he pulled the respirator's elastic behind his ears. The featureless mask of plain white celluloid covered his entire face, protecting him from the foul air outside.

For a few seconds he stood in front of the mirror, contemplating his pale *weiß* visage. The mask's anonymity was strangely comforting.

Satisfied, Joseph grabbed his coat, wound up his hat, and ran out into the murky Berlin night. Above him, a web of pneumatic tunnels, wires and steam vents crisscrossed the entire city, casting odd, angular shadows over the gas-lit streets.

Every so often, the sky would glow from a burst of artificial lightning, as one of the huge Photophone towers spoke wirelessly with the

Locomotives Aerostatique. Berlin, with its beacons of different colours and its blazing electric arcs, seemed to him like a gigantic monster, one with a thousand restless and distrustful eyes that glowered at him from every building and every street corner.

Joseph wished he didn't have to remove his mask. Everywhere he went, people stared at him. Without his mask's protection, the city's xenophobic populace would peer from windows or point as he walked past whispering *"fremde, außerirdische, ausländer, Asiaten, Japaner, Chinesischer Mann, Korean Mann"*—anything but his own ethnicity.

Of course, no one ever said anything. Orientals, especially the rich Chinese and Japanese, were nominally considered equals. His manners and good breeding meant he was frequently mistaken for their kind. Joseph knew, though, that in their heart of hearts, they considered all coloured people *untermenschen*, the unmentionable "undermen" of the world. He could sense the hauteur behind the eyes of every painted courtesan he slept with.

He wondered if his landlady would feel the same way if he ever found himself in her bed. At best, he thought, she would look at him as an exotic curiosity—a meal of rice instead of potatoes; at worse, he might simply be an occasion for her charity.

Joseph walked briskly, past the grounds of Charlottenburg palace, until he reached the somber façade of the *Berliner Gesellschaft für Anthropologie*. His destination was a simple grey building attended by a large cylindrical power plant that spun silver threads of steam into the sky.

The young man stepped up to the heavy wooden door and slipped a thin celluloid card into the glowing slot. A Euphonia's disembodied head was set above the lintel. The mechanical talking machine opened its glass eyes and announced his name in a ghostly, monotone voice. A small kinetoscope also sprang to life and verified his identity:

Name: Joseph Alonso y Mercado
Citizenship: *Reino de España*
Race: Oriental, Other
Member: Since 1895, Class C
Access: First floor public area only. Please note the restrictions on women, children below the age of 12, pets, and coloured people.
Sponsor: Ferdinand Blumenttrit @ Litoměřice, K.u.K. Monarchy

The door opened, and Joseph stepped into the building. He removed his accoutrements and went straight to the Brain's Head-End.

He greeted the machine's teletype attendant, an elderly Jew, who punched in his details into the room-sized mechanical computer. Joseph was not in the mood for conversation. To avoid small talk he stepped away and browsed the flickering displays.

The Society's Remote Projection Kinetoscopes were arranged in a circular, flower-like shape, held aloft by a mechanism that resembled an iron octopus. The numerous postcard-sized screens cycled images from the book *Art Forms in Nature,* by the artist and biologist Ernst Haeckel—orchids, diatoms, echinoderms, and all manner of strange and beautiful creatures.

In the center of the iron flower, a large urn-sized screen displayed text from Haeckel's philosophical treatise *Natürliche Schöpfungsgeschichte,* where he elaborated on the notion that the physical characteristics of a species determined its place in the order of Nature.

8

Joseph turned away from the screen. For a second he thought to himself that this was why he needed to return to Manila. He needed— all Indios needed—to succeed as a people and prove Haeckel and his kind wrong.

He closed his eyes to better hear the steam generator outside, growling like an Old Testament god. That was the sound of progress, of technology, he thought. It was a sound that divided the world into two.

The ill feeling came and went. Joseph sighed deeply and refused to feed his train of thought any further.

He left the displays and began to peruse the junk mail on the *bureaux plat*. There were several catalogues for Dresden porcelain, ads for *Luftbad* sanitariums in Bavaria, a testimonial by Alexandre Dumas for the cocoa-leaf tonic Vin Mariani and a flyer from a store that sold nothing but maps and atlases. A cryptic message was printed on the back of its quaint do-it-yourself map brochure:

> *"The lines that separate people are always artificial, as unnatural to men and women as they are to the birds overhead. As an author, what kind of country will you create?"*
>
> —Mr. Strabo,
>
> proprietor of Here Be Dragons

"Herr Mercado?" the attendant called out, interrupting his train of thought. "I believe this is what you had come for."

The old man handed him a pile of generic advertising materials.

Joseph thanked the attendant and prepared to leave when a sudden roar of laughter stopped him.

"It is best that you go *jung Mann*," the old man said, as he adjusted the card feeder on the multiplex Baudot teletype. "In the next room, the Society is entertaining the polygenist Dr. Karl Vogt and some American students of the late Louis Agassiz. They've brought with them their Human Zoo."

The attendant re-arranged the actuators on the Brain's switchboard, and a new set of pictures appeared on the Kinetoscopes: a pair of orangutans, a Samoan couple, a pair of Nubians, and two diminutive Aetas from Joseph's own island of Luzon. On the big center screen was a Hottentot Venus, a young Khoikhoi woman with large buttocks and unusual elongated genitals. The unfortunate men and women were exhibited naked, in the famous pose of the Vitruvian man. The orangutans, however, had been carefully dressed in the latest Prussian fashion.

"Your generic Asian features will pique their interest," the old Jew warned. "Unless you want to be poked and prodded in the name of Science, you had best leave."

"My family is rich," Joseph muttered reflexively, as he walked out of the Head-End. "The rules don't apply to those with money."

Joseph retrieved his mask, hat, and coat and returned to his lodgings. He disposed of the junk mail, save for a large fold-out map of Bavaria. He opened the illustrated pages carefully; at the center was a stiff card containing the decrypted message from Professor Blumenttrit:

Mein Bruder Joseph,

As we discussed last time, I have made arrangements for you to seek refuge at the Wolpertinger Luftbad sanitarium outside Minga. Berlin is no longer safe.

Anastasius Lebenskünstler is an old friend, and he will take you under his protection.

His Freikörperkultur philosophy will seem unusual or possibly even mad, but I guarantee it will strip you of what clouds your mind. It is my hope that, after this trip, you will no longer need to hide behind your usual masks. I am sure you will find your true destiny. The directions to his place are indicated below. Best of luck my young friend, and keep safe. This will be our last communication until you return to Berlin.

Sincerely yours,
Ferdinand @ Litoměřice

Joseph copied the sanitarium's particulars, ripped up the card, and threw it into a waste bin.

∞

"There is an ancient Tagalog legend about why the natives of the Philippines have short noses. It was said that Bathala, the chief of the Tagalog gods, sent a balangay boat carrying noses for every person in the world. Because the natives had short legs, they couldn't get to the shore fast enough. They were left with the squished, flat noses at the bottom of the hold.

To this day, Filipinos feel inferior to people from other lands because of their flat noses and their short stature. In Philippine legend, morphology equals destiny."

—Dolores del Mundo,
An Analysis of Guadencio V. Aquino's
"Philippine Myths and Legends" (2010)

∞

A few days later, Joseph was on a Locomotive Aerostatique bound for Minga, the capital of Königreich Bayern. From there, he boarded a Rail Zeppelin to Dießen am Ammersee, a few miles southwest of the city.

The young man alighted at a tiny train station, lost in the thick of the woods. Dießen am Ammersee was a tiny hamlet near the shores of an ancient glacier lake. The Wolpertinger Luftbad sanitarium lay some distance away from the village, in the very heart of a great Bavarian forest.

The grassy path was completely deserted, save for a lonely milk cart pulled by two large dogs. During his walk, he spied no steam engines, only windmills, lode-stone spinning wheels, and the giant sun-catching cones of solar concentrators, all of which were discretely hidden among the expansive trees. The air was crisp, clean, and pure. Berlin already seemed a world away.

After hiking for three-quarters of an hour, Joseph finally reached his destination. Professor Lebenskünstler's picture-perfect property stood by the shores of the bluest lake he had ever seen. The cottages of the sanitarium were nestled snugly between the proverbial loins of a small alpine hill.

He walked up to the front door and pulled the bell. After a few minutes, he heard laughter and the sound of softly padded footsteps approaching.

The door opened and Joseph was startled to see a beautiful young woman munching a red apple. She stood in front of him, naked as Mother Eve in that fatal second when she tasted the bitter Fruit of Knowledge.

"*Susmariosep!* I . . . I'm so sorry. I must be in the wrong house. I . . . I will take my leave," he stammered, as his face turned a shade three times redder than her apple. He bowed out of instinct, and his automatic hat tipped itself as usual. For some reason, the spring jammed, and his bowler moved up and down repeatedly, making a series of small embarrassing sounds before stopping at the "up" position. He apologized profusely, and to avoid further humiliation (as well as the overwhelming visage of the girl's perfect form), he quickly trained his eyes towards the cottage's peaked roof.

"*Guten tag.* Herr Mercado, I presume?" she asked. The young woman stared at Joseph with much amusement before looking up towards where her guest's gaze had been strangely riveted. She craned her neck in an exaggerated manner, as if to call attention to Joseph's embarrassment. Then she took another bite of her succulent fruit.

"Welcome to the Wolpertinger Luftbad sanitarium," she said. "The professor has been waiting for you. Will you not come in?"

Joseph stood still for a while, trying to make some sense of the situation.

"Did he send me all this way to clear my mind in a bordello?" he wondered silently. *"I could have done the same in Berlin and spent far less money."*

The young man nodded politely but kept his vision trained to the rafters. He searched in vain for the discreet red lantern that beckoned lonely souls from the dark seas of continence, but there was nothing there, save for a few potted petunias in need of watering.

He stepped inside and was led to a drawing room decorated by a multitude of statuary and paintings, all of which featured the nude as subject matter. The woman excused herself and went to find Professor Lebenskünstler.

Joseph took off his hat and fixed its mechanism. Feeling overdressed, he removed his coat as well. As he waited, more people passed through the common drawing room: two strapping young men and a quinqua-genarian lady shepherding a group of children. Despite the fact that Joseph was Oriental, all of them greeted him warmly—and like the art on the walls, all of them were stark naked.

"*Perhaps this isn't a bordello,*" Joseph worried. "*It's a bedlam or some manner of pagan cult. Dios ko po, what manner of horror did my old friend get me into?*"

The young woman returned and ushered Joseph into a well-appointed study bursting with books.

Dr. Anastasius Lebenskünstler had been eagerly expecting him all afternoon. Like everyone else, the sixty-year-old professor was dressed in Father Abraham's livery. His thick body was muscular and solid for his age. Apart from browned cheeks and stray liver spots, his skin was as youthfully white as pork fat.

Joseph averted his eyes once more to avoid staring at the professor's *sehr große* scrotum. He wondered if his own father's *cojones* were as big and as wrinkled, but realised that he had never seen his father naked.

"Delighted to meet you, Herr Mercado!" the professor said, gripping the young man's hand with a hearty handshake. "Professor Blumenttrit has told me so much about you. I do apologize for meeting you like this! We were on our way out."

"*Entschuldigung sie*, you are going out? Like that?" Joseph asked, clearly flustered. Despite being a doctor of medicine, he was extraordinarily uncomfortable being in the presence of so many unclothed strangers.

"Yes, we are having a swim by the lake," the old man answered patiently. "Didn't Professor Blumenttrit tell you that I'm a Doctor of *Freikörperkultur*? *Mein Gott*, you look like you're going to faint!"

"Herr Professor, I beg your indulgence," Joseph asked. "The Locomotive Aerostatique from Berlin was very crowded, and I have come from such a long way. Would you mind it very much if I just retired to my room to rest?"

"No, no, of course not!" the professor bellowed. "But only on the condition that you join us for dinner at 18.00!"

"Do you dress for dinner?" Joseph asked nervously.

"Bavarians are not savages; of course we dress for dinner!" he guffawed. "Klara here will bring you to your quarters," he said, pointing to the young woman with the half-eaten apple.

"Herr Mercado, may I present you Fräulein Klara Pölzl, of Waldviertel in Austria," the professor said. "Fräulein Klara, this is Herr Joseph Mercado from far-away *Las Islas Felipenas*. Can you kindly show him to his room?"

"I have heard much about you, Herr Mercado," Klara said.

"Good things, I hope?" he asked with some trepidation.

"Perhaps," she answered coyly.

Klara bowed and motioned for Joseph to follow her. She said nothing more as they walked out into the path towards one of the guest cottages. Once they reached the rustic, ivy-covered hut, she offered a quick goodbye and left.

Joseph stared at the monastic simplicity of his new quarters. It was even more depressing than his garret in Berlin. The floor was made of clay bricks, and the walls were rough logs, hewn and pegged into place. There was a small fireplace, also made of brick, straw chairs and a hard board for a bed. A thin mattress was spread on top, along with a pillow and a few quilts. A lonely washstand with a cracked basin shared a corner with an old chamber pot. He felt a great panic come over him and had to sit still for a second to calm down.

Afterwards, Joseph went to the window and watched as Klara walked towards the lake. When she disappeared from view, he opened his suitcase and took out his Stenhouse Lung Protector. He put on the white mask and, without bothering to get out of his clothes, succumbed to his personal demons.

After cleaning up, he dressed as comfortably as he could and dove under the safety of the covers. For some reason, Joseph started to weep, and his tears didn't let up until he finally fell asleep.

∞

"Spindle whorls and stone beaters to make bark cloth have been found in Philippine Neolithic assemblages from as early as 2740 BCE. Written records of first contact such as the Zhufan Zhi from the Song Dynasty indicate that the clothing Filipinos wore served decorative or ritual purposes, rather than as a means of protecting modesty."

—FRANCISCO PÖLZL,
THE FERDINAND C. ASHLEY ACADEMIC JOURNAL
OF ANCIENT HISTORY, MISKATONIC UNIVERSITY (1936)

∞

Dinner was not altogether unpleasant. Joseph was pleased that everyone was appropriately attired. The food was rustic country fare: *weißwurscht*, head cheese, and Brezen pretzels, finished with a syllabub of Bavarian cream, thickened with isinglass. In his honor, Professor Lebenskünstler had broken out some excellent silvaners of Franconian wine.

The vintage of the dinner guests was another matter. A school teacher from the village asked him where in the Caribbean was Las Islas Felipenas. A tall, bearded poet from Hanover tried to converse with him about Plato's *Republic* and the responsibilities of writers to the state.

Klara pulled him away, warning that the Hanoverian was an *urning*, one who would have gone Socratic on him in the worst possible way. Meanwhile, Professor Lebenskünstler lectured endlessly on social nudism and how it promoted fairness and equality.

The Hanoverian sidled by him again. Joseph felt mildly uncomfortable but did his best to conceal it.

"Do you know he is not really an academic?" he whispered conspiratorially.

"Do you mean Dr. Lebenskünstler?" Joseph asked.

"We call him 'Professor' and 'Doctor' out of respect," the man said. "His mother was Catholic and made him choose between University or the priesthood and his inheritance. Naturally, he chose neither. Herr Lebenskünstler lives for books, and he is very learned. Sadly, he never actually completed his doctorate."

"You seem to know a lot about him."

"I make it my business to know things."

"But do you believe in what the Professor espouses?"

"Ha! If people move past the barrier of looks and race, we humans will find some new way to draw lines. Perhaps it will be wealth or maybe sexual preference."

"If you are such a skeptic, why are you here?" Joseph asked.

"Ah, I myself am only sunning *au naturel* for my health," the Hanoverian replied. "Wolpertinger Luftbad is cheaper than Italy."

"I do not understand."

"The things that separate one person from another are so rarely skin deep," the poet noted, returning to his earlier point. "Do not tell me that is not the case as well, even in your distant islands?"

"My people are not like that. We are renowned for our friendliness and hospitality."

"Your delightful apropos of nothing is the bottle of *Bocksbeutel* talking," the Hanoverian quipped. "I'll have you know, I notice that you flinch whenever I come near. Are you afraid, Herr Mercado, that I will look at you with the same male gaze that you look at Fräulein Klara there?"

"What? No!" Joseph exclaimed in indignation. "I would never . . . "

"There, you are drawing up a new caste system already. Perhaps you should stick to the local beer," the man from Hanover suggested. "It will call far less attention to your charming naiveté. Good evening, Herr Mercado."

∞

"The Arumanen Manuvu of Cotabato believed that Ala-ta-Ala, the God of all Gods, and Magbabaya, the Creator, send messages to mankind through the Gimokud, who were disembodied sacred souls. These spirits possessed the Wali-an, the clairvoyant shamans of the Manuvu who spoke the word of the Gods.

They believe that people had no agency unless moved by higher powers. This relegated the concept of free will to an insignificant position, something still common to the people of the islands to this very day.

'Bahala na,' Filipinos like to say. 'The gods would always provide.'"

—DOLORES DEL MUNDO,
COLLECTED PAPERS, EVELYN T. CULLAMAR INSTITUTE OF
ANTHROPOLOGY & HISTORY, ADMU (2012)

∞

Joseph tried to spend his time writing in the quiet of his room. However, despite his attempt at self-isolation, the other guests insisted on inviting him to one activity after another. He played tennis with the Nordic-looking youths he'd met in the drawing room. The school teacher brought him to see the village of Dießen am Ammersee. The Hanoverian introduced him to some mawkish English writers of the Uranian persuasion. He indulged all of them, but always, always he kept his clothes on.

Klara had also come to call. She invited him for a picnic by the lake on the occasion of his third afternoon at the sanitarium. Much as Joseph was attracted to her, no words could persuade him to join her in the altogether.

"At least leave your coat and that silly hat behind," she insisted. "What have you to hide?"

Joseph smiled awkwardly and just shrugged his shoulders, flattered that she showed him some interest. He was usually very talkative and loved to dominate conversations. But with Klara, he seemed to run out of words.

When they reached the shore of the lake, the young woman turned towards him and unbuttoned his shirt to the waist. Joseph was too paralyzed to protest. He ate a simple meal of sausages and sweet potatoes in his *camisa de chino* undershirt. Afterwards, the smell of her skin and the softness of her touch lingered in his thoughts for hours.

∞

"Even under the guise of magic and tradition, the ancient Filipinos had some rudimentary knowledge of genetics and the selection of phenotypes. This was evidenced by the sacred Camote (Sweet Potato) rituals of Samar and Leyte.

After a field was burned and cleared, tubers were taken from a fruitful old field, and the farmers waited for the full moon to plant. They needed a waxing orb so that the sweet potatoes would become very smooth. If there were lots of stars out during the planting, this meant that the camote would be numerous and all joined together.

Before the planting was done, a young couple made love on the field, and the young man offered his first seed to Lakambakod, the protector of crops. Planting naked ensured that the camote skins would be thin. After that, the man made the woman ride on his back as he planted the rest of the tubers. It was believed that this would increase the chances of the tubers overlapping.

From an Ethnobotanical perspective this showed the complex relationship between Filipinos, their cosmological system, and the plants they grew. They knew that while a sweet potato would always be a sweet potato, there were many ways to influence the final form it could grow into."

—FERDINAND BLUMENTTRIT,
PHILIPPINE JOURNAL OF SCIENCE (1910)

∞

On his fifth day at Wolpertinger, Joseph noticed a large pile of logs stacked not far from his cabin. He asked the housekeeper what they were for.

"They are for back-up steam devils," the woman answered, as she hitched her dogs to a milk cart. "Sometimes, there is not enough sunshine for the collectors. The Professor needs to find someone to chop them into firewood."

"I could do it," Joseph offered. "I used to chop wood as a child."

"Herr Mercado," the housekeeper chuckled, as she picked up her distaff and a basket of wool for spinning. "*Danke*, but that would be difficult if not impossible for a young man of your frame and stature. Besides, you are a guest here."

"*A non-paying one,*" he muttered. "*Here in Europe I am a pauper and a weakling.*"

"Anyway, it is good you sought me out," she added. "It saves me the trouble of looking for you. The Professor has asked that you come by his study anytime you are free today."

Joseph thanked the housekeeper and went over to the main house.

"Professor Lebenskünstler?" Joseph asked, as he knocked on the heavily carved study door. A large wooden owl stared at him, as it sat on a reproduction of Spinoza's *Ethics*. A small banner curled around its taloned feet with the words: "*ut legitur, et illuminamini*"—"*To read is to be enlightened*".

The old man bade him to come in. As Joseph expected, the good doctor was sitting in his armchair, comfortably naked.

"How is your rest?" the Professor asked. "I trust you have not been too uncomfortable."

"I am sleeping just fine," Joseph replied, "and everyone has been unexpectedly . . . welcoming."

"Wolpertinger is an oasis of sanity," the old man said. "This is neither Madrid nor Berlin."

"I am grateful for that."

"Think of this as a '*Kreislauf*', that is an old Bavarian word for 'a bout of mental rest'."

"It has been all that and more, thank you."

"You are most welcome. Professor Blumenttrit has told me that Berlin is crawling with the men of *Conde de Benomar*. It is best that you stay here with us for a while."

"I had actually expected to join Professor Blumenttrit at Litoměřice."

"No, that is not a wise idea," the Professor warned. "Our mutual friend is a known agitator. There will be many agents watching him all the time."

"I realise that, sir," Joseph sighed.

"Well you are certainly safer here. After Leopold failed to win the Spanish crown, Bavaria has been no friend of Spain. The good Count will have trouble placing his men."

"Did Professor Blumenttrit tell you why he wanted me to come here?"

"He only told me that you needed a place to think and to hide."

"That is true. But why did he send me here in particular?"

"I am told that you are an author," the Professor remarked, ignoring Joseph's question. "Yet Herr Blumenttrit has told me that you've stopped writing. Why is that?"

"I am . . . not sure. There was a time I couldn't stop the words from flowing. Now I cannot even string a sentence together. At this rate, I will never write my third novel," Joseph lamented.

"Perhaps the time for writing is done?" the professor asked.

"When I started, anger stirred my spirit," Joseph continued. "My family was rich, and we were very comfortable. But in Las Islas Felipenas, even money was no protection. My family was persecuted. My brother was jailed for protesting a rice tax on the poor. If you were an Indio, your life had no true value. You belonged—body and soul—to the Church and to the Crown."

"Any one of those is a reason to take arms."

"So you say. But reforms must come from above. A savage insurrection will only end in blood."

"By 'above', you mean by the elites and intellectuals such as yourself? Is that why you chose to write stories instead?"

"Yes, I had sketched this idea for an alternate world—an alternate history, really—one without the distractions of our modern technology. I wrote a nested narrative about an author who had also written a book about yet another fictional writer.

In my story, a good man named Jose Rizal wanted to change the world using only words as weapons. He wrote two imaginary books called *Noli Me Tangere* and *El Filibusterismo*, where his protagonist, Crisostomo Ibarra, suffers great persecution from the Church and State. In the end, however, Ibarra chooses peace over armed struggle. Rizal himself would be arrested and executed. His death would become the catalyst for a doomed revolution. My third book would have focused on the nobility of my people, on their inherent love for peace. I thought also of extrapolating future events, perhaps from a hundred years hence."

"That sounds . . . interesting, if a bit too fantastical for my taste. I am curious as to why you wrote them as scientific romances," the old man asked. "Surely your message would have been more effective as proper, realist fiction?"

"Scientific romances are as marginalized as my people," Joseph answered. "Realism is neurotically obsessed with itself. It offers no norms, nothing to reach for. I wanted to get in touch with the masses, the common people who dream about better futures. Scientific romances are all about possibility, roads that move forward, not those that loop around in navel-gazing eternities."

"Yet all fiction is permutation. There is always change."

"Right now, all I want is for us to be treated as equals and have proper representation in the Cortes. The masses want revolution and blood. I need a third novel to correct this notion. Violence is never the answer."

"There is a time and place for everything, even fighting," the Professor insisted. "Your people are already taking your words and shaping their future with their own hands. Why would you change that?"

"What does it matter? I am a dead man, regardless. My two little books have caused great controversy, and my life now imitates my art. I am sure to end up like Rizal and face a firing squad. Although, if Benomar's *Hermandad* ever found me out, they wouldn't waste a bullet on an Indio—they would simply break my neck."

"So stay here," the Professor urged. "Write your other novel. Stay here and at least stay alive. Anyway, the ones who write eventually control the world."

"That would be nice if it were true," Joseph said. "You have treated me so well. I like it here. It's so different from everywhere else. But . . . it can't make up for what I've gone through, or the suffering of those I've left behind. This is just one place, one small thing."

"You are right, of course. However, everything starts with just one small thing," the old man mused. "The West has abused you and your people, but it has also sheltered and nurtured you. In my own limited way, I understand your conflict."

"I am not sure I myself understand it."

"And you have no wish to go back and fight?" the Professor repeated. "As I said, a handful of your words have already lit the fires of revolution. That makes you an ideal leader."

"I . . . I don't know about that. Are you sure my friend said *nothing*, Herr Professor?" Joseph asked, not wanting to speak his mind further, or disrespect his host. "I am honestly not sure what I'm supposed to do here."

"Well, he did ask me to tell you something else, something quite peculiar—'*Mene, Thecel, Phares*'. Does that mean anything to you?"

"Yes, I used it in my last book. It's a crucial line from Rizal's *El Filibusterismo*, but it was originally from the Book of Daniel," Joseph explained. "It was a mysterious message left on the wall of King Belshazzar's palace. One that he'd asked the prophet to interpret."

"Hmmm . . . I always thought the correct line was '*Mene, Mene, Tekel, Upharsin*'," Professor Lebenskünstler mused.

"Why did he tell you this? What did he mean by it?"

"I am afraid that was all he told me. I know of that phrase though. It's usually taken as an idiom."

"Yes, it is," Joseph sighed. "It means that the future is predetermined."

"I refuse to believe that," the old man said gruffly, "and neither should you. Seek shelter when necessary, yes. But make a decision on what you need to do. Do not bury your head in the sand forever."

With that, the conversation ended. Joseph thanked his host once more and returned to his room. On the way back, he saw Klara playing tennis. Beautiful Klara, strange Klara, a woman with whom every tactile moment intimated infinity.

For some reason, Joseph felt the void calling for him again. He was seized by the same darkness he felt in the brothels and bierbrauerie of Berlin. It was as if a great weight had suddenly pressed on his heart—the weight of a frozen life, the birth pains of a stillborn country, the infernal blackness of cities, and the oppressive insecurity of a brown body in a sea of infallible white.

He ran towards his cabin like a madman, stripping off his hat and clothes as he went. By the time he reached his quarters, he was completely naked. Joseph locked the door and shut the crinoline blinds. He jumped onto his bed and lost himself to the darkness. This time, he did not cry.

∞

That evening, Joseph skipped dinner. He slept fitfully, beset by troubled dreams.

I, Joseph Alonso y Mercado, found myself in an enormous library filled with nothing but books—books that different versions of myself, scattered infinitely through time and space, had always written. I saw thousands of volumes of poetry, historical annotations, meditations on women, language, moral values, mythology, prehistory, taxonomy, and others.

Feeling restless, I wandered about until I saw the shelves that held my precious novels. A great dread filled my soul when I realised that all of them were just the same two books—"The Social Cancer" and "The Reign of Greed", "An Eagle Flight" and "The Filibustering", "Noli Me Tangere" and "El Filibusterismo", different titles but always the same pair and nothing more. There never was and never would be a third novel.

Terrified, I ran towards a mirrored portal and found myself at the entrance of a cave on the peak of a mystical mountain called Banahaw. Eleven heroes of old, of the future, and of myth waited for me, toasting lambanog toddy and Vin Mariani.

They begged me to lead them to battle for I was a be-knighted National Hero, the greatest Medal of Honor which the Highest and

Most Honorable Society of the Children of Las Islas Felipenas could bestow.

Feeling inauthentic and hollow, I ran back into the cave, which for some reason I knew would lead me to hell. I fell endlessly, surrounded by an iridescent rain of burning dreams, until I realised that I was not falling, but flying. I was the Matanglawin, the great hawk of Philippine legend, whose eyes could see the ley lines of every possible future.

The voice of God boomed across the skies like a volley of cannon, and I discovered that God's voice was my own. I was the Christian God, I was the Indio Christ, and I was Bathala, the ancient God of the islands. I as God roared and sent lightning and thunder through the Heavens. I shouted: "Mene, Thecel, Phares", and then I finally understood the writing on the wall.

Do not touch me, I told Destiny. I shall choose my own Eternity.

∞

"Any life is made up of a single moment, the moment in which a man finds out, once and for all, who he is."

—JORGE LUIS BORGES,
BIOGRAFÍA DE TADEO ISIDORO CRUZ (1829-1874)

∞

Joseph woke up at the crack of dawn. He dressed and went to the main house for an early breakfast. The housekeeper told him she'd collected and washed the clothes he had so hastily discarded on the pathway. She also returned his abandoned hat, but the wind-up mechanism was now broken and needed replacement.

27

After borrowing an axe, Joseph walked back to his cottage. As soon as he got inside, he stripped off his clothes and folded them neatly on the bed. He took his Stenhouse mask from his luggage and put it on tightly.

He stood by the door, his hand on the knob, working up the courage to open it. After a few minutes, he decided to brave the outside world.

Joseph's first sensation was that of swimming, as if his body was slicing through the sea instead of the crisp mountain air. The feeling was heady and liberating, and he could not help but leap about like a child.

The young man walked over to where the pile of logs was kept and started chopping them into smaller pieces. All morning and afternoon he worked until everything was reduced to firewood. When he was done, he ran to the lake, threw his mask by the shore and dove into the clear, lustral waters.

When he returned to land, a small crowd had gathered to see him—the professor and his housekeeper, the school mistress and her children, the Hanoverian poet and his English friends. Klara was there, too, along with the two Nordic-looking youths.

Joseph hid behind a thin fringe of reeds. He lifted his eyebrows shyly at his curious onlookers. It was an unspoken greeting peculiar to his homeland, deep and pregnant with meaning. Unfortunately, it was completely lost on his European audience.

Klara handed him his mask. He put it back on and returned to his cabin. He wondered if any of them felt *Fremdschämen*—that uniquely German word for the awkwardness one feels for another's embarrassment.

At dinner he announced that he would be leaving the very next day.

∞

(Dearest Reader, depending on who you are and what you read into this story, there are three possible endings.)

1. *Mene: God hath numbered thy kingdom and hath finished it.*

The next day, Joseph boarded the Locomotive Aerostatique to Berlin. His short stay at the sanitarium had somehow swept the fear and doubt from his deeply troubled mind. Having steeled his heart, the young man quietly accepted his destiny.

As soon as he reached the city, he headed to the *Berliner Gesellschaft für Anthropologie* and messaged Professor Blumenttrit:

"I wish to show those who deny us patriotism that we know how to die for our duty and our convictions."

With great sadness his friend responded with just a single line: *"Consumatum est."* It was finished.

A week later, Joseph Mercado was on a clipper-steamer back to Manila, resolved to meet the immensity of his fate.

2. *Thecel: Thou art weighed in the balance and found wanting.*

After receiving a secret report from Joseph's landlady, Frau von Kusiemski, the Count of Benomar sent his best spy to the Wolpertinger Luftbad sanitarium.

The erstwhile "Uranian poet from Hanover" had hidden a small dictaphone in Professor Lebenskünstler's study. Its wax cylinder produced the proof that the *Reino de España* had been seeking—that the foreign student Joseph Alonso y

29

Mercado was Señor Laong Laan, the seditious author they had long been looking for.

That evening, the false poet sat next to Joseph and spiked his drink with laudanum. In the middle of the night, the Count's top agent crept into his room and silently broke the young man's neck. Afterwards, he burned the old cabin to ashes.

Joseph's name became a footnote in history. His books were all destroyed, save for a single set of copies in the Vatican's Index Librorum Prohibitorum.

3. *Phares: Thy kingdom is divided and is given to the Medes and Persians.*

Klara stole into his room that night, and the two made noisy, passionate love. In Joseph's fevered imagination, she was made of fire, and he was made of water. Water drowned fire, he reflected, and fire dried water. He knew that something in him had been irrevocably changed.

When they were done, she pointed to a trunk she had left by the washstand before disappearing into the darkness. In the nearby lake, the body of a tall, bearded Hanoverian quietly drifted towards the silty grey bottom, a trail of crimson flowing from a single bullet wound to the head.

Joseph opened the trunk. Inside were a Maschinengewehr recoilless machinegun and the plans for a small, steam-powered Babbage Brain. On the handle of the weapon was an inscription carved in Latin: "*Bene legere saecla vincere*"— *To read well is to master the ages.*

Joseph blew out his lamp and stared into the blackness, unable to sleep. He abhorred violence, yet he could not

deny that this kind of gun was powerful. It could be
reverse-engineered and even the odds for the 'savage insur-
rectionists' who were already fighting in his name. The
Babbage Brain could coordinate a military response and
spread his words to the world.

However, Joseph worried that even if his people succeeded in lifting the yoke of the white man, it would only be
because the white men themselves allowed it. What debt
would he owe his mysterious benefactors? When would
they collect?

The next day, he boarded the Locomotive Aerostatique
to Berlin. As soon as he reached the city, he headed to the
Berliner Gesellschaft für Anthropologie and sent a curt message to Professor Blumenttrit: "Thank you?" He signed-off
with the new name he had given himself, *"Matanglawin"*.

(Joseph Alonso y Mercado, Jose Rizal, and Crisostomo
Ibarra, as he knew them, were all dead.)

A week later, Matanglawin was on a clipper-steamer
back to Manila—resolved to fight his *Kastila* masters but
deeply troubled by what the future could bring.

AN EXCERPT FROM

THE PHILIPPINE JOURNAL OF ARCHAEOLOGY

(04 OCTOBER, 1916)

An Examination of a Megalithic Mass Grave on Mt. Pinatubo, Zambales Province, the Philippine Islands

By Francisco Pölzl & Ferdinand C. Ashley, Miskatonic University, Arkham, Massachusetts

Under the auspices of the Archaeology and Ancient Civilizations department of Miskatonic University, a team of archaeologists visited the site of a megalithic mass grave on an almost-inaccessible slope of Mt. Pinatubo, an extinct stratovolcano, in the province of Zambales, on the main island of Luzon in the Philippine Islands.

Mt. Pinatubo is part of a chain of volcanoes, formed over a million years ago through the subduction of the Eurasian Plate under the smaller Philippine Belt. No eruption has ever been reported in the modern era (at least during the island's official recorded history).

However, oral traditions chronicle several eruptions that would have certainly occurred during the island's dark pre-Hispanic past.

The site had been discovered in October 1913 by a team of biologists from the Philippine Bureau of Science who had been conducting the first comprehensive environmental survey of the area.[1]

The graves were located slightly more than a mile and a quarter from Tarukan village, on the left flank of the dead volcano. The area was primarily composed of andesite and dacite, as well as an assemblage of plagioclase, pyroxene, and hornblende. The andesite deposits were riddled by many small cave-like structures, many of which have collapsed, burying what appeared to be shell middens and other living areas, possibly during a major tectonic or volcanic earthquake.

---

1 E. Quisumbing, et al. (*Philippine Journal of Science*, March 1916) reported that their team was led to the site by a local Zambales shaman, an "*arbularyo*", who said that that spot had been cursed by "the old gods".

When the group first arrived at the small depression on the side of the volcano, they noticed that no plants grew among the stones, no animals lived there, and even the birds and insects seemed to give the area a wide berth.

Quisumbing reported that during their survey, the *arbularyo* sported an unusual wrist-to-shoulder ornament. The brace-like accoutrement was woven from pandan leaves and heavily decorated with seashells, old gears, and broken watches. The old man told him that it was an "*anting-anting*", a magic amulet that the shaman wore for protection as he believed that the site was "evil". He had also remarked to an American botanist accompanying Quisumbing that the former need not be afraid as "*everybody knows that monsters prey only on women and coloured people*".

These spirits were said to trap some people inside their dreams and devour the rest. This type of superstition was common among the natives and has been studied previously (Beyer, et al. 1914).

The anthropologist Ferdinand Blumenttrit (in correspondence) noted that he had seen a similar "magic" shoulder brace made of shark skin and studded with rare cabochons. It had been kept at the Berliner Gesellschaft für Anthropologie sometime in the mid-1800s but had since been reported stolen.

According to Blumenttrit, it had been bought by an Englishwoman from a bazaar in Shanghai that sold nothing but maps. The proprietor had sold it to her with the strange and ominous admonition that "*the dead bore a map of memories for the living*".

The remains of over 150 individuals of different ages had been found, encircled by a structure of standing stones and dolmens. This enigmatic circular structure represented the first evidence of megalithic architecture ever found in the Philippines.

Everything had been buried quickly, pointing to the likelihood of a catastrophic end to this fairly large and archaeologically important Paleolithic community.

One of the cone-shaped orthostats was partially reconstructed by the expedition team. It bore a striking similarity to certain prehistoric structures found on Nias, an isolated island off the western coast of North Sumatra.

The lack of stone-working implements anywhere in or near the site indicated that they were probably carved at their source. The plinths, each weighing at least an Imperial ton, had been carved from coral-rich Bolinao limestone, sourced from a quarry in the coastal province of Pangasinan.

It has not been determined exactly how the stones were transported over the 20-mile distance, given the lack of contiguous rivers to the volcano, as well as the site's challenging elevation (approximately 3,000 feet above sea level).

As reported by the 1913 survey team, there was also a startling lack of plant and animal life for a wide circle around the megaliths. This extended for about 3 yards in every direction from the largest of the standing stones. It has been theorized that the andesite cavities contained fractures or fumaroles that released poisonous fumes (most likely by advection). This was thought to periodically kill all life within a wide perimeter.

A preliminary dating of the monoliths estimated their age to be approximately 3,500 to 4,000 years. If verified, they would significantly predate the earliest Southeast Asian megalithic culture, the Kutai Martadipura of Eastern Borneo (from 4th Century AD), and make them roughly contemporary with China's semi-mythical Yellow Emperor and the late Uruk Period of Mesopotamia. Further and more accurate dating methods are required than what was available in the field.

Initial on-site forensic analyses also showed that most of the victims did not die from toxic gas, but rather from what appeared to be a ritual murder or execution.[2]

Significant damage was clearly evident on the cervical vertebrae of several skeletons, as if they had been garroted. The bodies were all found in a circle, radiating outwards from a patch of burned rock, suggesting perhaps that the killings served some religious or mystical purpose.

Professor Tyler M. Freeborn of the Miskatonic University's anthropology department speculated (in correspondence) that this may have

---

2 The authors could not agree on the exact cause of the deaths. Dr. Pölzl believed that this was an act of war, possibly by an invading force. He based his opinion on the presence of several deformed skeletons that were taller in height and did not conform to the Australo-Melanesian skeletal type (he called these odd skeletons the "Eaters" as some Negrito remains bore signs of cannibalism—an act that was completely taboo to most tribes on the islands).

However, Dr. Ashley pointed to the lack of direct evidence for such an assault, noting that the community was isolated and far from the coast. Also, he maintained that it would have taken a blade as sharp as a steel knife to make such deep cuts. This was clearly not possible as the remains predated the Metal Age, adding that that Negroid people in general were incapable of such sophisticated technologies.

A local Filipino doctor with the group had also remarked that the nicks on the bone could have been made by "a large carnivore of unknown origin" and insisted that they all leave immediately. However, he was curtly dismissed and reminded that no such predators were known from the Philippines. Dr. Ashley also wanted to put on record that this "disruptive individual" as he called him, was a *mestizo* (a half-breed product of miscegenation) who had graduated from a non US-accredited local university. His statements thus held no validity.

After this altercation, one of the guides suggested the victims were killed by an "*aswang*", a fantastical creature from Philippine lower mythology. This assertion caused half the porters to abandon their posts, hastening the team's departure from the site.

been some form of sacrifice to *Apo Namalyari*, the local mountain deity worshipped by the Aetas of Zambales. He noted further that human sacrifice was not unknown in the islands, citing the case of the Bagobos of Mindanao. This tribe had been much feared for their practice of dismembering slaves just before they sowed rice. This gruesome sacrifice served as a blood offering to their *Anito* spirit-gods to ensure a bountiful harvest (Frazer, 1890).

The actual identity of the people from the burial site has not been ascertained. Although their bone structures suggested affinity to the dark-skinned, Australo-Melanesian Aetas, there has been no known instance of permanent settlement in other similar communities—either in the Philippine Islands or further afield. Groups as diverse as the Orang Asli of Malaya, the Andaman pygmies from the Bay of Bengal, or the recently extinct Palawa aboriginals of Tasmania have never been known to progress beyond a simple nomadic existence.

Adding to conundrum was the discovery of late Paleolithic stone tools, bark beaters, and spindle whorls, as well as jade earrings and shell beads which had been unearthed in various other caves. It has been theorized that these were out-of-place objects, perhaps falling from more recent strata or buried at a later date by superstitious natives. Indeed, many of the items recovered were identical to those traded by Proto-Malays from almost a millennium later, although it was puzzling why the latter would provide offerings to a genetically inferior people who were obviously not their direct ancestors.

All the artifacts recorded could be spot dated with reasonable accuracy. However, it was very difficult—if not impossible—to prove that they were from the same time period as either the skeletons or the megaliths. Without the proper context, these detritus of ordinary life were simply ciphers, lacking a before, an after, or a when to determine their significance.

The expedition's most important find was a half-ruined cave wall, hewn from an ophiolite matrix and older than the surrounding igneous rock that was decorated with remarkable petroglyphs unlike anything seen elsewhere. The pictogram and logogram images seemed to be uniquely narrative in nature, although only a few logogram glyphs have been deciphered with certainty. One of the native porters suggested it was a record of an ancient supernatural battle, while another said it was a warning for the team to leave, precipitating the crisis that abruptly ended the expedition.

Some of the images were exceptional and intriguing—including what appeared to be representations of distinct stellar constellations (particularly the constellation of Libra which rises during the monsoon season), figures of mythical beings, strange hexagrams and creatures that resembled extinct animals, such as the recently discovered Philippine stegodon (*Stegodon luzonensis*).[3]

The existence of this particular cavern seemed to validate a controversial and long-debated footnote in Friedrich Wilhelm von Junzt's *Unaussprechlichen Kulten* from 1839.[4] In Chapter 5 of the original German-language volume, the author had spoken of "*a cult in Zambales that worshiped a cave with strange rock carvings on the slopes of Mt. Pinatubo*". How von Junzt was able to come to this knowledge a

---

3 The Philippine stegodon (*Stegodon luzonensis*) became extinct at the beginning of the middle Pleistocene, long before the arrival of humans in the Philippine Islands (Benitez, 1911).
4 The sole existing copy of the 1839 Dusseldorf edition of *Unaussprechlichen Kulten* is kept in the Special Collection of the Miskatonic University Library (Catalogue number PH-27041521).

full 78 years before its actual discovery remains yet another unsolved mystery.

Many of the petroglyphs had been coloured in with red ocher made from hematite ore containing large amounts of dehydrated iron oxide (Fe_2O_3). There were also marginal drawings (made from the same powdered pigment) all over the cave wall which appeared in a simpler, more haptic style.

A single set of human remains was discovered in the same cave as the petroglyphs—a pregnant female, superficially of Negrito lineage, approximately 16 years of age, with her unborn child still inside her uterus. Unlike the skeletons found by the megaliths, there was no visible damage to her cervical vertebra or any readily ascertained cause of death.

The young woman's sternum (breastbone) was keeled like a bird or a bat, indicating a previously unrecorded type of congenital deformity. Her bones were also dramatically light and hollow, exhibiting possible signs of early-onset osteoporosis.

A bag of pigment, the container of which had long since rotted away, was found by her right hand. At the time of this writing, her remains were the only piece of evidence linking the Australo-Melanesian skeletons (if indirectly) with the cave of petroglyphs. It has not been determined if she had lived or died at the same time as the first group, or if she was actually a descendant who had come at a later date.

Because the expedition's time had been cut so short, the team could not precisely date the rock carvings. From the wall's mineral composition and the actual paleographic content, both authors believed that they could be significantly older than the ocher drawings—possibly even predating the megalithic structures themselves (which had been carved from younger micritic limestone, with tuffaceous turbidite and minor chert). In particular, the carvings of the stegodons were remarkably detailed and seemed to hint at the possibility of direct observation by the artist.

From a structural perspective, the more precise arrangement of the ophiolite petroglyphs was a sharp contrast to the almost haphazard nature of the rock art drawings. This suggested that they were made at different periods, or perhaps even by a different ethnic group.[5]

Indeed the modern Aetas' unfamiliarity with the petroglyphs and their lack of even the precursors of a written language would seem to suggest this.

The mere possibility that the petroglyphs could have belonged to a people from earlier in the Paleolithic indicates the need for more thorough excavation of the deeper cave strata as soon as practicable.[6]

---

5 The authors have suggested that the carvings could have been made by archaic *Homo sapiens* from the Middle Paleolithic, as such remains have been found previously in Asia. The megaliths could have been added later by the ancestors of the Aeta.

Editor's note: After the much-publicized fall-out between the authors (already widely covered by many academic and professional publications so it shall not be reprinted here), Dr. Ashley had become more politicized and recanted the note above, stating that *"This kind of old art could not possibly have been created by the Aeta as their race is vastly inferior. There can be no question of this among contemporary and unsentimental biologists, eminent Europeans for whom the prejudice-problem does not exist."*

He also denounced Dr. Pölzl as a scientist whose views were "not objective" and coloured by the fact that the Bavarian was in fact a *"puffy-faced half-Asiatic with a brown native father"*.

6 With the United States Congress passing the Philippine Autonomy Act this August, it is vital that research continues even if the Philippine Islands should declare independence.

More pressingly, war has broken out around Europe and is spreading all over the world. With the sinking of the RMS *Lusitania* last year, it is likely that the United States will be pulled into the fighting, and all scientific funding will be suspended or diverted towards the war effort.

POSTSCRIPT:

A lone human handprint, decorated by what appeared to be representations of eagle-owls and stars was also discovered drawn on a wall opposite that of the petroglyphs. As the drawings were created from the same batch of red ocher that was found by the skeleton, it was believed that the anonymous woman was the artist. Also, the size of her metacarpus and phalanges were similar to the hand print, lending further credence to this assertion.

Although much work was yet required to determine the secrets of this enigmatic Paleolithic people, the remarkable structures they left behind, as well as the troubling question of how they died, the fragile yet defiant handprint and its lone creator—a mother, unspared by oblivion, with one hand reaching for her drawing tools and the other protecting her unborn baby—seemed to send a clear message across the shadows of time:

"I was here. My baby was here. We lived, we loved, and we died."

Because of the harsh tropical environment and the acute possibility of earthquakes, it is uncertain what will be left of the site if the excavation is abandoned for even a single year.

To mitigate this, the team collected as many bones and artifacts as possible, especially after most of the porters had fled.

As transport to Miskatonic University is difficult at this time, everything has been stored in a secure container inside a sealed vault at the US Army's storage facility at the Sta. Lucia Barracks in Intramuros, Manila.

Dr. Ashley believes that this is enough precaution as even a world war would never reach the backwaters of Southeast Asia. What little material the team has gathered would at least be safe for future generations to study.

"The natives here are good-natured but simple minded," he had remarked. *"It is a sad fact that it will be the burden of America to write their history."*

A ЅECRET MAP OF ЅHANGHAI

For a moment, GG seemed lost in ceaseless yearning as he stared out the old windows at the deep and endless sky. Outside, Xújiāhuì hummed with autumnal activity, with crowds of cardboard people, ants and bees, and sometimes even gods, architecting the destiny of the city. After eight months, eight days and six hours, he felt he had learned everything he could from her. He was a god of the city, and the time had come perhaps for him to leave.

He turned to where he had bound Mrs. Plimm, his teacher of Geography, the sweet-tongued annihilator of History. His foreign *Shanghailander* was stretched out like a map, held tight to the corners of a bridal bed, waiting impatiently for his next move.

GG pulled off his shirt, revealing a body that was no longer a boy yet not quite a man. Mrs. Plimm was already naked. He marveled at how her ancient hair and chilled skin wept with the sky's golden colour. Her bountiful breasts were cloudy towers, holy barbicans of slanted ivory and white. All around them the room smelled of orchids and ambergris.

He remembered his own first lesson. It seemed so long ago, yet every little detail remained carved in the eternity of his head.

"Shanghai is a man, a perfect, Vitruvian man," she had told him, as she spread him, unblemished, on her endlessly expanding bed, *"but you, my sullen boy, are still half-devil, half-child."*

She pillowed him with a carnality that hid an infinitely regressing imperialism, taunting him, enticing him: *"Listen my little godling. You natives know nothing of power. You need to dream you are a mighty, mighty city."*

He remembered the strange valise she had placed by his bedside, a shimmering mystery in pearly shagreen. Inside was a cornucopia of tools and implements, every single one of which had troubled and excited him.

"Sun Wukong, the Monkey King, stole this from a great city of books, and I stole it from him. With what's inside, I will tame your rough tigers, your insipid cranes, your pagan dragons. Never fear, my sweet little protectorate, I shall uplift and civilize you," she cooed. *"You are my special burden."*

Mrs. Plimm's voice was like a siren's, reminding him of the shape of abalones and the silkiness of tofu.

"Now then, to our first order of battle," she'd said to him, *"every city is an idea, and to conquer it, you must give it a name. You are my Shanghai. I shall name you; mark the ports that I shall enter, the roads that I shall tread."*

A murder of crows flew past the window and GG made an involuntary shiver. He remembered how she'd introduced him to a novel use for a bamboo ear pick, a weapon that bloomed in a ball of the finest, softest down. He was extremely ticklish, and he feared he'd simply die if she used it.

But his strange teacher had been gentle. She merely toyed with him, giving poetic names to every piece of exposed skin, teasing out each letter on his waiting flesh. Then she took away his ancient names, replacing them with cold epithets made of coal, steam, and iron. Every new word, every new verse summed up the vision of her perfect city.

"My man's head is at Qīngpǔ, pointing to Sūzhōu, the land of old dreams," she whispered sweetly. Back then, it had not mattered what she said. Her voice had filled his head and sucked his heart in her mouth, seducing him with myths and visions. *"That is why when you are asleep they say 'you have gone to Sūzhōu'. But forget the dusty past. In my name you will dream new dreams."*

Much time had passed since that first immaculate afternoon. Yet even now, when he knew he was free to just walk away, he still felt her fetters of velvet and iron. He knew he could not simply leave her. Besides, no other devil would miss him. No one ever would.

Mrs. Plimm had bound him fully clothed to her bed's *huanghuali* frame, an unbreakable skeleton made from the finest of woods. At first he'd tried very hard to escape, to break free of her heavy harness, especially when she'd pressed the cold, cold hilt of her sharpest scissors on his cheek. He remembered the flash of fear that had passed over his eyes, like the quick schiller of moonstone. He had never been so scared in his life.

Mrs. Plimm had cut away his shirt. Once his chest was bare, she called him her initiate and revealed her tools of magic conquest—a bouquet of the sharpest, fiercest needles.

"Please, no," he'd begged, regretting following her from school.

"My man's left hand is at Bǎoshān Qū, holding the hand of Māzǔ, the goddess of the sea." Mrs. Plimm continued, as she pricked his skin slowly, methodically with acupuncture needles.

"Here is a garden of ancient splendor," she whispered, as the first needle touched his skin. *"And there,"* she added, as she pinned another, *". . . is a temple worth eight hundred years."*

He remembered how she had lined his shoulders with generations of tiny swords. She had spiked both arms to the borders of his wrists, marking out her territory with unequal treaties. *"His right hand lies at Jīnshān Qū, crushing islands and mountains of gold."*

In the course of the next hundred hours, Mrs. Plimm had introduced him to her entire mystical arsenal—binding and claiming him under his thin, sallow skin. Like a cartographer, she uncovered and delineated Shanghai's borders on the contours of his young body, drawing from memory the *hútòngs*, streets, and avenues that were the capillaries, arteries, and veins of his beloved city. Then she walled it all up as her property.

When she'd reached the Huángpǔ Jiāng, the mighty river that bisected his waist, she returned to her infernal scissors.

"Don't, please," he pleaded, fearful he'd have to walk home in the nude. But his meticulous teacher had ignored him, cutting away indifferent trousers, peeling them away like a husk—as if searching for newer, deeper layers of secrets.

She stripped him inside and out, filling him with herself.

When she had cleared Pǔdōng, Mrs. Plimm stopped suddenly, pulling out another ear pick. Instead of down, this one was crowned with a fistful of eagle feathers. How dark was her smile, how ravening, he recalled, as she showed him her new toy.

"Oops, I forgot about the ring, our wedding ring."

And then there was the ring—he could never forget it—a curious black girdle that she said was made from the eyelashes of goats. Once she put it on, he found that he could not remove it.

"Men and guns are not the seat of Shanghai's strength. Words are its true power, and I am a woman of the Word," she declared, as she pulled the veil shut across their bridal bed.

"So now we return to literature," she announced, at his torment's denouement. Mrs. Plimm pulled a poetry book from her bag and said: *"I will coax the sacred mollusk out of Pearl Tower with the ninety-two characters of the poem* 施氏食狮史, *the 'Lion-Eating Poet in the Den of Stone'. Then I shall set you free . . . Shíshì shíshì Shī Shì . . . "*

The young man remembered how the darkness danced on the face of the silk-floating sky, chiaroscuro, as if it were a shadow play where the gods were both puppets and puppet masters. He closed his eyes and imagined repeatedly how the *Dōngfāng Míngzhūtǎ*, Shanghai's most famous landmark, had burst forth from fertile river soil, like a shoot of the thickest bamboo (and he knew, like all proper city gods did, that when they moved, the wan earth moved with them).

Mrs. Plimm was true to her word. At the end, she had set him free.

Yet for the eight months, eight days, and six hours they had been together, he never once tried to get away. Not once. Instead, he returned again and again to her devil bed of exquisite humiliations.

She was now part of his history. He could not erase her, nor forget her memory, even if he wanted to. He knew that a city like him drew from his life, and from the lives of his people, successive fictions—each no less true or false than the last. Veracity, she had told him, was slave to whoever sat on the temple's jade throne.

Mrs. Plimm was a goddess of the West, the direction of sunset, death, and age. GG was a thousand years old, but he was of the East, the direction of sunrise, of birth and youth, and he knew that in Youth, there was power. Yet with their every entanglement, every battle, he had grown older while she became younger and younger.

An eastward wind blew in from the windows, carrying the ancient air of deserts and the scent of drying jujubes. GG returned to the present and shut his eyes tight.

When he opened them, no time had passed, yet he had aged two score years and five. Mrs. Plimm had become a plum young maiden, freshly budded, an eternal bride hiding beneath the cloudy silk sheets.

"Let me show you my dream of Shanghai," he whispered to his former master, in the tender flowing tones of a true Shanghainese. *"There is a hollow in your soul that my city will fill, my once and future teacher. You made me, and now I have unmade you."*

"Whatever do you mean?" she asked, impatient for a new experience, pure and cold-edged with dear-bought youth.

"Turnabout is fair play. My Shanghai will take from you whatever it was you took from it," GG said, as he rummaged through her bag of pearl-ray shagreen. For the first time, he noticed the writing burned on its ancient leather—*"Here be Dragons"* in oracle-bone script—and he smiled.

"Yes, here be dragons," he said.

Mrs. Plimm speared her occupier with curious eyes, craving a force that shakes empires. In the soft twilight, he looked every inch a Chinese god of war.

"Shanghai is a woman, a beautiful Vitruvian woman," GG whispered softly, as he traced the city's contours on her smooth body. *"Her head is at Qīngpǔ, pointing to Sūzhōu, the land of old dreams. Her left hand is at Bǎoshān Qū, holding the hand of Māzǔ, the goddess of the sea. Her right hand is at Jīnshān Qū, crushing mountains of gold. Then there is Pǔdōng. Pǔdōng starts where her jade wheel crushes dew and ends with her toes touching the endless, restless water."*

He stared down at his former captor, a porcelain girl of mixed heritage—American, Russian, French, and British. He gazed at her jade wheel, the territory he must reclaim, a single pool of ocean he needed to drain with a single cup.

HERE BE
DRAGONS

In the long days before her sister was born, Isabella went to the *panaderia* every afternoon to buy her mother's favorite bread.

The young girl was sent out at the same time every day, carrying the same amount of change (two heavy one-peso coins or a blue two-peso note), given the same admonition not to tarry or talk to strangers and to buy the same *pan de coco* that her mother loved to eat at exactly 4:00 p.m. with a warm glass of milk.

Nothing exciting ever happened on her daily walks. She would always step out of the gate slowly—only after taking a cautious peek at the world outside. She would walk only on the left side of the driveway, not wishing to disturb the lovely carpet of pink *niyog-niyogan* flowers that fell from the arbor above. Once on the street, Isabella would assume a quick trotting pace, as if expecting rain to fall at any moment.

Her mother teased that Isabella always chose the longest road in the universe. Her favorite path took her from the *Puerta del Sol* convenience store, just next to their house, past the Milky Way Café midway in her journey, to the *Estrella del Norte Panaderia* at the other end of their block. She never varied her route, except if their neighbour Mrs. Mapa and her cat stopped her for a chat.

One very unusual day, a new shop opened in a row of old houses between the Milky Way and the North Star. The store had a peculiar name, *Here Be Dragons*, and it sold nothing but maps.

When she first laid eyes on the store, Isabella felt as if a veritable swarm of butterflies had taken residence in her belly. It was like her birthday, Christmas, and the first day of summer vacation had all been rolled into one.

Isabella loved maps with a great passion. Her father owned a dog-eared copy of *The Hammond Atlas of the World*. She had staked a claim on this cartographic treasure and kept it hidden, behind the thin taffeta of her ruffled bed skirt. Every night, she would stick her finger into the middle of the book and imagine herself in Addis Ababa, Saskatchewan, Ulan Bator or Llanfairpwllgwyngyll.

But Isabella could not bear to enter the strange store that called constantly to her heart. Her parents offered to take her there, but she always refused, afraid that once she had seen every map there was to see in the world, there would no longer be any place for mystery and imagination.

"The proprietor, Mr. Strabo, is a very nice old man," her father said. "I told him that you loved maps, and he invited you to come by and take a look at his merchandise."

Isabella would only shake her head.

One rainy day, on the week before her sister was born, Isabella finally tired of her father's atlas. After buying her mother freshly baked *pan de coco*, she decided to walk past the shop and brave a furtive look inside.

As she got near the door, she turned up the hood of her rain coat and hid behind her umbrella like a spy. For a few minutes she waited uncertainly, watching the rain paint the street with the sky. Finally, she made up her mind and poked her small head inside the shop.

She called out softly to the proprietor, but no one seemed to be around.

Here Be Dragons seemed much too old to be new. There were framed antique maps that lined the walls, globes piled over dusty desks, atlases stacked on heavy wooden shelves, and rolled-up maps strewn carelessly on the stone floor. There were two doors behind the overloaded front counter—one that led to a small kitchen and the other to a large library that seemed oddly bigger than the house itself. Isabella's curiosity got the better of her, and she slipped behind the counter to take a better look.

The library was huge! It seemed to extend forever, with many rooms like honeycombs connected by staircases all stacked up farther than the eyes could see. Just as Isabella was about to step inside, a large, furry hand closed the door, and someone tapped her shoulder from behind.

"Excuse me," said a young boy wearing a curious outfit. He reminded her of a circus ring-master, with his plaid vest, bowtie, and black, striped long johns. On his head was a large top hat with aviator glasses wrapped securely on its brim. A strange metal watch with many dials covered his entire left arm.

He seemed to be the same age as Isabella, and she noticed that he had a nice smile.

"You're not allowed in there," he warned.

"I'm sorry," she apologized. "I was looking for Mr. Strabo."

"You must be Isabella," the boy said, tipping his hat.

"How do you know my name?" she asked suspiciously.

"You told me," he answered, with a cheeky grin that only the smartest of children could carry.

"There must be some mistake," she said, deciding that her father must have spoken of her. "Where is Mr. Strabo? Is he your grandfather?"

"I am Strabo," he said, waving his hand in the air like a magician. "Not Mr. Strabo, just Strabo."

Isabella was normally a chatty sort of child, but the strange circumstances made her unable to carry a proper conversation. She turned to look around the shop instead, as she waited for something to say.

"I'm pleased to meet you, Strabo," she said eventually. "If you don't mind me asking, who would need all these maps? There are so many."

"Everyone needs a map," the boy answered. "Maps are like books. They help you build your world and find your place in it."

"I already own an atlas," she boasted. "It contains everything there is in the world."

"Maps can show more than just continents and oceans," the boy said. "There are maps to heaven and hell; to happiness and sadness; maps of music, of loves lost and loves found. There are maps to imaginary places known only to dreamers and mapmakers like me. I can even make a map of you, if you'd like."

"What do you mean a 'map of me'?" she asked.

"I can create a map with a one-to-one correspondence between you and my special paper. I will chart everything from the tip of your toes to every last hair on your head."

He pointed to a painting on the wall and explained.

"My bird, Animaxander, will record everything you will ever see and hear. My bear Eratosthenes will do the same for everything you will ever touch, and my apple Ortelius will map all the things that you will ever taste in your life."

"Oh! How much will it be for my map?" Isabella asked, excited at the prospect of a new cartographic adventure. "But I don't have a lot of money."

"A map like this is not made in every lifetime," the boy said. "But for you, the cost will be one bag of *pan de coco*, payable in advance."

Isabella made a mental calculation of the coins she had been saving in her piggybank and decided she had enough to buy more bread. She turned to Strabo and said, "All right, it's a deal."

"You have to give me time to make the map," he said. "Come back to the shop when you face your greatest uncertainty."

"How do I know that you will make me a real map?" she asked astutely.

"A map is true only if you have been there before," Strabo answered.

∞

Time passed swiftly. On her one-hundred-and-eleventh birthday, Isabella sent her great-granddaughter to buy *pan de coco* from the Multimegamart that now stood at the end of their block.

"On your way there, you will see an old shop called Here Be Dragons. It's a place that you have never seen before, and you will probably never see again," she explained to the baffled child. "Go inside, my dear, and ask the owner Mr. Strabo for my map. I have paid for it already, so all you need to do is to pick it up."

Eleven-year-old Sophia was the spitting image of Isabella when they were the same age.

Sophia skipped down the street and found the store as instructed. Inside, she asked the young boy who greeted her for her great-grandmother's map.

"Thank you for being so prompt," he said, handing the girl a rolled-up parchment. The map was secured by a small purple ribbon with a label that read: *On the Exactitude of Isabella Ocampo, age 11*. "We had just finished mapping everything a few minutes ago."

Sophia returned to their house to see an ambulance wailing by the driveway.

∞

Somewhere in time, Isabella stepped out of a curious shop called Here Be Dragons and felt a sense of déjà vu.

She remembered what Strabo said—was it just a few minutes before, or was it a lifetime ago?

"A map is true only if you have been there before."

ƧYNCHRONICITY

For the third time since he had crawled out of the wreckage, Felix pressed the power button on his phone. He hoped against hope that something, anything, would happen, but nothing did. It was exactly the same as the last time. His phone was inert, impotent.

"Why am I even alive?" he groaned, oppressed by the silence, of the shapelessness of evening.

Frustrated, he removed the back cover and took the battery out. He placed it between his palms and shook it desperately. For added measure, he prayed to St. Isidore, the patron saint of the Internet. "Help me," he asked softly. "Spare me one small charge please, just enough for a status update, just enough for a text."

The young man required only enough power to send a quick word for help—one small blip to tell the world where he was and that he was okay. But St. Isidore's help line, it seemed, was otherwise engaged. His phone remained stubbornly, obstinately dead.

Despite the rack of pain, he knew that he had no choice but to walk if he wanted to be rescued. "Forgive me," he asked his passel of precious saints. "But if you wanted to really help me, you should have just killed me. At least I'd be with her."

Felix had totaled his car on a remote and desolate stretch of highway. He hadn't gone on a road trip in a long while, not since he'd lost his wife in the nightmare of the previous year. Now his foolhardy journey had almost cost him his life. *You're not the type to travel by yourself,"* she'd once warned him. *"We're so used to being together. It would be hell to be on the road alone."*

He shook himself from the prison of memory and inventoried his things. The watch she had given him for his birthday had stopped ticking. There was a big, ugly gash on its beveled glass. His messenger bag, the one she had lovingly picked out from the recyclables store, was badly scratched but still intact. Nothing else in his car seemed worth saving.

Felix stared at the dark road that stretched out towards the horizon. The sodium vapour lamps had been spaced too far apart. They left only small islands of light in the vast ocean of darkness.

Before he took his first unsteady step, he made a sign of the cross and offered a prayer to St. Jude. Felix felt his soul sallow and threadbare. He needed to arm himself against the shadows. The night was still young, and he worried about what further troubles lay ahead.

"Stop using prayer as a good luck charm," his wife had chided him. *"It's not a religion for you anymore. It's voodoo."* His little leaps of faith unnerved everyone he knew. But he didn't really care about what anyone thought anymore. Pain and loss had a way of turning even the smallest of comforts into crutches, and somehow his constant calls for intercession made him feel less desperate, less powerless, less alone.

Felix squinted and followed the thin line of orange lights that seemed to lead towards infinity. To his relief, he spotted a bus stop about half a kilometre away. "Someone will pass by for sure," he thought. That would be his ticket back to civilization. The young man felt for his bus card in his pocket. He took it out and stared at it for a few seconds, as if to assure himself that it was really there. Satisfied, he started walking towards his lonely destination.

The night was neither cold nor excessively humid, but Felix turned his collar up as a precaution. He had walked about a hundred metres when he remembered that he'd left something of heartbreaking importance, something that he couldn't live without. He slapped his forehead in dismay and quickly ran back to his car.

"Where is that glove compartment?" he thought, as he searched the wreckage frantically. The front of the car was hopelessly crumpled. For a minute, he thought that what he was looking for was lost forever, and he started to hyperventilate.

"St. Anthony, patron saint of lost things . . . please, please help me find it. St. Jude, patron saint of lost causes. Please, please have mercy on me." He closed his eyes and repeated the litany in his head like a nervous tick. Felix forced himself to take deep breaths until his feelings of panic were checked. "I can't have lost it," he repeated, cracking his knuckles. "I won't ever lose it."

Felix took a step back to calculate where the glove compartment lay under the car's twisted frame. When he settled on a spot, he started to remove as much metal and plastic as he could. What began as a careful, studied process slowly escalated into a frenzy of destruction. He tore through the wreckage until he found what he was searching for—a woman's red turtleneck, carefully preserved in a still-intact plastic package. It had been protected from the crash by a magazine and an old rubber sleeve. The young man slowly pulled out his shrink-wrapped treasure. He opened the package, then gently stuck his nose in. His wife's sweet scent still lingered on the fabric.

Felix put the keepsake inside his bag and resumed his solitary walk to the bus stop. The terminal was unlike any he had ever seen. There was no sign indicating what station it was, nor, in fact, any identifying marks at all. There were no bus schedules detailing arrival and departure times, none of the billboards that cluttered other shelters. There was only a small laminated notice, attached to one post, reminding commuters to *"Select Option 2 for a return ride"*.

Felix didn't have to wait too long before something appeared in the distance. Like the stop it attended, the city bus that arrived was odd and strange. It was a heavy-duty Hino coach, with a low non-step floor and a spacious box-like interior. He remembered seeing a vehicle like this before, somewhere in the lumber of his grandfather's dusty photos. An unsettled feeling came over him, and he had to stop himself from running away.

The vehicle was painted sky blue all over, except for a white stripe that wrapped around the cabin, below the large plastic windows. A sign on the windshield said *"AIRCON"*, and above it was an LED board that read *"Non-Stop"*. Both flanks were decorated with three white hearts. The smaller ones said *"Save Gas"*, while the big heart had *"Love Bus"* in bold red-and-yellow lettering. As it pulled up in front of him, he noticed that, despite the vintage design, the bus seemed newly manufactured. So new, in fact, that the chassis was spotless, and the rubber on the tires showed no signs of wear. The surreal cleanliness added to his growing anxiety, and his body made an involuntary shiver.

He made the sign of the cross three times before getting on board. As he entered, he asked the crisply uniformed driver where the bus was headed. The man shook his head and did not speak. He pointed instead to the modern ticket reader behind him. Felix tried to engage him in conversation, but as soon as the driver's gaze fell on him, Felix shut his mouth. The man's eyes blazed like hollow furnaces, burning away all questions, cauterizing all speech.

Felix flashed his bus card. Two options appeared on a small screen, simply labeled with the numerals *"1"* and *"2"*.

"You are young. Choose Option 2, my boy," the coach's solitary passenger told him. "I've selected Option 1 already. That way, one of us will see where each one goes."

"Thank you, sir," Felix said as he moved uncertainly down the cabin. He sat opposite his fellow commuter, an old European man dressed in a black cassock, with a white Roman collar around his hearty neck.

The young man whispered another prayer of thanks. What luck that he was travelling with a priest. The presence of a man of God dispelled much of his naked fear, and for the first time since his accident, he felt the faint flicker of hope.

"Thank the Lord that you are here," the priest said. "I was slowly going mad by myself. What is your name, my son?"

"My name is Felix del Mundo," he answered softly, nervously, like a child's prayer.

"I'm pleased to meet you, Felix," the old man said, in a deep reassuring voice. "I am Father Vladimir of the Society of Jesus."

"I'm pleased to meet you too, Father," he replied, as he dusted the chair with his handkerchief. "There's something creepy about the bus driver. He didn't want to talk to me."

"I don't think he can speak. I've tried to converse with him for the best part of this ride. He simply took my last hryvnia and sent me to my seat."

"Do you have any idea where he's taking us? The sign on the bus says *'Non-Stop'*, but where's it nonstop to?"

"I wish I knew, my son," the priest said. "Your stop is the only one I've seen since coming aboard. The odd thing is that this isn't the same bus I started riding. I distinctly recall boarding a white LiAZ tourist coach."

"I'm not sure I get what you mean. But, yes, something isn't right," Felix concurred. His dusting became more frantic. "I've never seen this kind of bus before. What stop did you board at, Father?"

"I . . . I don't remember, actually," Father Vladimir muttered. "I was coming back to Estragon from a big semiotics conference. At some point, I think I was in a car accident. I still have my luggage with me."

"Estragon?" the young man asked. "Where on Earth is . . . oh my God! We're dead, Father. I think we're dead!" The young man said with a start, seized suddenly by the unforgiving inevitability of mortality. "I saw this in a movie once. Think about it. We were both in car accidents, in different countries! How did we get here? That can't be a coincidence. My God, *we're dead!*"

Felix hung his head with the grim realization and raked his hands through his hair repeatedly, trying to overcome a sudden urge to scream. "Here I was thinking how lucky I was to escape without a scratch." Felix took out his hanky and brushed the back of the seat in front of him. He cleaned it thoroughly before banging his head against the foam cushion.

The priest let a few moments of silence pass before speaking. "Calm yourself, my son. We don't know that for sure, do we? I certainly don't feel dead, but then again, I've never been dead before. There could be other possibilities."

"What other possibility is there?" Felix asked, befuddled by the unfamiliar logic of their situation. "We must be dead, and this bus is our hearse. It's too much of a coincidence to ignore."

"There is . . . there is coincidence, and then there is synchronicity," Father Vladimir continued. "When two things happen together, that doesn't always need to mean anything."

"Sorry, Father, I don't know what you're talking about," the young man said, cracking his knuckles anxiously.

"Sometimes things just happen together, and there's really no connection between them. That's called *'coincidence'*. However, if you do find something, like an idea or a plan, that connects the two, that's actually called *'synchronicity'*. I believe what happened to us was pure coincidence. My accident and your accident are not connected. Yes, we're on a strange bus heading to an unknown destination, but that doesn't mean we're on an omnibus to the afterlife. Think about it, if we're dead, shouldn't there be more people on this bus? Thousands of people die every day."

"Are you for real, Father? I'm sorry, but you don't talk like a regular person."

"Well, this is far from a regular situation," Fr. Vladimir said. "I'm not sure we are even in the regular world anymore. We could be dreaming or unconscious."

"So are you saying that this is only in my mind?" Felix asked uneasily. He looked out the plastic windows with uncharacteristic diffidence as the bus swept by endless fallow fields wrapped in darkness. The pall of night reminded him of the vacancy, the finality of oblivion, but something in his heart told him this wasn't death.

After a period of reflection he said, "Maybe you're right, Father. I always thought that there would be a big tunnel of light when you died and that the people you loved would be waiting for you somewhere. No, I don't feel like we're dead at all."

"Don't be too put out," Fr. Vladimir said quietly. "This is all much too strange, even for me. I wouldn't blame you at all for feeling moribund."

The old man droned on about death and the persistence of memory, but Felix just couldn't focus enough to listen.

"It's moving too fast to jump off," the young man remarked. "I just want to get off. Perhaps if we rush the driver together, we can overpower him."

"And then what?" the priest asked. "We would just be lost. It would be better for us to reach a destination first—at least before we contemplate such actions. I don't think either of us would like to be trapped out there. It's nothing but a brutal wasteland."

Felix said nothing. This had been the second time in his life that he had wanted to jump from a moving bus. The first was in New York City, a little more than five years ago. With his student visa expiring, he had no choice but to return to the land of his birth. The young man had been so used to life in America, that Promised Land for all Filipinos, that his trip back home had seemed like a punishment, an exile to limbo after his brief taste of heaven. On the bus, he had fought a great urge to run away, and he would probably have done so, if a beautiful young woman hadn't sat right next to him. Like Felix, she was also on her way to Manila. By some odd twist of fate, they ended up spending the next fifteen hours together. In those long golden hours, they became fast friends. Before they knew it, their relationship blossomed into something else. A year later, the two of them were married.

"We feel most mortal before dawn, they say," Fr. Vladimir said, trying to comfort his brooding companion. "Let us keep our wits about, and let us not lose hope. Who knows what destiny waits at the end of this ride?"

"Thank you, Father." Felix sighed. He knew that the old man was trying to make him feel better. "It's just that being trapped on this bus is driving me nuts. I wish we knew where we were going. It doesn't really matter where. I just want to get somewhere and get the hell off."

"I can't honestly say that I am not worried," the old man mumbled. "But Milton said that the mind is its own place. In itself, it can make a heaven of Hell, and a hell of Heaven. Perhaps we can lighten our mood with a change of topic. Let me think . . . hmm . . . my life's work, my magnum opus if I may, is a lexicon of dreams. I have been compiling it for decades. Shall we talk about dreams instead?"

"You study dreams?" Felix asked, momentarily distracted. He had dreamed of his wife every single night since her death. Different dreams, different situations, but always with one thing in common: every night, she would tell him to come and find her. His anxiety returned, and Felix took out his handkerchief and started folding it into a four-point pocket square.

"Yes, I study them, looking for a common language to define their meaning."

"So can you interpret dreams, Father?" he asked, tucking the pocket square back into his pants.

"In a manner of speaking, I can," the priest explained. "For example, according to my research, if you dream of riding on a bus to nowhere, it means that you feel you're being carried along by events beyond your control."

"So . . . you think that we are in a dream right now?" the young man said, looking around the strange bus and weighing the unreality of their situation. "I suppose that's possible. I could be in a coma somewhere."

"When you wake, or think you do, what would you say of this evening?" the old man asked. "I have an interesting thought experiment.

Let's say that we are indeed just dreaming, and you are dreaming that you're riding a bus to places unknown. What is your inescapable tragedy, my son?"

"I haven't said a prayer to St. Christopher yet," Felix said abruptly. He had wanted to ask the old man about his dreams but couldn't bring himself to open his heart to a stranger.

"Sorry? What are you going on about?"

"St. Christopher. He's the patron saint of travelers."

"And buses, I imagine," the priest added. "Forgive me, but I feel as if there is some truth that you are denying. However, I suppose Carl Jung can wait if you're not comfortable with confessions."

The old man looked out to the manifold darkness and became lost in his own thoughts.

After a while, the young man began to feel irritable and a bit light-headed. "Father," he asked," do you have anything to eat?" In his rush to drive back to the city, Felix had forgotten to have dinner. Now he felt the pangs of hunger, as his blood sugar started to drop precipitously. "Is it possible to feel hungry in a dream?" He thought, "If I die now, this won't be suicide. The saints will let me see her. Please St. Jude, St. Anthony, let me see her. We need to be together."

"Ah, hunger . . . another great *leitmotif*. Knut Hamsun used it well," Father Vladimir murmured, still lost in his thoughts. The priest had spent too much time on the bus alone. He succumbed readily to the temptation to forage his mind for conundrums and verities.

"Father, I have diabetes," Felix cried out. He knew that his wife wouldn't have approved of a diabetic coma, not after she had spent so much time mothering his illness. "I feel dizzy."

"Oh! I'm so sorry. Where is my head today?" the priest said, with much embarrassment. Fr. Vladimir opened one of his large valises.

Inside he had an enormous bag of chocolates, bottles of mineral water, and a crumbly cake packed securely in a sturdy Styrofoam box. "I was on my way to a party for the children of my orphanage. I suppose this is as noble a use for these victuals."

The priest took out some paper plates and used the handle of a plastic fork to cut the cake. He carved out a big piece and handed it to Felix, along with a bottle of mineral water. "*Smachnoho!*" he exclaimed, "That means *bon appetit.*"

"Thank you. That was surprisingly delicious," Felix said, gobbling his share with desperate gusto. "What kind of cake was it?"

"Kiev cake," the old man answered proudly. "It's a divine confection, isn't it? It's made of two airy layers of meringue with hazelnuts, chocolate glaze, and a butter-cream filling. It's very rich, like the culture of my people."

After they finished eating, the young man excused himself to take a nap. When he woke up, it was still night time. In the bus, he did not dream, and that bothered him greatly. He realised how deeply he needed the comfort of seeing his wife every night, even if it was just a shade of her memory.

The young man noticed that Father Vladimir had also fallen asleep. He wondered how long they had been travelling. He looked at his watch but remembered that it was still broken. He tried to recall the details of his accident, but his memory now seemed fuzzy. It was as if it had happened a very long time ago. He took his phone out of his bag and checked it again. "Please, I just want to see her picture," he prayed, but his phone remained hopelessly dead.

A voice boomed suddenly in the darkness: "Come, let's get to work! In an instant, all will vanish, and we'll be alone once more, in the midst of nothingness!"

"*Dios ko po!*" Felix cried out, startled by the old man's declamation. "Sorry, I didn't know you were awake, Father."

"Nothing like a quote from Samuel Beckett to start the day," Fr. Vladimir said gruffly. "Night and sleep came and went, but we did not dream. At least, I didn't."

"But it's still night," Felix protested. "In fact, I think it's still the same night. Everything is exactly the same. Nothing's changed since we ate and slept."

"Forget the night, my son! Beckett said that nothing matters but writing, and this applies to us now." The priest said, with a distressed tone and an odd, vacant look. "I think I have figured out where we are. We are not dead. We are not dreaming. We are in a story. Oh heavens, this would be such a contrived, self-referential plot if that were true!"

"We are trapped . . . in a story?" Felix asked warily, as he got up and moved a few rows behind his companion. The young man wondered if their situation had finally taken its toll on the old man's sanity. He started a silent litany to St. Dymphna, the patron saint of mental health, just in case.

"Yes, I believe so," Fr. Vladimir repeated, suddenly livid at their situation. "We are trapped in a cliché. I had hoped if someone ever put me in a story, I would be in something literary, not genre—some novel of ideas or lofty philosophical fiction. But two strangers trapped in a single point in space and time, waiting for Godot for all eternity? Maybe this *is* purgatory . . ."

"Father," Felix cut in. "I'm a business major with an MBA. I'm not so deep into philosophy. I have no idea what you're rambling about, and frankly, you're scaring me." He crossed himself silently and said another prayer to St. Dymphna. For good measure, he added yet another to the martyr St. Sebastian, the patron saint of cranky people.

"I . . . I'm sorry." Fr. Vladimir apologized profusely. The young man's worried tone had returned him to his senses. "It's just that I have dedicated my life to words and meanings. If my absurdist conjecture was true, then this would be the equivalent of hell for me."

"Hell on a bus? This is hell?" Felix asked. He hadn't thought about that possibility. Now it became his turn to get upset. There were things that Felix had done in his life that he wasn't proud of, and Catholic tradition wasn't particularly kind to sinners. Besides, there was no truer hell for him than any place where his lost love wasn't.

"This ride . . . this infernal ride has both of us undone," the priest reflected. "Let us talk about more pleasant things instead. I . . . I myself love to read. Do you like to read, my young friend?"

"Sometimes," Felix answered fitfully. "Business books on my tablet mostly. It's more convenient to read them in the toilet that way."

"Touché," Father Vladimir said, suddenly tired beyond belief and without a single word to say.

The pair remained silent after that. Felix felt that his fellow passenger didn't really converse, he lectured. Father Vladimir lamented the decline of philosophy in an age of restless, clueless youth.

The young man looked out through the dark windows, searching for the moon or the stars, anything that would help him determine the passage of time. There was nothing in all directions but a desolate landscape, one that mirrored the hollowness in his soul. "Just take me away, my love," he whispered longingly, forgetting which saint reunited soul mates and lovers.

After a while, the oppressive monotony of the road began to affect Felix. Without the company of his wife or the distraction of his phone, his mind started to root for something to do. Eventually, he decided to move back towards his companion and brave another conversation.

"Father, you mentioned *Waiting for Godot* earlier. I saw that play in college. Isn't it the one about the two bums who wait for this guy who never shows? I remember it well."

"You do?" the old man said, his face suddenly lighting up. "*Godot* is a difficult work. Not everybody likes it. Why do you remember it?"

"My wife played one of the characters, the one called '*Lucky*'. I could never forget it."

"Is that so? Where is your wife now?" Fr. Vladimir asked.

Felix absentmindedly reached inside his bag. He squeezed the plastic with her shirt tenderly, before continuing in a pained, halting voice. "She died of leukemia a year ago. Her scent is still with me though."

He pulled out the precious, shrink-wrapped relic and showed it to the priest. "It's like I've vacuum packed her ghost."

"Oh, I am so sorry to hear that, son," Fr. Vladimir said sadly, "and I am sorry for intruding on your personal life again."

"No, it's all right," Felix said. "I do like talking about her. It keeps her memory alive. Her life was all about that—keeping memories alive. She was an ethnolinguist, you see. After we came back from the US, we traveled around the provinces collecting stories from indigenous tribes. She had wanted to record them all, before they faded away forever."

"That is a worthy endeavor," Fr. Vladimir said solemnly. "Oral traditions are important, and they must be preserved."

"That's what she always told me," the young man went on. "She used to dream about a giant computer bank somewhere in the clouds. It was a place where she could store all these dying stories. In my own dreams, my wife keeps asking me to come and find her. I guess in a way, I've been doing that ever since."

"I have heard of such places," the priest whispered, "at least in literature."

"Anyway, going back to Beckett," Felix continued, somewhat embarrassed he had revealed so much. "I was thinking about what you told me regarding synchronicity. I don't think it's a coincidence that I'm in a situation that's just like the only play I can remember. I believe there's some greater design at work here. In the tribal stories my wife collected, there's always a man that goes on a quest to the land of the dead. Father, what if this wasn't coincidence, but synchronicity?"

"That's . . . not how it works. How do you know," the priest asked, "that you aren't only looking at what you're looking for? Besides, these Orpheus-type stories always end up in tragedy. Haven't you suffered enough? She's dead, my son. Let her go."

"I can't do that, Father," the young man said, turning towards the darkness. "I have nothing but my faith left. I'm scared out of my mind, but I have faith that this bus is where I need to be right now. I also have faith that I will find my beloved Dolores again, no matter how long it takes me."

"'*Dolores*', what a lovely name," Fr. Vladimir noted thoughtfully. "It means '*sorrow*' in Spanish, and your name '*Felix*' means '*happy*' in Latin. Happiness is searching for Sorrow. That is all so tragically poetic."

Felix said nothing more and excused himself. He couldn't tell if the priest was being sympathetic or condescending. He grabbed his messenger bag and moved again to the rear of the bus. After he sat down, he took out his phone once more and removed the battery. He warmed it in his hands, praying to St. Jude to give him one last burst of power. He returned the battery to his phone and hit the power button. It was still dead.

The bus continued on in the darkness. There were no other stops.

After their third cycle of sleep, Felix finally saw something that looked like a destination, a gigantic tower looming in the distance. As they got closer, he realised that it looked oddly familiar. In fact, it looked exactly like something from his childhood prayer books, a picture of the Tower of Babel.

"Incredible!" Fr. Vladimir exclaimed. "It is Brueghel the Elder's painting come to life!"

The digital signboard above the driver flashed three times. The words changed from *"Non-Stop"* to *"The Infinite Library"*. Finally, the bus passed through the building's soaring gates and came to a halt near a low parking garage. There, a group of monkeys were waiting with a notice board. The sign read: *"Welcome Father Vladimir of Estragon, SJ—Semiotician, Philosopher, and Dream Bibliographer"*.

"I guess this is our stop," the priest said cautiously.

"Father, those monkeys are dressed like people," Felix said. "Who are they? What are they? What is this place?"

"Hmmm . . . our bus says we are at a place called the Infinite Library," Fr. Vladimir ventured.

"Those creatures, they seem to be expecting you," Felix said. A pang of suspicion began to gnaw at his mind. "Did you know that we were headed here?"

"This is as much a surprise to me as it is to you, my son," the old man answered. "But as it happens, I do know where we are. I first read about this place a very long time ago, when I was but a child. My family had a complete set of the *Anglo-American Cyclopaedia*. It was all there, in a thick volume for the letter *'I'*, along with *'India'*, *'Idiom'*, and the *'Immaculate Conception'*. I remember that the *'Infinite Library'* is where all that has ever been written and all that will ever be writ has been recorded and preserved for all eternity. If that's true, I cannot wait to step inside."

The LED display flashed three times before changing to *"Please wait for the Return Bus"*. All the lights powered down, and the driver stepped out for a smoke. It was then that Felix realised that the man on the wheel was almost skeletally thin, a shadow of death himself.

The leader of the monkeys boarded the bus and greeted them in perfect, if archaic, English, one pregnant with meaning and epic formality. He extended an invitation for the old man to visit the library.

"I must follow my guides," Fr. Vladimir said, collecting his luggage.

"What about me?" Felix asked. Though he was terrified of the strange creatures, the young man refused to be left alone in the dark. "You can't leave me, Father, please."

"You chose Option 2, did you not? That means you have a return ticket. Just wait for the bus to be ready," the priest reminded him. "My son, I'm afraid that your grief is still very much in a state of denial. Your beloved wife is gone. This is not your story; go back to the real world. Find yourself someone else. Don't let your tale end in tragedy."

"No. There must be a reason I was brought here," Felix insisted. "Take me with you, please. Someone here may know how to find Dolores."

"Well . . . I don't see any reason why I shouldn't," Fr. Vladimir said, turning to ask the monkeys for permission. "However, if you miss your bus, you may not be able to go back."

"I'll take my chances," the young man insisted.

"It's a fair bet," the priest said. "In a place like this where only infinities matter, I suppose your bus can wait indefinitely."

They stepped into the library together. The interior was even more massive than the building itself, with endless rows of galleries and hallways that seemed to extend all the way to the clouds. Each gallery, in turn, was connected by a multitude of pillars and spiral staircases that linked everything together into a gigantic labyrinth of knowledge.

Felix noted that each hall and gallery had a brass nameplate over its entranceway. He did a quick survey and read some labels at random: *"English 51st Century Fiction"*, *"Flash Fiction"*, *"Algorithms and Equations"*, *"Internet Memes"*, *"19th Century Erotica"*, *"Maps and Cartographic Materials"*, *"Songs and Song Lyrics"*. He could not find any sign for an Oral Traditions section. He tried to ask directions from the monkey guides, but each creature pointed to a different doorway.

Their motley group walked across to the central rotunda where each of the halls for the living languages radiated like spokes. Their group stepped into a mirror-like portal, and suddenly, the signs in the library changed. Instead of language families, the two of them now passed row upon row of galleries dedicated to individual authors. Fr. Vladimir stopped by the entrance to one of these collections, a doorway with a brass plate that read *"The Works of Karl Rahner"* and spoke to one of the librarians.

Felix wondered where the priest's own writings were located. From his companion's great eloquence, he imagined that it would be a huge gallery. He tried to ask the librarian a few questions, but he seemed only interested in theological polemic. The strange man barely even acknowledged his presence.

Felix left the gallery and began to wander aimlessly through the labyrinth. Everywhere there were strangely dressed ghosts, impossible creatures and all manner of anthropomorphic beings. Above the central hallway, a conference of birds flew round and round, twittering silently: *"Manasu marugudhey, kanavu uruguthey. My heart bleeds, my dreams are shattered . . ."*

"What does it mean?" he wondered.

Eventually, he came across the room that housed Fr. Vladimir's work. Unlike Rahner's numerous lexicons, this collection consisted of only one bookshelf. There was a thick encyclopedia of dreams and various books on Faith and Theodicy, as well as many slim folios investigating Liturgy, Charity, and the importance of Sacrifice. He noticed that for some reason, there was not a single volume on Love. Felix wondered if the old priest had ever known true love in his life.

He stepped into another mirror-like door and found that the hallway signs had changed to modes of communication. Felix found himself in a gallery called *"The Cradle of Literature"*, where to his delight, there were hundreds of music players laid out neatly on the tables. He picked through the gramophones, Walkmans, iPods, and strange listening devices that looked like quivering crystals, until he saw one whose power source was compatible with his phone. He pried the back cover open and removed the battery.

Just then, a librarian came out of a side door and accosted him. "Sir, you are not allowed to do that," she said. The young woman looked into the intruder's face, and her eyes widened in stunned recognition. "Oh my God," she whispered. "You found me."

For what seemed like an eternity, Felix and the librarian just stared at each other, not stirring, not talking, for fear that the other might suddenly disappear like a dream. They stood apart, separated by an asymptotic space, as if they could not touch each other without shattering.

Finally, his heart could bear no more, and the young man jumped towards his lost love. He gathered her in his strong arms. "Dolor," he cried softly. "I've missed you so much."

No words or explanations were needed. The two remained locked in an embrace, cocooned in the library's strange twilight, when Father Vladimir and the bus driver found them.

"I am truly sorry to break you up," the priest said, "but I am told that Felix has to go back now."

"Can I stay, please?" he begged the bus driver. But the skeletal man just shook his head, face impassive as chalcedony as he pointed a bony hand towards the exit. Felix felt a shiver that chilled him to the marrow.

"Father, help me! We can't lose each other again," Felix cried, his tears now freely flowing. He got down on his knees and took the priest's hand. He whispered a silent prayer to his favorite, St. Jude, and to St. Raphael, whom he now remembered to be the real patron of soul mates and lovers. His mind composed a desperate canticle to his beloved saints, calling for their intercession and the compassion of their sacred thaumaturgies. "You said my story shouldn't end in tragedy," he said to Fr. Vladimir. "You have the power to change that."

The priest heaved a deep sigh and looked away into the distance. He seemed suddenly older, a man filled with the melancholy regret that came with age. "Have you seen my gallery?" he asked. "It's not as big as I'd hoped. I suppose I still have much work to do before they compare me to Rahner. Right now, I feel like that Kiev cake we ate on the bus, all filling and no substance. After watching you and your wife here, maybe I should go back and write about Love."

Father Vladimir held onto the young man's hand, contemplating the fragility of existence and the resilience of lovers.

"It's *my* story that's not yet complete." He said finally, "Give me your ticket, son."

Felix wiped the tears from his eyes and fished the bus card from his pocket. He picked up the battery he had dropped and slipped it into his phone. It turned on with a full charge.

"This is a multi-band satellite phone," he said, as he handed it to the priest. "Wherever you are in the world, it will pick up the nearest signal. You should be able to call for help. Thank you. Thank you so much!"

"I am a man of the cloth and a soldier to St. Ignatius. To give and not to count the cost is our motto," Fr. Vladimir declared. "Besides, what fool will not do this for true love? That trumps all religions and philosophies. Your Godot has come, my son. I must go and find mine."

As he was about to leave, the old man started chuckling out of character. He turned back towards Felix and said: "Do you know why your batteries ran out? You had your music playing in a nonstop loop."

"Yes, I know, Father. I forgot to switch it off," Felix answered. "I think I was listening to The Police."

"How prescient," Fr. Vladimir mused, as he read out the album's name from the music player: *"Synchronicity"*.

BIG ENOUGH FOR THE ENTIRE UNIVER/E

DAY 2—20:00 HOURS: SOMEWHERE IN A BUKIT GOMBAK
MILITARY INSTALLATION

"Love is like earth," Madame Semangat said softly, as she adjusted her tudong and drew her thin shawl closer. The impromptu medical exam had left her visibly shaken. "She said you need to cultivate it constantly to grow anything."

"Is that it?" asked the investigating officer, a thin Peranakan man who wore a crisp, olive-drab uniform and a pair of thick, black-rimmed glasses.

"No," the woman continued. "She said that having a family was like growing a garden. Then she asked me what I would do if my garden was destroyed."

"What did you say?"

"I said that plants could be grown from seeds. Life comes from tiny beginnings. I would simply begin again."

"When did you have this conversation?"

"A few months ago," the primary school teacher replied. "She wrote that note about love and family on a Post-it and left it on my door, along with a small plant as a gift."

Madame Semangat was anxious to finish the interview. She gave her inquisitor a long, pleading look then quickly changed the subject. "Please officer, my family doesn't know anything. Please, let us go home."

"How well did you know her?" he asked, ignoring her small protests, looking instead at the long list of questions on his tablet. "What kind of person was Madame Xīn?"

"She was . . . a very private person. She hardly spoke to anyone after the accident," the woman recalled. Her voice had become very small and defeated. "When can I see my husband and my children? Are they all right? My youngest will need milk, and my husband needs his medications."

"They are undergoing medical evaluation in the other rooms. Not to worry, their needs will be attended to," he answered coldly. "How often did you talk to each other?"

"Not often, mostly when she watered her plants in the common corridor. Although, to be honest, she talked to them more than she ever spoke to us. Still, she was nice enough I suppose, especially on the birthday of her boy. She would give my children rice cakes and watermelon seeds. Or was it lotus seeds? I don't remember right now."

"Did you know what kind of work she did?"

The woman ignored the officer. "When can we go back home, officer? My children will be very frightened without me."

Madame Semangat tried unsuccessfully to appeal to the officer's sympathy. She looked at the expressionless young man in front of her and decided that he would not make a good father.

"Did they . . . did they find her body yet?"

"I do not have that information," he noted mechanically. "We will let you know when your family can move back to your unit."

"*Inna lillahi wa inna ilahi raji'un!*" she exclaimed, bowing her head. "We all belong to Allah, and to him we will all return."

"Did you know what kind of work she did?" he repeated.

"I thought she had a job in IT. Why?"

The middle-aged Muslim woman had grown tired of the long inquiry and began to get agitated. She tore the questionnaire she had been given into small, evenly sized pieces and piled them into a white mound. "Please, we were just neighbours. We don't know anything. My husband has diabetes, he cannot *tahan* this stress. We just want to go home."

"Just a few more questions," he said more gently. "Please be patient. Did you ever notice anything strange or unusual about her?"

"Have you seen her plants?" she exclaimed unexpectedly. "I teach science to primary three students, and I can tell you that it is impossible for them to grow in Singapore."

"Which plants are those?"

"Love-lies-bleeding, bleeding heart vines, love-in-the-mist, and her favorite, a beautiful purple hyacinth called *Lost Love*. So strange and . . . *poetic*, I think that's best word to describe them."

"You said she gave you a plant with the Post-it note. What was it?"

"Oh, she called it a *Resurrection Plant*, something you'll never find at a *pasar malam*. It looked like a little brown ball when she brought it to our door. She told me that, if I placed it in a bowl with some water, it would come back to life—and it did. It was so amazing. The dead plant actually turned green again."

"Did she ever tell you what she was working on?"

"Do you mean what she was doing in that awful room?" Madame Semangat said, recalling disturbing scenes she had seen from their corridor—heavy boxes being dragged, things lying under white sheets.

But she was unsure if these had meant anything sinister. Madame Xīn had always seemed so nice. Her voice betrayed her nervous uncertainty. "No, I don't think so."

"Are you sure?"

"Yes . . . no, I mean, yes. Double confirm, officer, yes, double confirm," she repeated nervously. "But, you know, I always felt that, without her family, she had *gone case*. Her eyes, there was nothing in her eyes but *sudah mati*, death."

"Did she ever talk to you about math or anything involving numbers or computer programming?"

"No. Not that I can recall. Why?"

"Joyce Xīn had a doctorate in advanced mathematics. Think hard, Madame Semangat," he insisted. "If you give me something I can use, perhaps we can all go home earlier."

The old teacher leaned back and scanned her memories.

Suddenly her eyes lit up with a surprise recollection. "Wait, yes, I do remember something. A few months after the accident, I remember now. I saw her wandering in the void deck looking confused. I've never seen her *blur like sotong* before; she was always such a clever woman. I walked her back to her flat, and she said the oddest thing. *'Do you know what an algorithm is, Rauddah? It's a step-by-step procedure for calculating numbers, a formula,'* she said. *'Life is made up of numbers, Rauddah,'* she kept telling me. *'People are made of numbers, all of us. Perhaps I can recreate them using an algorithm, Rauddah.'* She said that or something like that. That's all I remember, officer, truly."

"Thank you, Madame Semangat."

"May we please go home now?" she insisted. "I need to see my family."

"I'm afraid we have a situation at your HDB. Your family will have to be relocated for your own safety."

"What? What is the emergency?"

"Let me show you," he said, tapping a video app on his tablet.

DAY 2—22:00 HOURS: SOMEWHERE IN A BUKIT GOMBAK MILITARY INSTALLATION

"Yes, she said something like that. How did you know?"

"What did she say, Madame Shén? What exactly did she say?"

"It's *Miss* Shén," the thin, bespectacled woman corrected him. "I was divorced last year. That *chee ko pek*—that pervert left me for his student intern. She's less than half his age. I should have known when we stopped sleeping together. All men are *buaya*, no offense. I go by '*Miss*' now."

"Okay, let's stay on topic, Ms. Shén, shall we?" To calm her down, the officer enunciated his words slowly, as if he was talking to a small child. "What did Dr. Xīn tell you?"

"She said that '*Love was like air; without it you cannot breathe.*' What garbage. Her brain is spoil after the accident."

"Did she say anything else?"

"Afterwards she said that Alan was like air to her. He was her spirit, her '*breath of life*' she said. Everyone with kids would forgive her, she kept repeating. I had Sanjeev, she said I would understand. She just *talk cock*, lah. "

"When did she tell you this?"

"My son used to play with her boy," she narrated. "They used to play every day on the void deck. He was a nice one, very polite, not like other kids. His name was Alan. He used to help my boy Sanjeev with his maths homework. I was too busy at work, never had time to tutor him. Have you ever been a single parent? *Aiyoh*, so hard, I tell you, and all these idiots at my office, always making *sabo* . . ."

"Ms. Shén, you are off-topic again."

"Sorry. Anyway, after their accident, Sanjeev would keep knocking on their door. He looked for Alan every day. It was embarrassing *lor,* he *dun* understand, my poor boy. I guess I was neglecting him. All he knew was that his father was gone, and now his playmate was gone *oso*. I never did tell him why I left his *lan jiao* of a father . . ."

"Let's go back to what Dr. Xīn said, please," the officer repeated. Beads of frustration had started to form on his brow.

"Sorry. It happened during a school holiday. Sanjeev was still missing Alan. He ran to knock on her door again. I came out to apologize to Dr. Xīn. Poor girl. She just stood by the metal grating, drinking something *chao*, and talking nonsense. That's when she told me that thing about love. I knew she *gone case* already. "

"Are you familiar with Dr. Xīn's work?"

"She was involved in maths—correct or not? I think it was something with computers. I sat next to her during our MP's last visit."

"Have you ever been inside her house?"

"Of course not, *meh*; the windows were always covered. But I peek through the door a few times. Everything was ordinary, like my house, except for the wires on the floor."

"Wires?"

"Yah *lah*," Ms. Shén explained, "wires everywhere, covering everything."

"What did you think was going on inside?"

"*Aiyoh*, I am not *kaypoh*," she said, getting irritated by the questions and her interviewer's droning monotone. "I mind my own business, okay? Not like that whore in 42-D. That one, *aiyoh*, when her *ang moh* boyfriend come over, no one on our floor can sleep!"

"Do you know anything about what's in Dr. Xīn's bedroom?"

"Eh, how I know?" she grumbled as she fumbled for a cigarette in her handbag.

"I'm sorry, you cannot smoke here," the officer said. "So you have no idea what was happening?"

Ms. Shén muttered something under her breath. It sounded like a really crude word for fornication in Hokkien. She decided that the man in front of her was an officious asshole.

"You cannot hold us," the woman continued, tapping her hands nervously on the plastic base of her chair. "We've done nothing, what? I demand to see my boy!"

"Answer all my questions, and we will return him to your custody," he offered. "Now, when did the power start fluctuating in your unit?"

"*Wahlao*, ask Singapore Power!" she exclaimed, unleashing bile peculiar to those born in the year of the wind-dragon. Ms. Shén closed her eyes and imagined whacking the officer with a big stick. "I don't know, six months ago? Everyone complain, nothing happen. My boy, ah, he naughty sometimes. He opened one of her bills by mistake. I saw the SP one—she was paying more than $4,000 a month for power. You mean the *gahmen* never notice that?"

"The government does not keep track of people's bills, Ms. Shén. But, thank you, that information may be useful."

"I want my son!" she cried, as her false bravado started to crumble. "I cannot *tahan* this anymore. We want to go home."

"We will release your boy soon," the officer said, in the puerile tone of someone hiding deep secrets. "But you cannot go home. Not yet."

"Why not, ah?" she screamed, releasing another stream of colourful Hokkien invectives. The biting words seemed to hang around the room like fine soot.

The investigating officer pressed something on his tablet and showed Ms. Shén the images on the screen.

"This is a live feed of what's happening at your block," he said.

The woman glanced over the top of her spectacles and stared at the moving pictures in disbelief. Her eyes widened, and her jaw dropped. For a full sixty seconds, no words would form in her mouth.

The gravity of the situation hit her like a car crash.

"Wha . . . what is that?" she muttered. "It's so big and so . . . so *chim*."

"Now you understand why we are extremely cautious," he said quietly.

Ms. Shén collapsed into a heap on the swiveling office chair. "She worked with numbers. I'm an accountant. I work with numbers too, ah. How can numbers be dangerous?"

"We are all just pieces of information," mumbled the officer, a former IT specialist, as he, too, was caught up in the tablet's disturbing images, ". . . and all information can be processed."

DAY 3—00:00 HOURS: SOMEWHERE IN A BUKIT GOMBAK MILITARY INSTALLATION

"What is your relationship with Mr. Borges?" the officer asked.

The painted woman adjusted her too-short skirt and tried to hide her legs under the interrogation table. She looked around the holding room and noticed that everything was grey—the carpet, the table, the chairs, and even the mirrors on the right wall. She decided that the glass was double-sided, just like the television procedurals, and moved her legs towards the opposite direction.

"He's my fiancé," she answered curtly. "Where is George? Are we under arrest?"

"You are both here for your own protection, Ms. Ài," the officer explained calmly. "As I said earlier, we need to ask you a few questions."

"I need a shower," the woman said, removing a piece of grey slime that had stained her thin, sarong-party-girl dress. "Why are we being held? I demand to be released now. Your medical exam was humiliating, and my mascara is running."

"Just answer a few more questions, and we will see what we can do," the officer said, handing her a packet of tissues. "How do you know Dr. Xīn?"

"She lives two doors down from me, at 42-B," she answered brusquely. "My parents know her better, but they're in Perth for the next six months."

"Are you familiar with her work?"

"I only knew she was some kind of math genius," the young woman said, making small irritated noises. She looked at her chipped nails and mentally added a manicure to her list of must-do items. "I thought hotshot IT folks were paid well. What's she doing living in an HDB?"

"Your block is in an executive HDB. It's like a condominium."

"I know that," the woman snapped, as she cleared the dark smear from her eye-bags. "I live there."

"Do you know anything about the programs she was working on?"

The young woman stared at her interviewer with wild, dagger eyes. Just a few hours ago, she and her boyfriend had come from a hot date, and she had been looking forward to another night of steamy lovemaking. They had been walking along the corridor, in front of Dr. Xīn's flat, when it—for lack of a better word—exploded. A quick response team hauled them from the slimy rubble and brought them to Bukit Gombak in separate vehicles. There, a team of faceless doctors examined her, took samples of the slime, and brought her to a holding room where she had waited hours for someone to talk to.

This was not how things happened in movies, she thought. She was a Singaporean citizen. She had voted for the ruling party. This was not how she should be treated.

"No, I have no idea. I have absolutely no effing idea what's going on!" she cried, wanting to throw a chair at her infuriatingly calm interviewer. "Where is George? Is he alive? Where is my phone? Where is my bag? It's a Louis Vuitton!"

"Mr. Borges is alive, and like you, he seems surprisingly unharmed," the officer noted. "He is being interviewed in another room. We did not find your things when we rescued you under all that err . . . techno-organic matter."

"I just want to go home! I already told the police and the SCDF what happened," she demanded, deciding that her officious interviewer had tiny reproductive organs. "Who do I have to talk to, to go home?"

The officer pulled out his tablet and showed Ms. Ài the live video feed from her HDB block.

The young woman stared at the screen with a bewildered look. She leaned back against the swivel chair, stunned into silence.

"May I have some water, please?" she said finally. "I don't understand. Is that real? What is that . . . thing?"

"We don't know," the officer said grimly. "But it's growing exponentially. It now covers three whole blocks. We may have to evacuate the whole of Bukit Batok. We need to find a way to stop this, Ms. Ài, please."

"It," she stuttered, "it probably has my mom's LV. Shit."

Another officer entered the room and brought a plastic cup filled with water.

"Let's try this again," he said. "Are you familiar with Dr. Xīn's work?"

"Not really," she said, knowing that this was only a half-truth. A mental polemic raged in her head. "How can I share what I know?" she thought, "Without destroying my relationship?" Her fiancé George had gone to visit his parents in Argentina for two weeks. That was too long a time for her to go without sex, and Ms. Ài had decided she needed a substitute.

Dr. Xīn had an assistant, a programmer from Manila who helped her with her strange machines. Ms. Ài had met him in the lift, and she invited him for a drink. She usually preferred potatoes to rice, but the little brown college boy was cute, and she treated the whole affair as charity work.

"You need to find this Filipino guy, Ghabby Marquez," she said. "He's a student at the National University. He moonlights as her assistant, and I . . . I have something else to tell you."

The officer scribbled the name on his tablet and excused himself for a minute. She resumed her story when he returned to the holding room.

"One day, I passed her doorway, and the gate was open," Ms. Ài continued. "She was standing there, reeking of whiskey. She spoke to me with that cold, dead voice of hers—*'You play with fire, girl.'* She said, *'Love is like fire; it burns you until you are consumed and there is nothing left. You are in the chicken business, selling meat, not love.'* I got scared and ran back towards my flat. She'd called me an effing prostitute."

"This Mr. Marquez, did he tell you what they were working on inside?"

"Yes, but I didn't believe him."

"Why, what was it?"

"He said they were writing an algorithm for the soul."

DAY 3—06:00 HOURS: SOMEWHERE IN A BUKIT GOMBAK MILITARY INSTALLATION

"Will I get deported?" the young man asked.

"That is a matter for immigration to sort out," the interrogating officer answered. "Now, Mr. Marquez . . ."

"Please, Mr. Marquez is my father," the student insisted. "Call me Ghabby."

"Okay . . . *Ghabby*. Tell me everything once again."

"Wait, I need you to know that I only took this job because my mother is sick," the young man explained, staring at his open palms. "My family is poor, and I needed to remit money every month for her treatment."

"Tell me about the monkeys again," the officer prodded, pointing a video camera towards Ghabby's direction. "You said that the source code came to her in a dream. Try to remember every detail."

"But I already told you everything."

"Please repeat it for the camera and try to remember everything she told you."

"But it was just her dream," the young man insisted. "Why are you taking it seriously? It doesn't even make sense to me."

"What's out, there right now is what makes no sense. We need to figure this out, and you are our only lead. Let's do this again, please?"

"Yes, sir." Ghabby nodded nervously. The camera's dark lens reminded him of the evil eye. Subconsciously, he made the sign of the cross.

"Like I told you, Dr. Xīn's family died in a car accident. She told me that, a few weeks after they were buried, she had this really strange dream. She wrote it down in her journal; maybe you can find it among her things."

"You were telling me about this dream?" the officer repeated.

"For a while, please, for a while," Ghabby said, wiping off sweat from his sideburns. "Sorry. Umm . . . it went something like this:

I found myself wandering an enormous library, which was as big as the universe itself. It looked something like a honeycomb or a warren, made up of an infinite number of identical galleries, separated by vast airspaces and connected by an innumerable number of staircases.

I wandered aimlessly for what seemed like months or years, marveling at how every book I ever read and every book I ever imagined could be found among its shelves. In the impossibly huge centre of each gallery, I saw a huge beacon of light, which for some reason reminded me of a lighthouse—a celestial beacon to the heavens.

At some point, I found a gallery different from all the others. It was painted crimson instead of black and was as large as the entire library itself.

Inside were an infinite number of monkeys, each one hitting the keys of a typewriter which filled endless reams of paper. Running between each row were even more monkeys, gathering the discarded sheets. The runners were wearing little shirts, each embroidered with the word 'inquisitor'.

One of the monkeys looked quite familiar. He was a stocky, big-eared creature who looked just like a miniature English college don. In fact, he looked like my favorite mathematician Alan Turing— the man I named my son after. I called him out, and the other monkeys told me that he was the leader of their troupe.

'I am Translucia Baboon,' he told me. 'I can provide any text that can possibly ever be written, no matter what the length, no matter what the language.'

I explained to him that math was a language and that an algorithm was just like any piece of text. I challenged him to write a code that would recreate my family. I asked him for the equation for life and the algorithm for creating souls.

The universe wasn't big enough for my pain, I told him. I wanted to plant a new seed. I needed to begin again."

A high-pitched cry interrupted Ghabby's story. The plaintive sound was so loud and forceful that it shattered all the windows in the complex. (Later on, the young man would discover that it had in fact shattered every window in Singapore.)

"What was that? There's something happening outside. Shouldn't you be trying to do something?"

"Whatever it is, I'm sure we are already addressing it," the officer answered in his usual manner, without haste and with great care. "Now, keep calm, and let's carry on. Did you see the source code?"

"What's wrong with you?" The young man began to get upset and started to raise his voice. "That sounded like . . . I don't know, that sounded like someone giving birth."

"Let's focus shall we?" the officer repeated. "Again, did you see the source code, Mr. Marquez?"

"Yeah, she gave me a weird code that came from her dream. I had to translate it into machine language," the young man answered, tugging at his hair nervously. "Basically, it was a set of simple reaction–diffusion equations for pattern formation. But I never had access to her bedroom or the machines she kept there. I was only allowed to use the test servers."

"Can you recreate what she did?"

"Only the parts that I worked on."

"What did you think you were doing in there?"

"I'm just an exchange student, sir," Ghabby sighed, deciding that the officer was probably a robot, a machine that had no soul. "I needed money, so I responded to her ad for a part-time programmer. I don't really know what she was doing. She never gave me the full picture."

"Filipinos are a generally nosy folk," the officer said, somewhat offensively. "I cannot believe that you were never curious about your employer."

"I was, at the start," the young man sighed, looking down at his shaking palms once again, "especially when I saw the freezers in the bedroom. Anyway, Dr. Xīn rarely spoke about personal things . . . except, I guess, on birthdays or special occasions. She told me about the monkeys on the anniversary of her family's death. The money was good, so I didn't want to rock the boat. My mother has lung cancer. I swear I didn't know the doctor was doing something illegal."

"Is that everything you can tell me?"

"Well, she kept on repeating something the last time I saw her."

"What was she repeating?"

" '*Love is like water*', she said. '*It always seeks its own level. Nothing can stop it.* '"

DAY 3—13:00 HOURS ONWARDS: BUKIT BATOK AND VARIOUS LOCALES IN SINGAPORE

After being released by the authorities, Ghabby G. Marquez, Filipino exchange student, devout Catholic, and world-class hacker, went to Geylang and decided to blow his mother's chemo money on a prostitute. His grim situation had given him an undiscovered thirst for life.

Ms. Ài and her fiancé Mr. Borges were given a change of ill-fitting clothes and dropped off at Holland Village. There, in front of a store that specialized in wedding bands, they had a major fight and called off their engagement. In the many hours she was kept in the quiet of the holding room, Ms. Ài had sorted out her life and reordered her priorities. Now it was time to burn bridges. She called an aunt and borrowed money for a ticket to Australia. She left that very same evening.

In the meantime, Mr. Borges went to a nearby pub and drank himself under the table. When he finally sobered up, he joined the long queue of expats desperate to leave Singapore. There would be no more flights available.

Ms. Shén collected her son Sanjeev and fled with him to her parents' flat in Hougang. There, in an HDB estate where the lifts failed to operate properly, they waited for their fate. Oddly, the harrowing experience had released all of her pent-up bitterness. She realised that her divorce had made her most scared of being scared—scared of loneliness, scared of pain, scared of losing control after building a life with someone else. Now, in the face of imminent apocalypse, it somehow didn't matter.

For the first time in over a year, she was able to breathe a sigh of relief. She sat her young son on his bed and finally told him why she had left his father.

On that same afternoon, Madame Semangat and her family cashed in their life savings. They went to the West Coast Car Mall and bought a cheap secondhand van, stocking it with new clothes and groceries. After a hurried meal at a Malay cooked food stall, they drove towards her family's relatives in Johor.

There, next to the house where her grandmother was born, she and her family started a vegetable garden. She could not explain to them the hows and the whys, but she knew that Bukit Batok's creeping destruction meant that the world they knew was ending and that something new was taking its place.

At exactly 13:00 hours on the third day of the crisis, the special agent overseeing the witnesses sat alone in his cold, featureless room. A murder of crows flew across his small screen, and the officer felt that he had seen enough. He shut off the video feed and rubbed his tired eyes.

He went to the bathroom and sat in the stall to think. Everyone in the office had been sent out on a mission or had already fled. He thought of going home as well, but there was no one to go home to.

After half an hour of ruminating, the officer returned to his room. He pulled up a browser window to check Dr. Xīn's blog, *The Fake Timaeus*, and read her last post from three days ago:

"Love is the demiurge that builds substance from the elements of our lives."

He dwelt on these, her last words, and thought about his own meaning and purpose in the universe. He tried to think of a word that described his life, but the only thing that would come to mind was an old UNIX command—/dev/null, a special file that discarded all data written to it.

He opened his dossier and scrolled through the transcripts, reading passages that caught his eye.

"Love is like earth; you need to cultivate it constantly to grow anything."

"Love is like air; without it, you cannot breathe."

"Love is like fire; it burns you until you are consumed and there is nothing left."

"Love is like water; it always seeks its own level. Nothing can stop it."

Haunted by a dark animus he could not fathom, the promising young officer took out his service pistol and—without haste and with great care—shot himself in the head.

Outside, just a short train ride from the secret military complex, a giant blob of grey goo in the shape of a human heart was expanding slowly but relentlessly over everything. Inside were millions and millions of rapidly evolving nanobots, programmed to consume and rebuild the entirety of creation.

With every heartbeat, the nanobots replicated a mother's unconditional and infinite love—a love big enough to contain death and the entire universe itself.

ENTANGLEMENT

Months later, I can still see you from the corners of my eyes, stray pixels of your face burned into my retinas, fragile and cruel as ghosts. I can't sleep. I can't eat. I sit all day drawing, painting, doodling, clawing your memory on every surface, every canvas, every wall. If I stop, you'll disappear forever, and I don't think I could carry on.

I don't trust my memory. I don't trust myself.

∞

"I loved that book." That was the first thought you placed in my head, as I sat reading Borges' *The Maker* on the brick perimeter of Blumberg Library.

"I . . . I love this book too," I stammered, startled by your sudden appearance. Back then, you had absolutely no clue how desirable you were. You had no idea just how many people were looking—hunting—for someone like you, for someone *exactly* like you.

But, shit, you came to me first. You were gathered so tightly then, bursting with righteous possibility, like a thundercloud. Yet there was something oddly vulnerable about your presence. Something about you was both there and not-there, something a preacher would've called *'immanent'*.

You had the most oceanic eyes I'd ever imagined.

"Sorry, do we know each other?" you asked, staring at me like a lost calf stares at a new gate. Your eyes, your sweet almond eyes, were the

first thing I ever made. I willed them into existence with a word, and they were there, like magic.

"My favorite story in this book is *El Testigo* . . . *The Witness*," I said, suddenly confident, hoping that would get your attention. "I saw you first. I can help you, please. Anyone can tell you I'm really dependable. Trust me."

In my mind's eye, I never saw you as the shapeless mass of energy that you were, or a lost ghost made from uncertain, unsettled numbers. Through the human eyes I made for you, I could see the power of infinity—of absolute and utter potential—and I knew I could hew your rawness into a true shape.

But on that first meeting, no amount of my deliberate and studied gazing could induce you to entanglement. I remember that you just looked at me strangely, saying nothing. Instead, you drifted away, tracing the edge of the building's perimeter.

"Wait!" I yelled, as I fumbled to collect my things. But you had already rounded the corner and disappeared. There was nothing in the distance but grass, a ragged patch of bluebonnets, and one of the janitor's calico cats. Somewhere beyond my sight, a train of big rigs rumbled on the I-10. It sounded almost like a storm was coming.

∞

I saw you again four days later. You were in front of the mathematics department at Emma Frey Hall, staring at an empty bulletin board. Even back then, I knew you could be everything I ever wanted, everything I ever needed.

"Hello," I blurted nervously. I'd felt skittish again, like a long-tailed cat in a room full of rocking chairs. "Are you lost? Why are you looking at an empty bulletin board?"

"It's not empty," you said, pointing to a fragment of a poster by the Heart of Texas Country Music Association. I could barely make out the announcement for a Johnny Cash tribute. Only one song title, "Mean-Eyed Cat", was readable, and the last four digits of the ticketing line, 5-3-5-4.

As softly as a blackbird's wing, you whispered: *"Where I come from, that's a bad sign. It means that I am . . . coalescing . . . bleeding into one."*

"Johnny Cash is a bad sign? I suppose, he only wrote sad songs," I said. I was determined to learn more about you, to groom you for myself. "So where are you from? I've never seen you around campus."

"I guess you could say I am from Singapore," you murmured absent-mindedly. *"5-3-5-4 is very unlucky. In Cantonese, it sounds like 'neither dead nor alive'."*

"Did you just transfer recently? I can't believe I hadn't noticed you before," I said carefully, trying not to be distracted by your ethereal form and your beautifully endless eyes. "I'm an American-born Chinese myself. I thought I knew all the Asian kids at school. Dang, I would've definitely noticed a fresh freshasaurus like you."

"Do you like cats?"

"Err . . . yeah, I love cats. I have one at home. Why?" I was amused by your attempt at misdirection.

"Cats dislike change without their consent. I think we end when I follow a cat."

"So did you have a cat where you're from, um . . . Singapore, right? Are you Singaporean Chinese?"

"No, I am Filipino Chinese," you said unexpectedly, confident of your mythology, *"but born in Singapore, raised in Singapore too."*

"So does that make you Singaporean or Filipino?"

"Both and neither, does it matter? I am like Schrödinger's cat."

"Yeah, well, in these parts, your identity's very important. I mean with the new immigration laws and everything," I said. "You are a gorgeous Chinese girl. You're now American and living in America. Let's fix on that before someone else is all over you."

"I am Filipino. I am Singaporean . . . I am confused," you told me, as your inner light started to dim. When you looked into my eyes, I knew I had your soul dead to rights. We were now entangled.

"Just listen to my voice," I repeated gently. Programming deep structures was about repetition, iteration, introjection. "You are a girl, a dang pretty one. You're also an ABC like me."

"I . . . I am a . . . I am a gorgeous Chinese girl. I am an American in America."

Truth to tell, I first thought you had Asperger's or some weird mental wallering going on. To deal with your baggage, the remains of your mind, was challenging. Yeah, you were quite the cattywhompus, playing your shattered angel bit very, very well. I guess it was your way to firewall me, to resist me, a smoke screen to keep your pretense of identity.

Too bad for you, I knew you were a blank slate, and I was *El Hacedor*, The Maker.

∞

The days stretched to weeks and then to months. Every time I saw you, we became closer. You became more fixed, more real. By nature, I was a loner, but your mystery drew me irresistibly towards you. I was addicted. I could never get enough of you.

Do you remember that special evening last July? We were walking by the abandoned railroad tracks, watching fireflies fool around the bluebonnets.

"I fear being forgotten," you told me, as we watched the cold yellow flashes appear and disappear into the darkness. *"No one remembers the fireflies of Singapore. They're not part of the program anymore."*

"What program?" I lied, trying to lose myself in your eyes once again. "You can trust me. I'm an English major, so the only program I know is Word."

"Then you can know me," you said. *"I am flesh turned into numbers, turned into words. But are you certain you are certain you want to know me?"*

"Hell yeah, I'm certain. You know, I've been wanting to . . . um . . . '*know*' you for months now."

That was the night you finally became a real girl, my perfect girl.

I led you to a quiet spot under an ancient live oak. Beneath branches dripping with Spanish moss, mistletoe, and resurrection ferns, we made love like cats in the night.

"What do you know about what happened to Singapore?" you asked, as we lay naked on the damp grass.

"Very little . . . I just read about it somewhere," I fudged, hoping my fictive chickens would never come to roost. I had to hold on to you, to the here and the now of you. God, how I quivered all over from the strange sensations we shared. Your hands, your body felt so . . . electric. I could hardly talk.

"I remember something about a nanotech incident; grey goo exploded on the island. I reckon a couple of million people died, serious shit."

"No, no one was killed," you told me cryptically. *"It was genocide by mathematical singularity. We were all turned into something . . . something else, numbers, equations, algorithms. An island of standing*

wave form . . . floating, drifting Hantu Raya, nanotech sprites moving in and out of time and space . . ."

"No need to think about that, my love," I said softly. I had never called you my love before. That night was the very first time. "Just stay with me. If you think too hard, you'll disappear. I'll be your physical memory. I *will* be your witness, girl. Be here, be real."

And for a while you did, and I was happy. We were happy.

∞

Then came Chinese New Year. Why did I ever bring you home with me? I kick myself every day for doing that. The night, that *damned* night, when we went home to 5354 Cat Spring Road was the worst one of my life.

Please understand, baby. I'm a proud American, but my parents are still Chinese. I am still Chinese. It's written all over my face, branded and burned into my genes. I can never erase it, not completely, even if I wanted to. You *know* that Reunion Dinner was just as important as Christmas, and I needed to bring my mother and father the perfect Chinese girl.

∞

And it had all gone so well, at least at the start. My folks loved you.

"Where is your cat?" you asked me after dinner. I pointed you to my black shorthair, Pruflas.

"His name, what does it mean?"

"Oh, that one's a game baddie from Ogre Battle 64. He's the demon of discord and falsehoods. I thought it was a cool name. Just call him '*Proof*' for short."

"It is a most appropriate name."

Why, oh why, did you follow my fool cat to my room? You should have waited for me, respected my privacy.

(Or maybe I should have remembered to tell Mother to hide my books away.)

- *The Dangers of Nanotechnology: The Singapore Grey Goo Disaster*
- *Big Enough for the Entire Universe—A Story of Lost Singapore*
- *A Computer for the Mind/An Algorithm for the Soul: Reconstructing the Work of Dr. Joyce Xīn*
- *80 Proven Techniques for Building Your Perfect Mate*
- *Creating Identity—A Hantu Raya Sprite Programming Manual*
- *The Dummies' Guide to Hunting Singapore Nanotech Sprites*
- *Reprogramming Singaporeans for Fun and Profit*
- *Possession, Ownership, and Rights of Digitized Humans*

Yeah, so you found me out. Yes, I lied. So sue me, beat me like a hired donkey, I don't care. I lied for love, and I'm proud of it. You know I would do it again and again and again.

But your milky face turned stormy. Your body flared so brightly, it burned out pixels from my eyes. Whenever I close them now, I see the cold ghost of fireflies, our fireflies; each one holds a fragment of your precious, perfect face.

"What have you done? You have reduced me to looking at myself through your eyes. This is not me at all. I must delete this form."

"Don't, please. I saw how alone you were. Do you really want to be alone again? Everyone in love creates the one they love, don't they? Don't they?" I challenged. I changed you, and you changed me."

Yet you ignored my pleas. How could you do that? You disregarded my feelings and collapsed into the amorphous blob of energy I first saw at Blumberg Library. God, how you made the air around us crackle with strange electricity. I remembered how scared I was when, in the distance, there came the low rumbling of thunder.

"You . . . you needed someone to anchor you to this world. I know you love me. You have to," I said, desperate to reattach to you. My hack was pole-axed, chomped, compromised. But still I persisted, still I held on to our tenuous umbilical cord of words. "I needed someone too. We both got something out of this. Did you know this was going to happen? How did you break my semantic encoding?"

I don't know who I am. I don't even know if I was a man or a woman, or if I was young or old. But I do remember random things. Before I was uploaded into the grey goo, I was in the middle of an identity crisis. Was I a Singaporean-Filipino or a Filipino-Singaporean? That was in my head when I 'died'. You cannot program over dissonance.

"But I love you. I'll just die without you. Stay with me, please. You'll be nothing without me, nothing again, you hear?"

"You pathetic man, this love was entirely your creation."

"Yeah, so I rewrote your history. So I reprogrammed your shell with my desires, so what? I truly love you. I can't live without you, not anymore. Don't you know we're entangled?"

"Then commit your version of me to memory. If you ever forget, the 'me' that you made will disappear forever. You said you would be my anchor, my witness. You are now El Testigo, *this form's eternal keeper."*

"But . . . honey, baby, does that mean if I keep remembering, you'll come back?"

"Perhaps," you said cruelly, as you disappeared back to infinity. *"I'm like Schrödinger's cat, a wave function, a supposition of probabilities. I am neither dead nor alive."*

Outside, in my parents' living room, an old radio began to wail a sad golden oldie. It was Johnny Cash singing "Mean-Eyed Cat".

∞

I haven't stopped crying since.

If I stop, if I forget, you'll disappear forever, and I . . . I don't think I could carry on.

THE OLD BLUE NOTEBOOK

She unlocks the door of your father's flat and motions you to come inside.

The landlady is mostly pleasant—sweet, yet subtle and reserved, like a stereotypical English grandmother. You realise you cannot tell where her shawl ends and where her cat begins. She leans toward you and assaults you with the smell of rosewater and cat feces. You raise a fist to your mouth to suppress a gag reflex. You really, really want to throw up, but you can't.

Instead you smile and say: "Thank you."

You had been to your father's quarters only once before, on the week his broken body was identified. Only, back then, you didn't know he was your father—just some distant Filipino relation who lived quietly in Hull and died a violent death.

You spent two hours and fifty-seven minutes on the National Rail because your great-aunt from Sheffield insisted you go. You remember wondering, why the bloody hell should you care? Who was this man who lived so utterly alone? Why did he leave his ancestral home in Pagbilao, only to die so far away from everyone and everything he knew?

You'd been sent to inspect his things and to find something of value—savings, investments, perhaps a deed to an exotic island property, anything that could be sold to defray the costs of his simple funeral.

You remember finding nothing of that sort. The flat was common and boring. No pictures, no bits 'n' bobs of sentiment or worth. Nothing but endless sheets filled with crude models of Dyson spheres, star charts, and linguistic analyses of dead languages with the most flawed Zecharia Sitchin/*Chariots of the Gods* methodology you've had the misfortune to read.

Nothing but the remains of a sad old man with bogus scientific obsessions.

Today, you want to look at his room with new eyes. He was, after all, your father. Every scrap was now a possible treasure; every leftover was pregnant with possibility. Perhaps there was a picture of you hidden in *Here Be Dragons*, a children's book you spied on his nightstand, or maybe there were some unsent letters at the bottom of that shagreen Shanghai valise he'd left by the door. You want to look through all the papers and charts you didn't bother to check the first time around. None of it had meant anything to you just two months ago. Now they were all you could think of.

To your dismay, the room was totally empty. You suddenly remember that the landlady had said as much over the phone. The men in the dark suits had taken everything during the inquest—every item that hadn't been nailed down. Somehow, what she said had not really registered. Not until now, at least.

In any case, you still had to come. You still had to see it for yourself. Idiot.

You close your eyes and look inwards. The people around you just couldn't understand how stumbling onto your roots made you feel so lonely. Your girlfriend was too obsessed with her mathematics dissertation to have a clue, and your superficial mates at work couldn't care less.

You long to tell the old woman how the inquest had shaken you to the core. You want to share with her how the coroner had required you to provide a DNA sample—something that told you more about yourself in a few days than your own family ever did during the last twenty-five years. You want to tell her that you now no longer speak to your great-aunt in Sheffield, nor to any of your mother's relatives.

Of course, what you'd really like to do is to pick a bone with your mother. You have a million different questions firing off in your head, but there was only one that really needed answering. Too bad your sainted mother had been dead for a very long time.

However, your father's landlady was alive and right here. Surely she must know something about him? After all, she was the one who told you about his old blue notebook.

"So you are really his son," the landlady says, stroking her bombinating cat. "I never pictured him with anyone, especially not with a proper English woman. No offence, off course. You look so normal."

"And so white," you want to add. Instead, you say something polite and reassuring. You want her to keep talking because you need information about the father you never knew.

Over time, you'd become quite inured to casual racism, especially the passive-aggressive kind. Strangely, you've always suspected it's because of that part of you that's indelibly Filipino.

Filipinos always could hide in plain sight.

"A son needs to have something of his father. Especially since you are also a linguist," she whispers over tea (as if worried that the men in dark suits were listening from the Aspidistra). "He left this with me for safekeeping."

You take the lab notebook into your hands, and you wonder why she didn't turn it over to the inquest. A Latin motto was stenciled on the cover *"Bene legere saecla vincere"*. Everything scrawled inside seemed as cryptic as the aphorism: a primer of Aeta syllabary, reaction–diffusion equations for pattern formation, linguistic statistics in Latin and L33t Speak, star charts of the Gliese system in the constellation of Libra, and copious margin notes that were written in Tagalog—a language you had always wanted to learn but never bothered to.

After tea, the old woman tells you that your father never found what he was looking for. She cackles with unexpected laughter before pushing you out the door.

On the train, you flip through the book searching each page for your name. Nothing. Not one note mentions you. You don't find your mother's name either. You feel hurt and angry, but somehow, you are not surprised.

When you get home, you feed some of the Tagalog notes into a machine translator. You puzzle over references to a story that infinitely cloned itself, hidden within an improbable place called the "TWw2N Nebula". Your father claimed that anyone who deciphered this strange, recursive story could read about everything happening in the universe—in every possible permutation, simultaneously, without distortion, overlapping, or confusion.

You google "TWw2N Nebula", and you find out that it doesn't exist.

"Gibberish," you say to yourself. "But what does it mean?"

Later, you notice that he repeatedly mentions a woman with two navels and think its code for some kind of worm hole. After half a bottle of the cheapest Asian whisky, you conclude it refers to the cow who replaced your mother in his heart.

A troubled month passes before you find out that most information about your father has been scrubbed from the Net.

You [insert appropriate verb/action word indicating panic]. You spend almost all your non-working hours trying to decipher the notebook before someone takes it away from you. Five months later, your long-suffering girlfriend finally wises up and dumps you. She returns to Singapore not knowing that she is pregnant with a child whom you will never ever meet.

You also never discover who the men in the dark suits were. But, then again, it no longer matters. They never come for your precious notebook.

Yes, it is all yours now.

Twenty-five years later, you decide to move near the Jodrell Bank Observatory. You sell all your belongings and let a small cottage in Lower Withington.

On the day that you finally decipher the old blue notebook, you decide to go to the pub. You believe you have broken the unbreakable code that had stymied your forgotten father. You believe that you—an invisible, half-breed, fucking-little-island-person—have seen Infinity, and it was so _____, _____, and _____. You have no words to describe it. A small part of you wants to gloat at his memory. A smaller part wonders if he would have been proud.

In any case, you knew you more than deserved to celebrate with a few pints.

You leave the old blue notebook with your landlady and her shag-pile of a dog. You tell her in half-jest that she wasn't to give it to anyone but to you or your kid in Singapore. The old bat laughs (probably thinking you're asexual because you're such a barmy recluse). She pushes you out the door.

You walk to the pub content in the conundrum that—due to circumstances beyond your control—you are now the master of your fate and captain of your soul.

At the Black Swan there are no other customers except for you and a large group of men playing boules. All of them are wearing dark suits. When you enter, all their eyes suddenly fix on you.

PYꟻCHRONOMETRIA,
OR THE BELLS ARE ALWAYS SCREAMING

"To loop," my father once told me, "is to repeat a set of instructions until a specific condition is met. If you're stupid enough to let that happen, it means that (1) you're an idiot, and (2) your system will loop infinitely."

10 BEGIN "LIFE"

20 GOTO 10

[0_o]

This is where the story ends: I am always at the shouting end of life.

Somewhere in the other room, my mother is always shouting. She shouts at my father as he dresses for work. She shouts at the maid when she forgets to feed the dog or neglects to water the fortune plants. She shouts at her mother when they talk once a week over the black rotary-dial phone.

Every day, she shouts for someone to set the kitchen TV to Channel 4. The rabbit ears on the black and white are forever broken; I don't remember when they ever worked. The picture is opaque and fuzzy; the only sound you hear is the Angelus and the carillon of canned bells.

(Ding. Dong. Ding. Dong.)

Somewhere in time, I am always seven, and my bed is a time machine. Young as I was, I already knew the awful and immense Truth that Space always ended wherever Time began. Somewhere in time, I knew that I could escape the shouting—I could escape the noise that filled my every day and night.

In my time machine, I would leave my room, with its suffocating plaster saints and its ugly pleated curtains that matched the ugly pleated underskirt of my bed. I would leave my mother and her shouting. I would leave my eternally distant father, a school principal/Mathematics professor, and his young secretary, a pale slip of a woman who wore tight clothes and gave me a slice of *pan de regla* every Thursday morning.

I would close my eyes, and my time machine would take me to a library at the end of the universe. In that library, there were no people—only books containing every story that had ever been written, every word ever spoken, every secret ever told.

My library was my secret, my escape, my soul.

∞

When I was twelve, my father taught me the honest truth about the space between everyone in the universe. He said that you could measure this, quantify it, using the same equation for measuring the length between any two points: The Distance D between two hearts is always D = Velocity of Life x Time.

["Therefore," he said, "the distance between your mother and I, no . . . the distance between you and other people can only grow with time."]

:{

One day, late in my childhood, I woke up polluted—a sinner without sin yet a sinner nonetheless. My mother saw the books I had hidden under my bed and said that I was wicked, godless, and profane. She said I was *just* like my father, the man who sat in a corner wearing a white Crispa undershirt, man-nipples poking out like Mother's pointed accusations of infidelity—infidelity to her God, infidelity to her marriage, and (looking at me, the devil-spawn) infidelity to the commandments in the Good Book that kept all good Catholic children from going blind.

"The snake Ahas-Bakunawa-Ouroboros tempts man with the fruit of knowledge," my mother warned, mouthing the words of her Born Again brethren (who spoke in tongues and fainted when strange men touched their foreheads).

Ouroboros. Ouroboros. Ouroboros. Big words from a failed theology-teacher-turned-housewife. On the kitchen's new coloured TV, there is a grizzled old preacher with a one-eyed python around his neck. Behind him, there is a big sign that says *"Ang Dating Daan: There is no Future except through the Past"*. Every five minutes, the hermit makes the Sign of the Cross. Mother does, too.

Father stands up to tell her he wants to go to New York for a divorce, but Mother ignores him. She shouts to no one in particular that she is a Filipino and a Christian, then turns to punish me instead.

Mother takes away my books, and I receive the Word of God through the grace of her holy *tsinelas* and the intercession of her blessed wooden ruler.

I never see my library again.

>:[

∞

Somewhere in old Manila, I am always seventeen.

When I was a teenager, I was always running. I thought that if I could just run fast enough, I could jump up and fly away.

Somewhere, anywhere, in the big wide world beyond the prison of words my mother built for me, I would find my own universe. I would build my own ontology of knowledge, my own Space and Time. My time machine would take me to a place where I would not hear her voice—a place where there would be no other voices save mine (because tongues were so small, yet they could destroy so much).

But a heart in motion was a greedy and needy monster. Instead of books, I filled my time machine with women who were *not* my mother. Together, I and my 1-random companions explored realms with no terminus, no destination, ending only in discarded clothes, empty condoms, and sometimes, suitcases. The bodies that shared my bed were always different, always transient, threading Markovian daisy chains of no commitment, no meaning.

But nothing lasts forever. Whenever one of them began to cling, whenever one of them started to shout, I ran and I ran . . . and I ran fast.

(In fact, I am still always running.)

∞

Just before he died, my father taught me about Entropy. In information theory, he said, Entropy was the average amount of information that we received with every message, event, or character drawn from a particular stream of data.

Therefore:

$$H(X) = E[L(X)] = E[-ln(P(X))]$$

Where:

> H = *Entropy or Life's baggage*
> E = *The expected condition of Life*
> L = *What Life really brings*
> P = *Whatever dreams you have left*

> X *is your age in years*

"*Dreams . . .*" *he mused (in the manner of someone who lived at the intersection between self-indulgence and narcissism), "dreams contract as Time expands. This is the most important lesson I can ever teach you.*"

o_o

Somewhere in New York, I am always forty-five. The city is fat, and my body is bloated with the pus of life. My feet feel far too heavy to run.

My new bed is big, big enough to be shared permanently. No longer divided by nothing, it is no longer free. No longer undefined, it refuses escape. It cannot time travel. Like me, it is fat and broken.

In my new universe, I am trapped in a cage that is the exact size and shape of a rent-controlled apartment. The walls are thin, and the rooms smell of bleach and dried fish. Unlike my father, I am merely a bottom-feeding programmer—but I like to think we look at the world with the same fearful consonance, in the same stochastic way.

Because of Mathematical Symmetry, I married someone just like my mother, a sensible, religious woman who made the Sign of the Cross every time we had sex.

Our love is a zero-sum game.

Every Thursday night, she sends me to a bakeshop in Gramercy to buy her favorite *pan de regla* (which my mother said was made from the odds and ends of a woman's disappointments). Every Friday night, we used to fuck. We stopped ten years ago. I don't really know why.

Every day, my wife likes to shout. When she shouts, she smells of tallow candles. Sometimes I wish she would just burn up so I could fly away, but I cannot bring myself to leave her.

She shouts at me as I dress for work. She shouts at my son, the promiscuous teen psychopath who sleeps with everyone, and my daughter, the girl with a hole where her heart should be.

My wife tells me that we will all go to Hell for our sins. Sometimes, I write down equations for our eternal damnation, and I post them behind the billboards on the 53rd Street Line.

"Putang ina!" she shouts as loudly as any Pinoy New York City Medea, but no one ever hears her. I know I never have. Perhaps I never will—because my poor, poor wife shouts too late. There was already a prior claim to the shouting, to the never-ending noise in my head.

Outside, the rain is always falling and falling. New York is a pissoir. I cannot breathe. I am drowning.

Every week, I want to call my mother, but I cannot. My mother is small and already dead. Somewhere in my old universe, she is having a stroke as she shouts at the dog (that is always biting the maid or peeing on the fortune plants).

:'-[

"Ceteris paribus," my father used to say, *"an organism's size is inversely related to its metabolic activity, which in turn is inversely correlated to its lifespan."*

["In other words," he said, "Life diminishes us until we die."]

[>_<]

One Friday night, in the middle of the novena to the latest saint-du-jour, time crawled to a shuddering halt during the longest decade of the rosary in all of human history.

The gates of Heaven opened, and I remembered that Time, like Distance, was merely a physical quantity, a fundamental measure of dimension that existed apart from my linear human perception. Every slice of Time contained the universe, and every slice could neither be created nor destroyed.

Because the paradox of Infinity, deep inside myself I find my time machine again—one slice of Time, one chance to go back.

I crossed myself to please my wife, and I ran. I ran through the city. I ran across oceans of Time and Space. Somehow, I ran and I ran until I returned to the place where Time ended and Space began.

Dyschronometria. Chronesthesia. *Putang ina.*

∞

I am in old Manila. I am always here. I have never left. Every day, I sort through a library of boxes—the hundreds of boxes of Mother's things, boxes and boxes that my random, Möbius strip of a father could not bear to throw away when he moved on to other secretaries (and other kinds of tight things).

Every day, I search endlessly for her cassette tapes, her videos, CDs, or perhaps an old 8-track cartridge.

I tell myself I need to find out if there was anything that came before the shouting.

I guess I have always been searching.

[*⌐m⌐]

Before he died, my father taught me that of everything strange in Mathematics, nothing was stranger than a Strange Loop. He said it came about when, by moving only upwards or downwards through a hierarchical system, you find yourself back where you began.

["The worm Ahas-Bakunawa-Ouroboros," he complained, "was senescent at dusk. Having forgotten how to let go, it bites its tail for eternity."]

0_0
+_+

I know there *must* be something in this rubbish of memories because, in my dreams, my mother's tone is always sweet. In my mind, her voice is low and profound, with diphthongs that round themselves in her mouth and very tenderly around my heart.

If I could only hear her forgotten voice, perhaps I could be happy again. Perhaps her voice would bring Revelation, that sacred instrument that would make me remember what I didn't even know I've lost.

Outside, a monsoon storm is raging, and I go to our old kitchen to find something to eat. On the time-worn marble counter, I notice two

TVs side by side—one black and white, the other coloured. Both are broken.

For no reason at all, I turn them both on.

Static. There is only grey screen static. In the distance I hear the 6 p.m. Angelus tolling from Mt. Caramel.

I don't know whether to laugh or to cry.

Because in the end, there are no cassette tapes, no videos, no CDs, no 8-track cartridges. There is only the sound of church bells ringing and the ding dong ding dong piss of rain on the roof.

<3

Error 404

</3

Fucking shit, in my mind, the bells, the bells, the bells—like my mother—are always screaming.

Shouting.

Static.

The noise refuses to let me go.

I M Þ 1 IN 1O

"Neque porro quisquam est qui dolorem ipsum quia dolor sit amet, consectetur, adipisci velit." (*"Neither is there anyone who loves pain itself since it is painful, and thus no one wants it."*)

—Cicero, *On the Purpose of Good and Evil*

They r coming 4 me, my Dev/Null executioners, I got no more tym left, so u, dear reader, have 2 fill in d gaps in my story. I don't know who u r, but if u value ur life, LISTEN 2 me. I'm a dead man talking.

Listen n listen closely.

LIFE HACK # X: SPEAK THEIR LATIN OR DIE.

"I signed up because I want only d best 4 my family"—d@'s d *only* safe answer if any1 asks u why u're here. B very careful wot u say n remMbR, always remMbR: *"Optimum est pati quod emendare non possis"*. It's best 2 endure w@ u can't change. Ur f*cking life depends on it. N don't ever speak ur mind. If u're a resident of d New Cities, ur mind's not urs, not anymore. So speak their Latin n b safe.

If they pursue conversation, stick 2 trivial topics. Rhetorical questions can n will give u away. U never know who u'll be talking 2. Let suspicion breed ur confidence. In d New Cities, d walls have eyes n every word is twittered by d wind. Speak only every1's truth. Think b4 u speak, n never ever post what u really feel. HIDE URSELF FIERCE, HIDE URSELF DEEP.

[<_<] = ☺

Here's a gud, innocuous subject 2 talk 'bout: *"D New Cities r d cleanest, safest, n most modern places 2 live on d planet."* Tell them d@ u're extremely grateful . . . no, privileged, 2 b so far away frm d famine n d filth of d rest of d world.

D@ isn't a lie, u know. 4 all intents n purposes, u'll b living in a virtual hotel, a fancy country club. Each n every1 of those New Cities is a high-tech dream built on d back of d world's greed—pasteurized n homogenized by a 1000 years of steady business. It's a society decorated by d rape of many old countries, a Frankenstein's monster built frm actual, authentic cultures d@ they just couldn't fake.

Each n every 1 of d New Cities is also a PRISON, 1 whose bars r determined by ur income n IQ levels.

Tell them something 'bout hoW ur kids will go 2 d top schools in d world. U have 2 paint ur spawn as d ambitious sort, or they'll b cast aside in d streaming process. RemMbR d@ they view ur children as ur contribution 2 d 5 FUTURES—Fecundity of Family, Felicity in Society, Freedom frm Fear, Focus on Industry, n Forever Prosperity.

If u're lucky, ur kids will become citizens—not a bottom-feeding drone like me. N if u r *really* lucky, 1 or more of them will b born w/ extraordinary genes. U'd have hit d jackpot of genetic destiny, d building of perfect little beasts: beauty + brains.

But @ least ur children won't have 2 join d 1 in 10.

LIFE HACK # IX: LOVE IS A GROUP THING.

I know we've never met, but if u're part of d 1 in 10, I know d@ u wouldn't have made it dis far w/o an approved Latin-speaking wife n @ *least* 2 kids. U wouldn't even b reading dis if u weren't born just like me. We rn't d children of d obscenely wealthy, those who could buy their way in w/ \$\$\$\$. We're d sons n daughters of a middle class family whose dreams reached FAR beyond their grasp of reality.

Like u, I was Mommy n Daddy's perfect little *hijo*. I was valedictorian all d way frm kindergarten 2 my university days. I slacked off a bit in law school where 2 d utter disappointment of my parents, I fell in <3 w/ another boy.

It wasn't really his P3NIS d@ bothered them. There were medicines 2 correct d@ minor inconvenience.

His family wasn't even really poor. Truth 2 tell, they were just as upper-middle class as mine. D real problem was d@ his family didn't have d same political leanings. My boyfriend n his family shunned d New Cities—n not wanting 2 live in d New Cities was perhaps *d* worst social sin imaginable. It left u socially CASTRATED, n losing ur social *cojones* was much, much worse than losing d real thing.

My <3r's father was an old-school journalist who blogged 'bout hoW AUTHENTICALLY FAKE d New Cities were, n hoW its shallow promise of wealth n prosperity was really nothing but a bit bucket 4 d soul. His mother was a rabble-rouser who encouraged workers 2 reap d benefits of their work, instead of exporting them cheaply 2 gated high-tech communities.

My mother couldn't understand my attraction. "They r so proudly proletarian," she sniffed. "Every tym I c them, I have 2 roll my eyes. Look hoW fat his parents are. Only poor people r fat these days. *Hijo*, think 'bout it, @ least they're not starving. No 1 is hungry anymore. Every1 who wants 2 be beautiful is beautiful. There's no need 4 revolution."

"But u don't really know them! They r not poor!" I protested. "Please, just meet them, just once," I begged. "I <3 him."

"*Hay naku, hijo*, being poor is not 'bout money; it's a state of mind. They r just sooooo déclassé. Understand me, u never <3 just *a* person, u don't get hitched to just *1* person," she said. "Relationships are always a group thing—people come w/ family, friends, etc, etc. These others r not always d best sort, so choose ur <3 wisely."

"So I can't <3 anyone I want?" I objected. "Is what I want n what I <3 important @ all?"

My mother didn't understand my question. "Well, I <3 u n there is no space 4 any1 else," she said. "Success depends on <3ing n hating d right people. Choose who u <3 n choose wisely. Ur life depends on it, n certainly ur INHERITANCE does."

My mother was not 1 2 threaten idly.

LIFE HACK # VIII: A GOOD BRAIN IS INCOMPATIBLE W/ A GOOD HEART.

What is d square root of existenZe? If u r 1 of d lucky 1s, u have no mortal fear of material discomfort, but not me. It was not enough for me 2 b alive. I had 2 LIVE.

(@_@)

I remMbR my fragile soul being scared all of a sudden, scared n uncertain 'bout what 2 do. Then, on my way home, I saw a stooped old man push an ice cream cart in front of me. He struggled uphill pushing his cart of 5000 Flavour Dodo Pops as d callous, UNCARING WORLD passed him by, f*cking dead-as-a-Dodo Pops. D@t was my future. D@'s when d light bulb turned on inside my head—my own DARK EPIPHANY.

What I really wanted in life, 4 myself, 4 my own happiness was *"non gradus anus rodentum"*. What I <3d myself was not worth a rat's ass. I had 2 <3 what every1 else <3d, want what every1 else wanted. If not, I'd be poor n pushing Dodo Pops up a very big hill 4 d rest of my miserable life

I decided then n there d@ I needed 2 make my parents happy, 2 apply myself n make something out of my future.

"Never decide 4 urslf," my mother always said. *"D wisdom of d crowds is infallible."*

I pulled out my phone n set up a poll on my profile page. Yes, I stopped being selfish n finally let d world decide 4 me. All it took was a Dodo Pop. D feeling was heady n liberating, like ur first orga$m.

Eow world! Wot shld I do w/ my life?
Go 2 post-graduate school
Trade-up d ball-n-chain
Nothing

My survey said d@ I shld dump my boyfriend, which I did d@ same evening. He tried in vain 2 tell me hoW much he <3d me, but somehoW d@ wasn't worth as much 2 me anymore. I needed 2 prove 2 myself d@ I could b like every1 else. I quit <3 cold turkey. Still, my ex didn't understand what happened. He made a very public, very n00b threat 2 take his life. Un4tun@ely 4 him, I was already plugged in 2 my new social world. All I wanted now was 2 b part of d SWARM.

I told him d@ he was yesterday's news, n I couldn't downgrade 2 my previous version. I left him crying by d side of d street. Once safely home, I tweeted him again 2 remind him d@ our little chapter was finished. I removed all my posts 'bout him. I even took down d sex tape d@ we'd been so proud of. It was now tym 2 move on.

Thick face = check. Black heart = on.

A few months l8r, I heard d@ something terrible had happened 2 him. 1 of my friends had posted it so gruesomely on his status update. I guess even back then I felt a little GUILTY 4 his tragedy, @ least on some level. Maybe I shldn't have dated so soon after we broke up. But what could I do? My mother had set me up w/ d son of her *amiga*.

We all make our own CHOICES in life. He made his choice when he jumped off d@ building. I made mine when I unfriended his memorial page. I couldn't bear 2 attend his funeral.

"Such is life. <3rs come n go, but Mommy will always <3 u," my mother consoled. Then she took me shopping.

My indiscretion was quickly hushed up. However despite my parents' best efforts, social media was a difficult animal 2 control. My ex's parents saw 2 d@. They flooded d blogs, d 4ums, n every online media outlet possible w/ stories 'bout hoW their son had been *so lucky* 2 have been w/ some1 who supported leftist liberal ideas, some1 who could think 4 himself n choose what's right. They posted n promoted every picture n every video where I lambasted d New Cities n made fun of my parents' social climbing.

My parents, my friends, n my school were all mortified. 4 my poor judgment n conduct unbecoming, I was duly punished, socially gang-raped by every1, online n off.

My wide circle of SCHADENFREUNDS n FRENEMIES all abandoned me. Every1 was still horribly polite, but no 1 sat next 2 me in d cafeteria. No 1 commented on my posts anymore. No 1 sent me any TXTs. No 1 wanted 2 have sex w/ me, no matter hoW much I sexted. I = SOCIAL LEPER.

My university debated 4 a loNG tym on what 2 do 'bout my case. Eventually they let me graduate. I was d best in my class, n I always had perfect grades, but it was d oldest, most prestigious feeder school 2 d New Cities. I shld have been d Valedictorian, but as it was, I was lucky 2 have been given *cum laude* @ all (or maybe it wasn't luck, but d new auditorium d@ my parents funded). I didn't care anymore. I was already starting 2 feel DEAD INSIDE.

K, so I know it's hard 2 feel sorry 4 a f*cking *cum laude*, believe me I know. But d reality was: 2 be selected 2 b in 1 of d New Cities, u had 2 have d best paper qualifications. My mother dearest, d broken-hearted parent d@ she was: said d@ *cum laude* was just not gud enough. I remMbR her crumpling my award n throwing it in2 a waste bin. Since then, I've always associated d noise of crushing paper w/ d sound of DEFEAT. It made me feel like d@ proverbial girl who lost 100 kilos but still felt fat.

It's been my pet paranoia ever since.

SERVICE ANNOUNCEMENT: PLS READ DIS END-USER LICENSE AGREEMENT B4 CONTINUING.

BTW, let me stop 4 a moment 2 remind u d@ if u are already in a New City, don't be a N00B; u have 2 keep dis rant 2 urself. Don't even share it w/ ur wife or children—not if u want ur family 2 remain residents. WORDS R DANGEROUS so bury dis as soon as u read it. Bury it deep in an encrypted file d@ they cannot open. No sense is far, far more common than common sense. U have 2 f*cking remMbR d@. If u get careless, it's not going 2 b on my head.

In public think gud thoughts, happy thoughts 24x7, n toe d line.

Oh, since u r reading dis, frm now on, u'll have 2 avoid d memory holes. U know, d hooded chairs they put in public places d@ look like they're frm a hair salon? D Ruling Party has placed these devices everywhere, so u can dispose of dangerous n unproductive thoughts. They will force u 2 use them if they find u reading dis. Sorry.

:-X

Funny thing is, in d New Cities, most people WIPE THEIR MINDS clean willingly, just as easily as they delete their browser history. But 4 d sake of d future, some1 needs 2 keep a record of unhappiness, of pain, of dissent. So whoever u r, if u can read dis Easter egg, keep it close n away frm those holes. Illicit knowledge, like illicit sex, has its own value.

I knew d@ my parents had entered me in2 d New Cities Lottery. However @ d@ tym I was certain d@ my indiscretion n my "poor" academic record would keep me frm getting in. Instead, I applied 2 a prestigious local law firm which hired me almost as soon as they read my resume. On d day I received my 1st pay, I brought my parents 2 d swankiest restaurant in town. I told them 'bout a huge litigation case d@ I'd been assigned 2 n hoW it would certainly get my name in d local media circuit. @ d@ point, I was so sure d@ they would be proud of me.

Sadly, dinner didn't turn out as I expected. Instead of being excited, my mother cried d whole tym, n my father just kept silent. They both fiddled w/ their silverware or looked @ what d other diners were eat-ing. They did everything 2 avoid talking 2 me.

Wotever I had achieved on my own wasn't enough 2 compensate 4 missing d Lottery. My education had been too expensive 4 me 2 f*ck up. My actions cost me my spot as valedictorian n being valedictorian all d way frm preschool would have ensured my place.

In dis overcrowded, hypercompetitive world, my parents said there was no room 4 youthful mistakes. *"Some1 will ALWAYS be ready 2 take ur place,"* my father repeated endlessly. N @ d@ tym, we all believed d@ I'd already forfeited mine.

Desperate 4 their attention, I offered 2 get married 2 a woman—any1 d@ they wanted me 2 wed—n d 2 of us would have sons d@ would carry my father's n mother's names, pretentiously hyphenated of course, as was d fashion among their set. But they just stared @ me blankly, hunched over their expensive, uneaten meal. They were weighed down too heavily by d burden of my FILIAL DISAPPOINTMENT, something d extent of which I just couldn't seem 2 fathom.

"Wot's d point?" I remMbR my mother asking, as she crushed a face blotter in2 a tiny ball. "By d tym they get old enough 4 d Lottery, I would b dead. Lourdes' daughter got her number 2day. Nestor's son n his family left 4 a New City last week, d@ chi-chi one on a cloud, floating 50km over d sea. Every1 I know has a son or daughter who got in. I don't even want 2 look @ their updates anymore. I just feel so small."

I don't remMbR hoW my dinner really tasted d@ evening. Wotever it was we had ordered, all I could recall was d metallic tang of BITTERNESS in my mouth. My words just trickled through their minds like water in a sieve.

Despite their disapproval, I actually enjoyed my brief working tym in d 3rd World. 4 once in my life, I actually felt like wot I was doing *meant* something. I fought corruption in d local government. I went after companies d@ polluted d environment, n I spent a lot of tym defending d man on d street. I was a proverbial big fish in a small pond, n despite my youth, I quickly rose 2 d rank of partner. On d side, I dated whomever I felt like dating, f*cked whoever I pleased. Of course, my parents pretended not 2 notice.

I guess u could say d@ @ d@ tym I was happy (although 2 be honest I never really understood wot d word *"happy"* really meant). Sadly, dis utopia of sorts wasn't meant 2 last. D philosopher Boethius once said d@: *"For in all adversity of Fortune, the worst sort of misery is to have been happy."*

It was certainly d case 4 me.

LIFE HACK # VII: YOUR WORST POSSIBLE PUNISHMENT IS TO GET EXACTLY WHAT YOU WANT.

I still remMbR d@ life-changing day when I got d note telling me d@ my number was up. I had just turned 19. It was a Thursday. I was reading *Consolatio Philosophiae* on my tablet when d mail alert popped up on my screen.

:O

"Congratulations!" d message said. *"You have been selected to be the One in Ten. Please find the Instructions for Residency attached. Read through the acknowledgement form and kindly tick the box when completed."* It was all very nice n officious.

Somehow I'd made it 2 a New City, even w/ just a *cum laude*.

D file size 4 d attachment was over 2 TB in size, n d@ was just 4 d TXT portion alone. F*ck, who had tym 2 read all d@, let alone on a screen? I had thought something so important would have @ least merited a hard copy, but I suppose there's a reason postal services closed so loNG ago.

I checked d acknowledgement box, n they assigned me a unit code: *Horse<3r Fat*. D@ was it. My future = made.

"We only have 5 years 2 prepare!" my mother shrieked excitedly, as her fingers flew over her phone. My parents' loNG n expensive investment in my education had finally borne fruit. Within 10 minutes, her entire social circle had heard of my selection. *"My son is d 1 in 10!"* bragged her 18st update. *"I have never been so proud of him!"* She was so overcome w/ emotion, she had 2 go shopping 2 calm down.

As 4 myself, I'd never felt so overeducated in my life. I spent an hour in d bathroom throwing up. I puked out wotever d hell was left of my soul. D@ was also when I started jacking digital narcs—Virtual Valium, Online Opiates, Electric Ayahuasca. It was d only way I knew 2 clear my f*cked-up head.

D first thing I needed 2 do was 2 get married. D New Cities were not homophobic. There were no laws saying u couldn't b a man D@ <3d men. In theory I could have still married a guy n had kids in vitro. But there were written laws n unwritten 1s, n usually, it's wot's not written d@ really matters.

My mother, d f*cking practical saint d@ she was, insisted d@ a traditional marriage would better my prospects. I didn't really care anymore, so I just followed her wishes. She rang up all d marriage bureaus she could find, asking them 2 send crawler after crawler in2 d ether of marriage-worthy dating profiles.

Eventually, my mother found 2 matches d@ she felt suited my temperament. 1 was a quintilingual, bisexual-leaning lesbian New Media artist w/ a Doctorate in Visual Media frm MIT. D other was a girl who held more degrees in advanced medicine than there were diseases 2 study. Her main selling points were (a) her Harvard education n (b) d@ she used 2 b a man.

I chose d self-identified lesbian. I felt d@, as an artist, she could commiserate w/ my situation, n I thought d@ perhaps we could @ least b friends.

Looking back now, I still think I made d safe choice. 4 d first decade of our marriage, I actually enjoyed my wife's company. Through d wonders of artificial insemination, we had a son after our 1st year. A year l8r, we had a daughter. On our 5th year together, our application 2 d Condominium Development Board was accepted, n we finally moved 2 1 of d New Cities.

LIFE HACK # VI: EVERYWHERE, LIFE IS FULL OF FAKERY.

I had been a high-flying lawyer in d Third World. In my New City, I worked as a "Paralegal Management Consultant" 4 a large multi-national applications-development company. D truth was they took in migrants like me 2 do d shitty, repetitive work d@ d Richie Rich citizens didn't want.

I was, however, paid quite handsomely. On my 1st payday, my mother revealed hoW many decimal places there were on my pay check, n there was a huge uproar in d virtual *tambays,* d hangouts where my old schoolmates lurked.

My new firm ran a subscription service d@ reviewed all d fine print of consumer contracts. We had a system 2 alert subscribers 'bout privacy or liability issues d@ they needed 2 b aware of. I specialized in d End-User License Agreements 4 software applications. Whenever u downloaded an application, we reviewed d legal fine print. Every day I managed a virtual team of lawyers who scanned through 1000s of

EULAs flagging any questionable terms n conditions, so lazy f*ckers like u didn't have 2.

D thing was I never did any actual work. In d New Cities, managers = work nannies. Everything was crowdsourced 4 peanuts frm 3rd-world lawyers. I got 2 do wotever I wanted 2, as long as d work slaves from d lower pecking orders did theirs.

Some days I just MAS2RB8ED in my cubicle. Mostly I jacked in2 my Virtual Valium n fell asleep. I never got scared of getting caught. My boss was always overseas, n d cubicle walls were so high I rarely saw my co-workers.

Sometyms, I just pretended 2 be asleep. I would lie face down on my desk pretending d@ I had died. It was my theatrical reaction 2 d endless permutations of emptiness in my life, a realization of 1 of my favourite mottos: *"Quando omni flunkus moritati"*—if all else fails, PLAY DEAD.

1 day I overdosed on my jacking, maybe I shldn't have mixed d Electric Ayahuasca w/ D opiates *after* my 8 high-ball lunch, or maybe I was just brain damaged. Wotever it was, I got looped in2 a really BAD TRIP. Somehow I had transformed in2 a monkey pounding out 1 sentence after another on an old Underwood typewriter. I was in a gigantic red room w/ 1,000,000s of other monkeys, all of whom were producing endless amounts of gibberish on a neverending supply of paper. D cacophony of clicking keys was deafening, n I wanted them all 2 stop.

>.<

Thank gudness I was used 2 managing chaotic monkeys. I did it every day @ work. D trick was 2 identify some1 in d local team d@ all d worker bees would listen 2, n then get him 2 do ur bidding.

I scanned d room looking 4 d tell-tale signs of leadership. In d dead centre of everything, I noticed a stocky monkey who sported bigger, more dignified ears than normal. When dis sexy beast stood up, he stood erect n tall. When he moved, his movements were relaxed n purposeful. All of which I knew were d nonverbal signs of credibility n competence. I called out 2 him n politely asked 4 his help.

He was indeed, d leader of d monkeys. He came up 2 me, n b4 I could speak he told me d@ I was his l8st special pr0ject.

"Never in my infinite years," he said, *"have I met someone with such an endless capacity for cognitive dissonance."*

"Ooooh . . . u can talk? Kewl accent, Mr. Monkey-face," I nattered, slipping in2 an odd sort of daze. "So . . . wot d f*ck does d@ mean?"

"It means that you have lived your life balanced precariously between conflicting ideas, beliefs, values, and emotions, too paralysed to make choices," he explained, in his quaint, archaic English. *"You simply hide your confusion brilliantly behind a façade of rudeness and apathy."*

"D@'s not true," I protested. "U don't even know me."

"Consider this." He asked, *"When was the last time you acknowledged something was your fault? When was the last time you actually took a stand?"*

In my drugged-out state, I didn't know wot 2 say. My f*cking Trip-Master Monkey was right. More than anything else, I knew d@ I had impeccable credentials 4 indifference. I wanted 2 punch his stupid monkey face.

"You are a veritable font of self-justifications!" he said. *"I am so excited to meet you because you are the paradigm for Everyman in your society. Like Holden Caulfield, you should be preserved for posterity."*

He handed me a sheaf of typewritten papers n told me 2 read it in d privacy of my home. A big red "Secret" sign was stamped across d top.

"Wot is it?" I asked. "More pop-psychology mojibake?"

"It's a summary of the Instructions for Residency you agreed to when your number came up. Read it, and you will know what being the One in Ten really means."

"I'd wanted 2 read it b4. But I figured it would take me @ least a decade 2 go through d fine print," I said. "It was easier 2 just tick d acceptance box."

"Then you better read this abridged version," D monkey said. *"You know what they say before making any purchase: Buyer Beware."*

"Dis makes no sense!" I yelled. "U don't make sense. U might as well b talking in Klingon or Hebrew!"

"No, that is all in order," he said dourly. *".siht ekil ti gniyas eb d'uoy, werbeH ni erew siht fI"*

"Wot?"

∞

When I woke up, I'd left a big pool of drool on my desk. Next 2 it was d sheaf of typewritten papers I had received frm d strange monkey. Somehow, it had made its way frm my narcodream 2 reality. I slid them in2 my bag n messaged my boss d@ I would leave work early. My jacking had really gotten out of hand. I couldn't tell wot was real anymore.

Bad, BAD MONKEY . . .

LIFE HACK # V: SEX IS WAR.

I came home 2 find my wife in bed w/ another man. I closed d door quietly n let them finish their business. D man left discreetly by d back door. He was our neighbour frm 2 floors below.

"I thought you were mostly lesbian?" I asked her, as she lit up an electronic cigarette.

"U n I have an arrangement," she said, blowing a fine mist of vaporized propylene glycol @ my face. "I have needs. U r never available, so I have 2 FIND MY WAY OR MAKE 1. It's really none of ur business."

"U have an arrangement w/ my parents," I corrected her. "But I thought we were friends."

"We r," she said, as she crumpled an empty refill in her hand. "He's not ur type. Otherwise I would have shared."

D@ night we ate our dinner of mystery meat in silence. My salary was huge compared 2 wot lawyers in d 3rd World were paid. But life in d New Cities was expensive. 2 b successful u had 2 put up appearances. Despite our double income, we barely scraped by every month. Mystery meat was 1 convenient way of stretching our budget.

No 1 really complained. In fact, no 1 ever said anything @ all during meal tyms. 4 d life of me, I can't remMbR d last tym we had a real family conversation. @ meals, I usually read my e-books or surfed p0rn. My wife was always glued 2 her gossip boards, while my kids seemed 2 have been born plugged into d SWARM.

I took a loNG look @ my son n my daughter n smiled. They would never ever experience wot I had gone through. Yes, I was 1 lucky bastard—both of them were beautiful. Somehow our imperfect marriage had produced 2 children w/ perfect genes. My mother really knew hoW 2 shop 4 anything—even potential DNA donors. It was a better legacy than any trust fund; n 4 us, they were our ticket 2 a cushy retirement.

As soon as they grew up n got married 2 full citizens, we needed 2 wait only 10 years. Then we could apply 4 citizenships ourselves. D Department of Social Development would take care of us in our old age. D kids would not have 2 lift a perfect finger. We just needed them 2 keep liking us, n more importantly, we needed tym.

LIFE HACK # IV: LIFE IS FAIR ONLY IF YOU HAVE MONEY.

Now comes d tym when I tell u wot being d 1 in 10 really means. Bullshit baffles d brain, so I will just go straight 2 d point. Do u know where d word *"decimation"* comes frm?

It's derived frm Latin n means d *"removal of a tenth"*. In Roman tyms it was a form of military discipline used by d army 2 punish mutinous soldiers. A unit selected 4 decimation was divided in2 groups of 10; each group drew lots, n d soldier on whom d lot fell was EXECUTED by his 9 comrades.

When u n I ticked d@ acknowledgement, d@'s wot we signed up 4. We r d 1 in 10 selected 4 sacrifice, a social class preselected 4 deletion shld d system run out of resources. It was all in d papers d monkeys had given me.

If there was a war, we would b d first 2 be repurposed, transformed 2 disposable anti-virus grunts. If overpopulation becomes a problem, we would b d first 2 get written over. If there was anything @ all d@ needed society 2 choose between a citizen n d 1 in 10, there was no argument—we had already "volunteered" 2 b selected.

D:<

Wait, there's more. There is Justice, n there is d New Cities' brand of Justice. Like most civilized places, all crimes demanded punishment. But if u had real money—d kind d@ got ur profile in finance magazines—*"Justice"* could b more flexible. No matter hoW serious d charge, as a valued member of d Cities' economic engine, u could choose 1 of our number 2 take d punishment in ur stead.

Don't worry, dear reader. If u are part of d 1 in 10, no 1 will force u 2 b a whipping boy. RemMbR d unit number u were assigned 2 when u first joined? Whenever there is a need 4 a volunteer, they will flash d@ unit number on all ur screens. If u click d banner, it means u accept. U will become *d* 1 in 10 4 1 final tym.

All of dis sounds awful, right? But if u are selected, ur family becomes f*cking SET 4 LIFE—immediate citizenship 4 ur spouse n children, free education 4 d kids, n a guaranteed pension 4 ur family. No waiting tym whatsoever. 4 many, it's an offer they simply can't refuse.

LIFE HACK # III: IF U WANT 2 LIVE, LISTEN 2 WHAT I SAY.

If u r d 1 in 10, never ever let ur guard down. Trust no 1. If there is 1 thing d@ I can tell u 2 save ur life, it's dis. Be as nondescript as possible: obscurity = security. Stop publicly liking things no 1 else does. Do not share ur true emotions. HIDE UR DESIRES.

When u're young, all u want 2 do is 2 get noticed. But listen 2 me. 1 day u'll pass a point when all u want 2 do is 2 be invisible, 2 blend in—2 disappear. U work so hard 4 d New Cities 2 pick u, then u'll spend all ur tym hoping they won't.

But above all, PROTECT UR IN4M@ION. N never ever leave ur equipment unattended. Not even @ home. No 1 is really ur friend or really ur enemy. In dis world w/ too many connections, real <3 n true hate don't exist. There is only d fatal static of indifference which paralyses ur soul like a neurotoxin. D@ numbness is d allegorical grass where all devil snakes lie n wait.

o_0

I was so busy w/ my unfulfilling work d@ I failed 2 c d@ my wife's career was imploding. Art was more vicious than contact sports, n if u were an artist n ur works were no loNGer in favour, u suffered d worst fate d@ could ever befall a creator: u became IRRELEVANT.

I hadn't noticed d@ her portfolio hadn't been updated in 2 years. She hadn't been featured in any exhibits 4 loNGer than d@. I even misinterpreted her growing addiction 2 casual sex as some new per4mance art pr0ject, instead of as d CRY 4 HELP d@ it probably was.

In hindsight, I shld have been worried when d f*cking mystery meat started appearing every week. I knew d@ money was tight, but I had no idea d@ her grant money had stopped. No 1 ever told me, n I never asked. We just sat together @ each meal twiddling w/ our devices.

I guess d@'s d curse of social media—we updated our profiles every day, but no 1 f*cking cares wot we post. We tell d whole world wot we think. But we're only interested in wot d world thinks of us. VOICES RANT ON. There is no f*cking CONVERS@ION.

We never really talked. I guess we still don't.

I woke up l8 1 morning, after a loNG night of drinking n sex camming online w/ a multitude of strangers. In my rush 2 catch d city shuttle, I left my old tablet on my nightstand.

My wife broke my password easily. I had no idea d@ my unit number was flashing on my screen. I had no idea d@ she had read d monkey's stupid papers (kids, never ever leave anything marked "Secret" in plain sight).

Worse, I had no idea she would ever click on that innocuous little banner . . .

LIFE HACK # II: REALITY, LIKE MORALITY, IS RELATIVE.

I once knew some1 who worked @ d Department of Defense. She told me d@ d New Cities had a worldwide network of satellites tracking each n every f*cking person on d planet. D@'s why they already knew d@ I liked 2 work l8. They knew d@ d early evening would be d best tym 2 pick me up. They knew there would be a minimum number of witnesses n d@ I would be so tired, I'd come w/ d least amount of fuss.

"Congratulations!" d officer frm d Department of Social Development said when he n his team showed up @ my cubicle. *"You are the One in Ten!"* ☺

In retrospect, I shld have felt mad or @ d very least—scared, but I felt nothing @ all.

EVERY1 knew I was in custody (even if they didn't know why). Yet no 1 called or visited. No 1 so much as posted an update 'bout me. No 1 said good-bye. Every1 just pretended I didn't exist.

D prison psychiatrist told me not 2 worry 'bout my kids. They were already busy reading d profiles of possible stepfathers.

"I suppose I shld be f*cking grateful 4 their resilience," I thought, as I crumpled their perfect pictures in my hand.

As a consolation, my jailers said d@ by "volunteering" I saved a child frm Death Row—some Billionaire's spoiled little 16 yo who suffered frm extreme affluenza. D boy got high 1 fine summer day n killed 42 people in cold blood.

I guess the moral here is dun do drugs unless yr daddy's filthy rich. Mine just wasn't rich enough 2 save me.

(So dis is hoW it ends. Not w/ a bang nor a whimper, just ur soul torn asunder w/ an Epic Digital Death Trip.)

RemMbR d@ drugged-out hallucination I had in my cubicle? On my last night on death row, I had another really bad trip. D thing was I hadn't jacked in 4 weeks, but strangely, I hadn't had any withdrawals. I knew my jailers must have been dosing my food. I wouldn't b surprised if my parents had bribed d guards to do dis. All things considered, I knew my folks still <3 me on some level.

In my final narco-nightmare, my Trip-Master Monkey came back 2 me in my cell.

"You don't seem to be too upset about your impending deletion," he observed.

"My LIFE SUCKS," I said. "Always has, n always will; @ least dis way I know d@ it ends cleanly n painlessly."

"That is too cynical for someone who has yet to reach his 33rd birthday."

"I will never reach 33."

"The vagaries of Fortune visit everyone, and you are by no means the worst of her victims."

"Who d f*ck cares? I never did anything bad. I did wot every1 told me 2 do, but I still got punished anyway. Now they've taken everything away."

"All the things you have been given—your place in this magnificent city, your high-paying job, your beautiful family—they were never really yours to begin with. You only have your mind. That is the one thing that is absolutely and irrevocably yours."

"Really?" I asked. "Well f*ck d@! We gave d@ up a loNG tym ago 4 d hive mind of d SWARM. Why shld I think when d world will do it 4 me? They r thinking 4 me right now."

"But you still ask questions. The faculties are still there. With your mind, anything is possible," he said.

"2moro I'll b dead as a Dodo Pop," I reminded him. "There r no possibilities 4 d dead."

"A good mind is a terrible thing to waste, the cliché goes, but it's true. There is a higher purpose to all of this."

"If there is, I can't c it," I mused, as I crumpled another photo in2 d most miniscule ball possible. "HoW much does re-purposing hurt?"

"The sleep algorithm mimics sodium thiopental. It will put you in a coma," he answered.

"No change then. My whole life = coma," I said. "I'm glad it'll b over soon."

"This is not necessarily the end," he said, handing me a strange computer tablet. *"Here, leave a message."*

"Why? Can u get me out of here?"

"This is a drug hallucination, a glitch in the system, and you are talking to a monkey," he reminded me.

4 some reason, I laughed; I laughed until my sides hurt. It was d first real emotion I'd felt in years. "Dis is like d@ old Terry Gilliam film *Brazil*," I said.

"No, it's more like a Philip K. Dick story."

"Who is Philip K. Dick?" I asked.

"He was a brilliant metaphysical writer," he answered solemnly, as he started 2 disappear back 2 wherever he came frm. *"One of his pseudonyms was 'Horselover Fat'. Quite a coincidence, don't you think?"*

I could think of nothing 2 say. But 4 once, d ballad of my narcocorrido let me down w/ a gud trip. 4 no real reason I could fathom, I woke up feeling oddly @ peace. Dis tym I was really awake, perhaps 4 d very 1st tym in my life. Now I knew who n wot I really was n wot my place was in dis sad, mad world.

LIFE HACK # I: U'LL NEVER GET OUT OF LIFE ALIVE—SO LIVE WHILE YOU STILL CAN.

Why d f*ck do they use Latin in d New Cities? Latin's a dodo-dead language, d@'s why. It's all 'bout FORM, all 'bout ELEGANCE, n most of all, it's all 'bout CONTROL.

Let me tell u a little secret. I have a secret affectation 4 Latin. It was my favourite subject @ school. I have always been fascinated by hoW a dead language could somehow be subverted n live on after d death of its civilization. If I ever wrote a script 4 a zombie movie, I would have d zombies speak only Latin. It's d lingua franca of d living dead. Let me tell u another secret. Just like zombies, Latin is not really dead. Language = Life, n life always finds a way. Someday WORDS will find a way 2 break d system n f*ck them all.

I 4got 2 tell u d@ my Trip-Master Monkey offered me a job after I died. HoW weird is d@? He said d@ I could come n work 4 his *Infinite Library*, an impossible place where everything d@ has ever been written n will ever be writ was kept 4 posterity. If I wanted 2, I could become a junior inquisitor 4 his *Lingua Mortuus* gallery. Too bad it's all just a hallucination.

But hey, if u r reading dis, then perhaps dis last trip wasn't fiction @ all. Maybe my nouveau riche parents slipped me dis tablet hoping I'd say goodbye. Or maybe I'm just f*cked up in d head. Maybe u—my dear reader of dis sentence—exists only while reading me.

But wot do I know?

If u r reading dis death sentence, dis DEAD SENTENCE is my body. But something of me is alive, I hope, dancing in d electricity of ur brain. It's my last WORD.

May my flesh turn in2 words n dwell among u.

Jejejejejejejejejejejeje . . . .

I don't believe in an afterlife. I don't believe in happy ever after. Sometyms u just die, n there's NO F*CKING REDEMPTION @ ALL.

Stay out of d New Cities. Don't be a bit in d Swarm's noösphere. It's not worth wotever it is u consider ur soul. Just live now, <3 now, n (if you want to) f*ck ur brains out. D@'s all u really have. D@'s all u will ever really get.

B4 uploading to d New City, my ethnicity was PINOY. My ancestors used 2 greet each other w/ d phrase *"Mabuhay ka!"* which sadly, no 1 ever uses anymore. I use 2 <3 d@ greeting as a kid; it means 2 *"Live!"* n I think it's d best wish u could ever give anybody.

Eow dear reader, *"MABUHAY KA"*.

Live free, n live like u mean it.

My name was Allan Walang-Turing. I was a 5-year conditional resident of d New Cities. My unit number was *Horse<3r Fat*. I worked as a paralegal consultant 4 a multinational applications-development company. I had a wife, a son, n a daughter. But who I was—who I m—is inconsequential. I'm just migrant slave labour, an immigrant 2nd-class citizen. I'm a placeholder. I am filler text.

I could have been any 1.

Lorem ipsum dolor sit amet, consectetur adipisicing elit . . .

I M D 1 IN 10.

My Dev/Null executioners r right outside my door. *Ave atque vale.*

EXIT QUIAPO STATION

"As stars with trains of fire and dews of blood,
Disasters in the sun . . . "

—Hamlet, William Shakespeare

"Annie?"

"Yes, Nanding."

"Can I ask you a stupid question?"

"What's the stupid question?"

"Why is our Liftport called *'Quiapo Station'* when we're in orbit thousands of kilometres from Quiapo?"

"I don't know. I guess it's because the boom tube exits near the old church I suppose."

(There is a beeping sound over the comms.)

"Hang on. Sorry, Annie, I need to report. New Tundon, this is Quiapo Station Gamma reporting. All systems nominal. Tether Section One is free and clear."

(There is a series of muffled pulses, the sound of platforms making a status check in the background. When her turn comes, Annie begins her report.)

"New Tundon, this is Quiapo Station Mu reporting. Tether Section Fifty is free and clear. Liftport Climber *Adarna-12* is now in Section

Forty-Eight, safety rollers engaging in T-2 minutes. Manual QA check is nominal on all systems. Ascent is a go."

(Annie reaches down and releases a locking mechanism. The hatch of her observation deck opens like a giant clam, casting an arabesque of shadows on her nut-brown skin. She peers past the radiation shielding into empty space, looking for signs of the approaching Climber, a vertical train shaped like a flatworm, carrying a dozen well-heeled passengers. There is silence over the comms for three minutes.)

"Annie?"

"Yes, Nanding."

"I wonder what it's like in New Tundon. Can you imagine living in a city floating fifty thousand kilometres above the Earth?"

"You'd have to marry someone with serious creds to find out. All-Asia Entertainment ran a feature last week. Have you seen it? There was even a three-second Holosonic—imagine, for three seconds, you'll look and feel so Imelda Marcos."

"Really? I'll check it out after my next e-cycle."

"You should. By the way, how's your back?"

"The constant low-level pain reminds me that my vertebrae are separating. At least space will make Pinoys taller."

"Stupid. It'll make everyone taller."

(Silence)

"Hey, Annie?"

"What?"

"Can I ask you a personal question?"

"Sure."

"Quiapo Liftport's got over two thousand employees. How come you've never hooked up with anyone?"

"I don't know. Depends on what you mean by *'hookup'*."

"Is it because you're only into rich kids?"

"Nanding?"

"Yes?

"*Tangina mo.*"

Like a force field of words, Annie's crisp, curt curse blocked further conversation.

∞

Lance Ayala stared out his window at the solitary figure manning Way-Station Mu. Climber Adarna-12 was ascending at over two hundred fifty kilometres per hour. However, the platform's observation deck was open, giving him a clear view of its cramped interior. Everything seemed to whizz by in a substance-less grey blur, but he was certain that the person he was looking at was a woman.

Liftport tours of duty often involved months of isolation, with operators spending their days and nights plugged into a central womb of massive shared-world offices. Actual monitoring duties, recreational and social activities, exercise, and even toilet breaks could be done while immersed online. There was never any need to physically leave their stations. There was no need for any other kind of life.

Lance wondered if that was enough for the girl on the platform. Was it enough for her to feel truly alive?

He didn't know how or why, but he was attracted to her. Somehow, he could sense a kindred loneliness, something that stirred all sorts of strange desires.

The young man turned towards his companions in their small but well-appointed Sleeper. His husband Henry Jr. was spooning their wife Imee in the lower bunk, their naked bodies entwined like porcelain snakes. His other wife Kris had fallen asleep after a long afternoon haranguing everyone else. She had barricaded herself in the upper bed with a fortress of pillows, curling herself towards the wall like a fossilized embryo.

The four of them had been living together for the last three years and married for the last one. Two months ago, on the evening of their anniversary, three of them voted to have children.

Kris had strongly objected but was over-ruled, blighting their special moment.

"I won't do it unless I'm the egg mom," she'd cried, after throwing the mother of all tantrums. Afterwards, Kris impulsively fired servants at random and obsessively arranged and rearranged their small collection of vintage Leeroy New sculptures.

"Punyeta, fuck medical stats! My mitochondria are just fine. I'd make a really good mother," she repeated endlessly, as she dusted odd pieces of furniture. Later that night, she unsuccessfully attempted to bake a cake. It smelled of rancid coco jam.

None of them understood why she'd been so upset by what was, by all accounts, a rational decision. Or even if they did, no one said anything about it. Whenever Kris ranted, they simply ignored her until she got tired and (inevitably) fell asleep. In the mornings, she'd always pretend that nothing happened.

Lance walked up to the sleeping bunks. A part of him felt like climbing up and joining his oft-troubled wife. Instead, he just stood by the foot of the sleeping area, watching her breathe.

"They need the four of us to make perfect, disease-proof babies. Mixing and matching genomes is just like building Lego super-sets,"

Henry said softly. Lance hadn't noticed he wasn't asleep. "She has to grow up and stop being so selfish all the time."

"Sweetie, sweetie, you have to learn to let go," Lance said, reaching up to caress Kris' pale arm.

"You never call *me 'sweetie'*," Henry complained, nudging Lance's tummy with his bare toe. "You're getting soft in the middle, L. Tomorrow, let's hit the gym. I hate fatties."

The young man bent down and kissed his husband's foot.

"I can't sleep, Hen," he said. "I think I'll go to the bar for a little while."

"You sure?"

"Yeah," Lance said, as he quickly threw on some clothes, "Look after the girls while I'm gone."

"Lance?"

"Yes?"

"Don't drink too much. You have a family history of alcoholism."

(There is a hissing sound of the door sliding shut.)

∞

"Nanding?"

"What?"

"The Command channel's asleep until the next Climber comes. I've sandboxed us a private room. Your video-feed's on. I want to see you naked."

"Annie, I'm not in the mood. Quiapo Control warned about a possible meteor shower tonight. Check your messages; it just came in. We have to investigate."

"Station Gamma, Station Mu is lonely and horny. Let me see your long tether."

"Haha."

"I mean it, you stupid jerk. Do you want to keep camming with me or not? Strip!"

"Okay, okay . . . wait," Nanding yelled. He picked up the plaster statuette of the Black Nazarene from his console. He said a little prayer and made it face the other way.

(There is the sound of a zipper being unzipped, as well as softly crumpling cloth noises.)

"Hey, why aren't you naked?" Nanding asked. His smooth, skinny body shivered a little from the cold.

"Shhhh . . . you'll ruin it."

"Annie . . . what are you up to?"

"Close your eyes. What do you think about when you beat off?"

"You."

"Only me?"

"Yes."

"Nanding?"

"Yes?"

"Station Gamma, your tether is stretching."

(There is a sudden beeping sound.)

"Hang on. Station Lambda just reported a falling star."

"Make a wish and shut up. Focus on me."

"Annie!"

"Now, I want you to touch yourself thinking you're touching me."

"What?"

"Do it. Do it now."

Annie watched Nanding's awkward efforts on screen as if he were some creature on a natural history channel. Bored, her thoughts drifted to the man she'd seen staring at her from Climber Adarna-12. She wasn't sure how she knew, but Annie was certain that the stranger had the most beautiful face she'd ever seen.

"So perfect," she thought.

Annie closed her eyes.

∞

"My great-great grandmother was a *mangkukulam*, a witch," the bartender told Lance. "But she believed in God and went to mass every other Sunday. She had a stall just outside old Quiapo Church."

"What kind of witch was she?" the young man asked, as he slowly nursed a glass of Macallan 1926. "What could she do?"

"Here, take a look," the bartender chuckled, scrolling up a screen that had appeared on the long, luminous countertop. "My family still has her business sign. We've kept it all these years for luck."

(A picture of an enamel signage appears on the table screen. It was the kind of homemade advertising that itinerant plumbers used to leave on street posts.)

Miracle *Hilot* Healing	– P1,000
Pagtatawas Demon Banishing	– P2,000
Unisex *Gayuma* Love potion	– P3,000
Chat with the Spirits	
5 Minutes	– P500
15 Minutes	– P1,000
Unlimited Chatting	– P3,000

"Did she have anything that could make you happy?"

"Hang on," the bartender said, as he emptied his jacket pockets. From his personal effects and miscellaneous detritus, he picked out a vintage medicine bottle. Inside was an amber liquid steeped with bark from a *palaypay* tree, preserved *susong kalabaw* fruit, bony stems of black coral, a moss agate shaped like a heart, and a small brass amulet of a couple in a sexual embrace.

"I only have this. It's the last bottle of her gayuma. I'm told the *kambal tuko* figure can bring you lots of good sex partners."

"Sex doesn't bring happiness."

"Well, I can dose your Scotch with serotonin-producing bacteria. It won't affect the dryness or the flavour."

"No, thank you."

"If you don't mind me asking," the bartender continued, "you're young, rich, good looking—and from the look of those three rings, well married. What's wrong with your picture?"

"I don't know."

The bartender poured Lance another glass of the same single-malt Scotch. He had a degree in psychology, a requirement for bartending in New Tundon. But all he really did, he thought wearily, was babysit in-bred brats—little emperor-monsters who liked to create their own problems. Although in this case, he thought, the young man in front of him was a particularly good-looking brat.

"So ... do you want to talk about it?" the bartender asked. "That's ... um ... what I'm here for."

"Doctors, we have so many doctors. What do you think happens to genes when you try to keep fortunes within the fewest families for generations? The docs sort out whose genes should be paired with whom safely. From the time we're babies, we've known our partners. There's no escape. Our families seal the marriage deals depending on politics, economics, or who hates whom less. Then they raise us all together to make perfect babies."

"Is there a problem with that?"

"Money is the worst mutagen."

"So, what do *you* want?" the bartender asked, leaning closer towards Lance.

"I saw a girl manning one of the way-stations today. I don't really know what she looks like. She's probably from the wrong kind of family, poor genes and that sort of thing, but I'm so drawn to her."

"Oh," the bartender said, disappointed. "You are on your way to New Tundon to have kids. Doesn't that mean anything to you? I'm sure you can afford to bond with any man or woman of your choice. But if this girl's manning a platform, it'd be impossible to reach her."

"Why?"

"Don't you know that Liftports only hire the descendants of call center employees? You know the type—generations of lower middle-class wage-slaves addicted to being plugged in."

"I'll never really know her. That's why she's perfect," Lance said. "All the same, though, reaching her is just *improbable*. There's a difference between *improbable* and *impossible*."

"For them, everything is virtual reality," the bartender ventured. "They're living fake lives."

"As if mine is any more real," Lance mumbled.

The bartender began to say something but held his tongue. He hated rich people and their strange, rich people games. He wished he could go home or at least attend to the other patrons, but he'd been paid to tend to Mr. Ayala alone. He turned towards the drink taps feeling oddly embarrassed.

"Stop judging me. My money pays your bills," Lance remarked. "What would your great-great grandmother do?"

"Would you like a snack with your drink?" the bartender asked, trying to change the topic. "We have cocktail Pili nuts, Cornik by Berco's, and three flavors of gourmet Chippy."

Lance looked him straight in the eyes.

"Oops, I'm so damn clumsy," he said suddenly, letting go of his drink. The Glencairn glass shattered on the marble part of the floor, spreading a web of shards across the carpet.

"Let me get that, sir," the startled bartender grumbled, leaving his things on the countertop.

Lance quickly grabbed the gayuma and the bartender's ambient access bracelet, secreting them in his blazer.

"Can I get you another drink?"

"No," Lance said. "I want you to call the dining cabin now. I want *crispy pata* made from grain-fed pork, upland red rice, and *laing*, but you need to make sure that the rice and taro leaves are certified organic. I also want *leche flan* for dessert, but you need to tell the kitchen that I want them to use authentic buffalo milk, not cow's milk. I hate cow milk flan. I want to eat right here at the bar, so don't leave this room. Did you get all of that?"

"Yes, sir."

"Go get everything ready. I just need to use the toilet.

"Yes, sir."

Lance left the bar and his confused bartender. He headed straight for a staff service hatch that he had spotted earlier.

∞

"Henry?"

"Yes, Imee?"

"Where's Lance?"

"Insomniac and indulging his Impulse Control Disorder, he's at the bar."

"Oh, God, I hope he's not screwing the help."

"Who knows? We're still a day and a half from New Tundon."

"Is Kris awake?"

"No, she's out cold. She's still jealous of you, though. I can tell."

"Well, she has a 50% probability of getting three yucky mitochondrial diseases. I have to be the egg donor. She can carry the babies though, or you can do it."

"Naaah, growing a synthetic womb takes too long, and I'll get fat."

"Well, Lance doesn't want to get pregnant. Given his ICD, maybe that's a good thing."

"No, he'd never carry babies. He doesn't think it's manly. Getting a surrogate was a good idea."

"Hmmm . . . I wonder if that that makes it officially three moms now?" Imee wondered. "Seriously, I'm worried about Lance. It's like he's always pulling away from us."

"The man likes to keep his secrets."

"I'm surprised he agreed to have children at all. He's got a 50% chance of Parkinson's."

"Well, he's rich, and he's paid our folks his share of the Bad Genes dowry."

"What I'm surprised about is that Kris is still so upset. We'll use my egg, but that doesn't mean she won't be a mom. *Ano ba*, mito-mom, geno-mom, what's the difference? Anyway, we're having quadruplets, one kid each for us to spoil or scar for life."

"You know she's the mother-hen type, and her family's the richest in Cebu. She's used to getting her way."

"No, she's just a bigger brat than all of us combined. Oh well, it's too bad we won't get to fuck to make those babies. What makes Kris so annoying makes her so good in bed."

"You're not allowed to make babies by fucking anymore."

"Hey, did you see that?"

"See what?"

"Outside the window, I saw shooting stars."

"Where?"

"Oh my God, those aren't shooting stars!"

(There is the silent rumbling of distant explosions. An alarm goes off on Climber Adarna-12 and throughout the entire Quiapo International Liftport.)

∞

"Annie? Annie! Station Mu, this is Station Gamma, please respond. Annie, talk to me!"

"Station Gamma, this is Quiapo Control. Please report your status."

"Control, this is Station Gamma. I am whole and undamaged. All systems remain nominal; Tether Section One is free and clear.

"Roger that. Please initiate emergency protocol FAO-04-07-98 and remain on standby for extraction."

"Control, what happened? I am unable to raise Station Mu."

"Quiapo Liftport's sustained multiple bollide collisions. The swarm's estimated orbit is thirty degrees from 2013 TV135. We've got major damage to the Climber and Tether sections Fifty to Seventy-Five. Ascent is aborted. I repeat, ascent is aborted."

"Oh, God, but we're outside the major risk corridors. Do you mean we didn't see them coming?"

"No. The self-healing walls are overwhelmed. Standby for extraction."

"Please, I need to know what happened to Station Mu!"

"Station Gamma, keep this frequency clear, and for fuck's sake, you've got your video feed up, please throw some clothes on!"

"Control, is Station Mu all right?"

"Station Gamma, the rescue team is en route to your location. Please prepare for extraction NOW!"

"Oh, God, Annie . . ."

Lance skimmed the bartender's heartbeat pattern from the access bracelet and used it to open the service hatch. He struggled against the Climber's linear acceleration and the wind that whipped the tether moorings like a troop of hired mourners. He climbed down several floors until he reached the berth for the Liftport's maintenance spiders. Lance opened one of the hatchback-sized pods and climbed in.

His family manufactured the special smart chips that secured the systems of practically every vehicle in Southeast Asia. He himself had developed the Constructed Language used to encrypt them. Within minutes, he'd hacked into the guidance unit and locked it on to Station Mu, five thousand metres below.

As the spider descended the service tether, Lance felt a familiar rush of excitement. His heart was pounding; his mouth was dry. He felt the pleasant tingling sensation of blood rushing through his loins, and the young man smiled.

Suddenly, a swarm of small meteors struck the service tether just in front of his spider. They punctured the carbon nanotube ribbon as if it were a curtain of wax. The safety rollers ripped off violently as the spider tumbled free and began to hurtle to the ground.

For what seemed like an eternity, he let the spider free-fall. As he tumbled from the heavens, the young man felt no panic, instead an odd dream from a week before intruded his thoughts.

Lance had found his dream-self wandering the strange halls of an enormous library. In one of the corridors, he met an old Ukrainian priest.

"Hello, I am Father Vladimir of the Society of Jesus," the priest greeted.

"I'm Lance, Lancelot Ayala, CTO of Ayala Industries. Where is my mommy?"

"Sorry, son, I don't know where your mother is."

"Oh. It's okay; I never knew my mommy."

"Is there anything I can help you with?" the old man asked.

"Father, I always feel empty and alone, but how can I love if I can't quantify it?"

"Goodness, what a strange and random question to ask, even in dreams."

"Is there an equation for love? Is there a mathematical function where I can just solve for x?"

"Son," the priest said gently, "you are not asking the correct question."

"What is the right question?"

But Lance never got to finish his dream. He had woken up that morning to three warm bodies eagerly pressing against his flesh.

As he restarted the spider's rockets, Lance wondered about the nature of Love and whether he actually even knew what it was. He looked up towards the heavily damaged Main Tether and the Adarna-12 carrying Kris, Imee, and Henry. On the rear-cam, he could see Station Mu damaged and on fire. For a second, he hesitated to pull up. He had already fallen a very long way, and it would be an easy thing to just let the spider crash to the ground.

∞

"Quiapo Control . . . New Tundon . . . any station . . . this is Way-Station Mu. Mayday, mayday, mayday! Tether Platform Fifty is on fire; I repeat, my platform is on fire. My escape pod is destroyed. I need an extraction team immediately."

(The crackling sound of static bursts over the comms like a swarm of angry bees.)

Annie climbed into her space suit. After initiating a shutdown protocol, she made preparations to zip down one of the service tethers.

Something in the rear of her way-station burst into flames, and Annie practically leaped out of the airlock. She slammed her pulley's gas jets to maximum just in time to escape the LOX tank's staggering explosion.

The service tether she was using snapped and flayed itself into a million incandescent ribbons. Annie found herself hurtling down to Earth like a fallen angel.

(*During particularly depressing nights, she had often wondered how she'd feel if Death ever stared her in the face. Would she feel scared? Would she feel sad? Would she feel numb and alone like she usually did?*)

Annie closed her eyes, realizing she felt vaguely horny and absolutely nothing else.

Suddenly, a portion of the tether material wrapped itself around her body, coiling around her like a shroud. Annie panicked as she tumbled down blindly for several hundred metres. She screamed and screamed, but not a single soul could hear the sound of her terror.

As quickly as it began, her uncontrolled descent was arrested. A maintenance spider came out of nowhere and snatched her up with its emergency hook. The vehicle hit the brakes hard, and its liquid-fuel rockets howled like a wounded animal.

Lance dragged Annie's struggling form into the spider and cut her free with a laser knife.

A message crackled from the dashboard comms: *"Quiapo Control, this is New Tundon . . . zzzzt . . . zzzt . . . confirming Climber Adarna-12 is destroyed. There are no survivors. I repeat, there are no . . . zzzt . . . zzzzt."*

Annie adjusted her visor and stared at her rescuer. Her eyes betrayed a look of frightened, sheepish recognition—it was the man with the perfect face.

Lance sat in his bucket chair, quietly oblivious to his tears. Despite his present predicament, he marveled at the intricate choreography of chance required to bring him precisely to where he was right now. Was any of it due to his agency, he thought, or was he just a boat being carried by some huge existential river?

A part of him was surprised that he was crying.

The pod continued its slow, steady descent.

Annie wanted to reach out and comfort her rescuer, but she recoiled at the thought of actually touching someone else.

Instead, both of them kept silent, staring at one another, until an alarm on Annie's space suit beeped, indicating that it was now safe to make a jump.

"This spider has no chute, and the fuel is low," Lance noted calmly. "It's best you go, you can't carry us both. I'm . . . dying anyway. This is the third body I've downloaded to that's got cancer, and I've been paying a fortune to keep it a secret."

"I thought you rich kids were bred to be perfect."

On the spider's speakers, her disembodied voice sounded like a ghost trapped in an air duct.

"Only our first few bodies are. Then you crash your Ferrari too many times. You OD, or you play whose-suicide-is-cooler. My wife Kris once drowned herself in a tub of Perrier-Jouët. That cost a million creds per bottle. God, that makes us sound like total shits, doesn't it? I've got the Holosonic though. Do you want to see it?"

(Annie shakes her head.)

"After a while though, every new body gets some kind of generation loss. Damn it . . . I was on my way to New Tundon to have kids, you know. I wanted to leave something behind before my DNA got corrupted further."

Annie looked away from the man's increasingly sad eyes.

"Before you jump, I'd like to give you something," Lance said, tossing the witch's bottle towards her.

"A gayuma?" she asked. For some reason, her palms began to sweat with anxiety. "I . . . I haven't seen one of these since I was a kid in Quiapo. Why . . . why are you giving it to me?"

"You look like you need some magic," he said. "Life's short, despite all our technology. Reach out and touch someone."

Annie wanted to ask him *Who the hell do you think you are? I don't know you, and you don't know me.* A million hostile thoughts went nova inside her head. She wanted to let him know that she wasn't a weirdo for not wanting physical contact. She wasn't sad or anti-social. She simply liked being alone, and it was absolutely none of his business.

However, as Annie looked past his perfect face and his seemingly perfect life, she began to feel strangely guilty, although she didn't know why. In the end, she decided to say nothing and checked her altimeter instead.

"Take this as well," Lance added. A series of small slots hidden just beneath his hairline opened on his forehead. The young man ejected and replaced a few memory chips before finding the correct one.

"I'm sorry for the loss of your colleagues. I hope they had insurance. No need to worry about the other passengers. All of them were backed-up before this trip. Their PAs just need to download them into new bodies. Ha! No one with money dies permanently. Although . . . giving this brain-chip to you means that I won't get resurrected."

"What is it?" Annie asked. She carefully took the chip from his hand and examined it as if it were an insect.

"It's me, or at least it's a fragment of me that I've partitioned and freed," he said. "It's the only part of me I like. Just jack it into an AI compiler. If you ever decide to take another Liftport job, I'd like to get to know you and keep you company on your long, lonely nights."

"You'd rather be an AI than be meat again?"

"If you want to kill someone," Lance answered cryptically, "you have to murder him in parts. When you get too rich or too successful, you'll understand."

"But this you, the real, complete you, will die."

"I'll tell you a secret—I don't really know if there ever was such a thing as a 'real' me. We're all just the sum of the fucked-up illusions we create in our heads. Besides, life's not fair, right? This is me flattening the bell curve a bit."

"I don't understand. Why are you doing this?" Annie asked. She zipped his brain-chip and the gayuma into her pocket as she prepared to leap from the doomed spider.

"I don't know," he answered. "You don't need a reason to love. You don't need a reason to die. Not every story needs a reason."

As Annie jumped towards the waiting Pacific Ocean, she thought about her rescuer's curious words. Her mind withdrew into its deepest of sanctuaries and imagined that his makeshift hearse was a great cloud filled with longing and pregnant with warm, comforting rain.

For no reason at all, she imagined that he was happy.

PANOPTICON

"The illusion of free will is itself an illusion."

—SAMUEL B. HARRIS, NEUROSCIENTIST AND AUTHOR

I woke up in a dirty public toilet, white noise fogging my head. The stink of urine and cigarettes choked the dead air. A broken sink in front of me lay thick with organic crust, ashes, and ancient spittle. Overhead, an incandescent bulb flickered uncertainly.

"Mr. Salazar?" a voice behind me asked. "Try not to move so much, you're not complete yet."

I glanced up at the mirror and saw the reflection of a woman in a tight white jumper, slender and tall like a huntress. I knew immediately that something was wrong. Her face was familiar, too familiar. It was a face that I had seen hundreds of times before, the 1970s screen siren Marrie Lee. She looked as if she'd stepped out from the movie *They Call Her Cleopatra Wong*.

I balled my hand into a fist. I knew she couldn't possibly be real.

"No need to fight, Mr. Salazar. Your reaction is all the confirmation I need," the strange woman replied. "Cigarette?"

"Who are you?" I asked, gagging at the assault of cesspool smells. "Where am I?"

"It's me, Pai Kia," the woman said, her voice dropping suddenly to a baritone. "I'm Ms. Esperanza's agent, remember? Let me adjust my HI."

"H . . . HI?" I stammered, as her body morphed into something more androgynous.

"*Aiyoh*. H-I, Haptic Interface. It allows you to touch me," e explained. "Anyway, we spoke at Golden Acres. I'm your caseworker, at least for the next few minutes. Sorry for the rough landing. This is my cheapest loading program. You did travel by steerage after all. Welcome to Alt.Tundon."

I threw up.

"Isn't it wonderful? That's your system getting rid of unnecessary information," Pai Kia said, as e took a drag from a long Djarum Black. "Feels so real, correct or not? This place is almost the real universe. You won't see any pixelation, not even on the quantum level. This hack is *that* good. You *gone case,* uncle. But soon, very soon, you won't even remember transitioning."

I kept throwing up until my knees gave way. My face slumped onto the dirty sink, straight into the puddle of my own vomit.

"Listen, I'm paid by the second, so listen and listen closely," the agent said. "You just came back from the dead, and your algorithm's still broken. She wants you to find her. This time, she said there's less bullshit, no guns and no restraining orders. Find her. She's waiting for you."

"Where am I? What . . . what is this place?" I asked.

"Alt.Tundon's a Hacker Town. It's a cloud of parasite spaces called *Gimokud* hidden beneath the New Cities. Are you sure you don't remember? The New Cities are what passes for Paradise for the affluent deceased."

Pai Kia fished for something in eir pocket and tossed it to the floor. It was an old Casio Databank watch.

"Since you're not part of the 1%, you have to wear one of these. Your identity and your credits are inside until you're re-skinned. Don't lose it, or you'll be purged. If you need more credits, you'll have to sell something. If you got nothing, sell yourself. Good luck."

"Wait . . ." I whispered hoarsely, struggling to get back on my feet. "Please wait."

When I finally managed to stand, the agent was gone. Only the smell of clove cigarettes remained, pungent as rotting fruit.

I moved to a clean sink and washed my face. When I looked into the mirror, an impossible face stared back. Somehow, I was young again, probably 41 or 42. That was about how old I was when I first met Esperanza. I had a feeling something would happen to my form when I transitioned, but I had not expected this.

"Damn it. Why is she torturing me? Why now, after all these years?" I asked myself, feeling a familiar flood of pain and self-loathing. *"Why did I even come?"*

In my old age, I had tried my best to forget about her, to erase what had ripped my heart out. Our love broke me to the point where I couldn't deal with relationships, not anymore, perhaps not ever.

It took a very long time, but over the years, I honestly believed my nightmare was behind me. Why the hell did I agree to see her again? Why the hell did I agree to tear old wounds wide open?

It hadn't been easy. My stupid heart refused to forget past sins. To move on, I had opted to misremember everything. Memory was never perfect anyway, and false memories were just as good as real ones, if you wished hard enough.

I dried my face on my shirt of *piña* cloth, a luxurious *Barong Tagalog* reserved for weddings. The telltale static of Nanotex fabric on wet skin, a glitch actually, told me it wasn't a real shirt. I put on the watch she'd left me and checked its digital signature. Every single thing I was wearing were hand-me-down downloads, pre-owned by her dead husband, the industrialist Julio Salas.

A message scrawled across the *calado* embroidery on my shirt cuffs, a helpful reminder of my indigent humiliation:

"Good evening, ~~Mr. Salas~~ Mr. Salazar, this shirt is best washed with Mr. Clean digital detergent. Removes vomit and all simulated organics."

A detergent ad? I noted with surprise. Biofilms and ultrasonics cleaned everything now, and I hadn't seen real soap in decades. I decided it was probably a skeuomorph, a virtual anachronism designed to make people—old people—more comfortable being digitized.

What the hell is this place? I wondered.

After a while, I staggered out of the toilet. Night had fallen, and I looked around the deserted alley, wondering where I was supposed to go. A bicycle had been propped on a wall just in front of the lavatory entrance. As soon as I stepped towards it, the bike began to flash its lights, illuminating layers of advertising graffiti with a frail white fluorescence. The lights kept blinking until I put my hand on its bamboo handlebars.

A message popped up on its digital odometer:

"Thank you for choosing a Shimano Intelligent Bicycle, ~~Mr. Salas~~ Mr. Salazar. The seat has been automatically adjusted to your height. Your route has already been preselected. Please climb aboard and simply pedal."

I heaved myself up to the gel-padded saddle and kicked off. The bike guided me through the dark and narrow alleys that snaked through the labyrinth of tenements. Everything in Alt.Tundon lay in the shadow of its sole skyscraper, the neon-lit Torre Paraiso.

I passed through the slums like a ghost. Through the yawning windows, I saw people leading seemingly normal lives—playing mah-jongg or the card game *pusoy dos*, eating dinner, or simply gathered around their living rooms, plugged into a legion of electronic devices. This was a town of old people, permanently idled, permanently trapped in the amber of unstructured time. Not a single child was in sight.

The faces of certain strangers looked disturbingly familiar. I passed a *panciteria* where I thought I saw Harrison Ford drinking San Miguel beer with Jonathan Pryce and Bembol Roco. Nearby, on a street-level TODA station, a woman who was the spitting image of the actress Hilda Koronel waited patiently for a hover-cyclo to come.

I wondered how many of them were actual *real* people, not background SIMs or in-memoriam programs. If they were human, I wondered if this was their idea of heaven.

The bicycle took me away from the maze of small streets to a wide, tree-lined boulevard bustling with shops and post-modern apartments. My ride stopped in front of a garishly lit clothing store called *The Way We Wear*. There, an oddly dressed man waited for me expectantly.

"Welcome to Alt.Tundon, Mr. Salazar," he said softly. The old man was wearing a circus ringmaster's outfit. On his head was an elegant top hat with large aviator goggles that hung carelessly from its brim. A strange watch, encrusted with many dials, covered his left arm like an armature of metal eczema. I imagined it could keep time for the entire universe.

"I have been asked to dress you and guide you to Paraiso."

"Thank you, but this looks like an expensive place," I replied, as I stepped in to view his merchandise. The store smelled of spikenard, incense, and myrrh, the stink of gods and rich people. "I'm not sure I have enough credits."

"Don't worry about that, Mr. Salazar," he reassured me. "Your re-skinning has already been paid for."

Inside the store, I realised that there were no actual clothes, just an infinite library of paintings, photos, and video screens displaying clothing styles from every time period and from all over the world.

"Now then," he announced theatrically, "a *Gimokud* is a world where heart and mind are one."

"Hang on. What is this place?" I interrupted. "Where am I? Am I dead?"

"I understand that you were a filmmaker once," he said, cryptically. "You were a director, a scriptwriter. You were once a *Creator*."

"Yes, but what does that have to do with anything?"

"Can you not recognize art when you see it? Some creators can build worlds from words and images. Some can create an entire universe. Your mind is what the philosopher Anaxagoras called *'the intellect that builds reality'*."

"You're not making any sense." I said, "Who built this? Who is responsible for this place?"

"I was under the impression that *you* were responsible," he announced without emotion. "I suppose if you want to know more, you will have to ask Mrs. Salas."

"Where is she?" I asked. "Is Esperanza really here?"

"She is waiting for you at Paraiso. I am afraid you are running very late."

I wasn't sure if it was my traumatic transition or simply the thought of seeing Esperanza again, but I felt suddenly faint. I sat down on a huge Persian carpet in the center of the store and buried my head in my hands.

"I'm sorry. Please get up," the old man said gently. "Paraiso checks for broken souls and will frown on your second-hand clothes."

"I have nothing else."

"Oh, that is not true. Even here you have some measure of agency," he said unexpectedly. "I will use your Nanotex canvas to craft a new outfit that will map the man you used to be. I will cut it from the cloth of your pain, that buried fabric spun from the love you've lost, and sew it with the dark threads of your forbidden consummations. Finally, I shall embellish it with the future fruit of your final, bittersweet meeting."

"What are you talking about?"

The older man was much stronger than he looked. He raised me up and ushered me to his workstation.

"Does that outfit sound about right to you?" he asked. "After all, our clothes are guideposts to our feelings. Your outside will now match what is in your inside. How are you feeling now, Mr. Salazar?"

"I don't know," I answered. A swarm of 3D printers, buzzing like paper wasps, stripped me down to my bare Nanotex frame. There was absolutely nothing underneath.

"You are dressing me with emotions that I have spent a lifetime forgetting."

"Ah, but that is who you are," the old man said.

The tailor's curious machines repaired my algorithm, then created code by code, thread by thread, a beautiful new suit of grey merino wool—one that did not have *"Mr. Julio Salas"* crossed out on its digital signature.

"Perfect," the old man exclaimed. "As they say, clothes do make a man. You are now a perfect simulation of your old self. Perhaps this time you will find the right words to say."

"What do you mean?" I asked. "What do I need to do now?"

"Just a piece of advice—the body can become young again, but the soul: never. When the hurt is strongest, we must watch what we say," he cautioned. "Now go, please, there is a Personal Air Lifter outside, waiting to take you to Paraiso. Mrs. Salas is already there."

I thanked the old man and left feeling as grey as my suit. I wasn't really sure what he'd done, but it felt like I'd been prepped for a funeral.

"Hello again, Mr. Salazar," Pai Kia greeted cheerily, as I climbed aboard the sleek red aircraft. E was still dressed in Cleopatra Wong's tight white jump suit. "You clean up very nicely, uncle. I could fancy someone like you."

I said nothing as our autogiro lifted up towards an indifferent brown sky, past the grid of wires that stretched over the slums like a garrote. The highway in the heavens was teeming with sky jeeps, floating hawker stalls, hover-cyclos, air tuk-tuks, and giant advertising dirigibles. The latter's Holosonic displays bombarded my head with hundreds and thousands of advertisements, factoids, and subliminal purchasing suggestions.

I closed my eyes to escape, letting the lights of the airborne traffic blur into hazy constellations. Every few seconds, a small group of vehicles would peel away, puncturing the smoke-choked clouds like dying meteors.

"I don't get it." I asked, "If people pay to be here, why does it look like a retro-future dump? It's like we went back in time, to some old Third World country."

"*Wah liao*, every time the same questions," Pai Kia said. "Let me tell you all you need to know. *Aiyoh*, everyone has three possible afterlives. If you're rich, you stay in the clean, ultra-luxe New Cities. If you're poor, you just die, end of story. For everyone in between, if you're in the know and you've got something in the way of credits, you can pay soul-hackers like me to build an afterlife. But hey, as they say—*no prawns, fish also can.* Do you understand, *lah?*"

I nodded for some reason, even though eir answer made no sense.

"Of course, your level of comfort, your level of reality, depends on the size of your wallet. Ms. Esperanza has a very big wallet."

I studied my strange companion, wondering how e really translated behind the HI. Was e even real? I couldn't tell anymore.

"Listen," Pai Kia said suddenly, with a voice that slid out viscously, like snails gliding on glass. "I don't know why, but she instructed us not to complete you. I'm sure you already know. There's no *ku ku* bird down there."

E pointed to my crotch, a sad, flat affair devoid of any protrusions.

"I can fix that. We can work something out."

I was way too tired to hide my emotions. I looked straight into eir eyes, sharing a yearning and a heartache that words simply could not convey.

"So drama! Lucky woman, that Ms. Esperanza," Pai Kia laughed. "*Heh*, the mosquito dies, but the itch remains doesn't it? Nevertheless, my offer is there if you change your mind. My contact's in your watch."

We flew towards our destination in silence.

Torre Paraiso was a private Integrated Resort that rose seven kilometres into the heavens. The enormous building tessellated into separate sections that celebrated Christianity's Seven Deadly Sins: *Envy*, *Greed*, *Gluttony*, *Sloth*, *Lust*, *Wrath*, and *Pride*. Pai Kia dropped me off at the rooftop landing pad and blew a kiss for luck.

Esperanza was waiting for me at the Immersion Gallery, an eight-star lounge at the highest penthouse level. Everything inside was done in the old Filipino style called *Earthquake Baroque*. The rooms were hewn from pig-fat marble and solid *piedra china*, gaudy, and over-the-top with decorative *calabasa* motifs. The transoms, fixtures, and room detailing were all gilded with mother-of-pearl and electrum ormolu.

On the walls were Holosonic reproductions of early masterpieces—Lunas, Hidalgos, and Amorsolos, each one radiated terabytes of synesthetic information and shared emotional content. A large Luna, *The Spoliarium*, filled my mind with images of dying gladiators and left the unwelcome taste of blood in my mouth.

This was an area reserved exclusively for the most important of VIPs, the world's one percent mega-rich that were members of an exclusive club called *Pride*.

Esperanza sat almost preternaturally still, like a porcelain doll, her small frame entombed within the red womb of a rare Cobonpue Ball Chair, woven from the finest, palest bamboo.

"Hello, Alfredo," she whispered softly.

I said nothing and looked around the room until I found another Ball Chair to curl into. I hid my head in the cold shadows, not wanting her to divine my feelings. Esperanza looked exactly like she did when I first fell in love with her. Her short brown hair was cut in a bob, framing a delicate face that looked not unlike the Singaporean actress Marrie Lee.

We sat across the room staring at each other for what seemed like hours. As each second passed, I pressed myself deeper into the chair's embrace. The weight of her presence slowly turned every bone in my body to glass.

"What is this place? Why did you bring me here?" I said finally, yielding to the oppressive stillness. "I was happy at Golden Acres. You should have let me die in peace."

"You'd rather be in a hospice ship?" she asked. "Death has no angels, you know. It has no dominion. There are no tunnels of light. There's just this or oblivion."

"This is nothing but another prison."

"Yet you still came when I called. Why?"

"I don't know."

"Do you still have feelings for me?" Esperanza asked. Behind the grottoes of her eyes, I sensed the vague shine of emotions I thought she'd long forgotten (or maybe it was just a trick of the light?).

I took a deep breath and decided to say nothing. When I was alive, our past had kept me in a cell without walls. Words bled, words betrayed. I let the silence tell her everything she needed to know.

"Really, you have nothing to say to me?" Esperanza pressed. "After all this time?"

"Why am I here?" I whispered finally.

"Let's recap, shall we? I married Julio the year after you and I parted. He was so much older than you. He had money, and best of all, he never, ever hurt me. After that, I had . . . I have a beautiful child. In fact, my baby is having his own baby soon. For the last thirty years, I've lived a blessed life, a life most people can only dream of."

"Why am I here, Esperanza? Why can't anyone give me a straight answer?"

"Shut up and listen," she said. "That's always been your problem. You like simple answers because you don't like to listen."

I bit my lip and just stared at her.

"Anyway, after Julio died, he transitioned to the New Cities, and he left me with so much. I hadn't planned to join him so soon, but there are things that no amount of money can control."

"I know all of this. I tried to come back to you, but you took out a restraining order," I said cautiously, nervously. My skin wrinkled around me like a chrysalis. "I should have known enough to stay away."

"We left a lot of things unfinished, didn't we?" she added.

I tried to search her eyes for a hint of what she was up to, but she quickly turned away.

"Anyway, that money's what brought you here. I paid to capture a star that's keeping you alive."

"This storage facility's a town for hacked souls, true, and you're just a squatter under our New Cities. But you won't die, not for a very long time, and you'll never age. I can watch you whenever I want to, just like how you used to watch me."

"Hang on, you *bought* me a star?"

"Yes, isn't that the kind of over-the-top melodrama you used to like?" she said. "Do you know how much processing power your brain needs? It takes the power of an entire star to store a single mind. That's why only the rich live can live forever."

"Why did you do this? This is really messed up, even for you. Did you even think to ask how I would feel?"

"I was seventeen, you were forty-two. That wasn't messed up? Did you ever consider me or how *I* would feel?" Esperanza snapped. Her eyes rolled up to the ceiling, as if looking for something solid to hang on to. "You were my film teacher, so I had this place built just for you. Doesn't it look like a set from your favorite movies? What were they again? I only remembered *Brazil*, *Blade Runner*, and *Manila in the Claws of Light*. You've always wanted to play the tragic hero. Well, my money can buy a lot of things."

"Why are you doing this? Why am I here?" I asked again. "It's not as if we have anything anymore. We made a mistake . . . I made a mistake, but Jesus, that was a lifetime ago."

"And Jesus said we must pay for our mistakes."

"The truth is," I said crossly, "you were never the type to love anyone, Esperanza. You just liked to own people."

"Hah! Now who'd like to own a loser like you?" Esperanza yelled, losing her carefully constructed cool. She closed her eyes and began to laugh.

"Stop it. Stop laughing, please."

"As it happens, I *do* love someone, and the one that I love is my son," she declared, getting up from her chair. She snapped her long, slim fingers, and a viewing screen appeared on one of the filmy silver walls. "I promised him he would meet you one day, but I had an unscheduled aneurysm. I guess this was the next best arrangement. At least now, he can see you exactly as I once did."

A dark figure flickered on the screen, throbbing like a haunted memory.

"What happened to you, Professor Alfredo? You threw your life away, a burned-out basket case in a nursing home. It was lucky my agent found you before you died," she said, shaking her head in the manner parents did when scolding children.

However, Esperanza's tone had become a little less angry, unexpectedly softer. "I took out that restraining order to save your life, you stupid idiot. That's one more you owe me. Julio's extremely jealous. He would've killed you if he knew what you'd left me."

"What are you talking about?"

"Jun—*Julio Sales Jr.*," Esperanza addressed the dark figure looming through the static. "Speak now. You can translate into this Haptic Interface when I'm done."

The screen blinked like the eye of a god, exact and infallible, revealing painful truths. I had never seen her child. Esperanza paid big money to keep her family out of the press. But as soon as I saw his face, my knees started to buckle again. Jun looked almost exactly like I did when I was in my thirties.

"As you already know, this old man is your real father," she said haltingly. For a moment, her voice seemed to betray the pain of a great, long-hidden loss. I waited for some real change, for forgiveness, but Esperanza just pressed on coldly. "I would have rather you never met. But I made you a promise, and your mama always keeps her promises. Take a good long look, sweetie."

I tried to open my mouth, but no words would come. My sentences seemed to stall in mid-thought.

The past belonged to the past, yet here we were now. Through the cybernetic agency of the *Gimokud*, a network of Dyson bubbles— huge, star-eating computers storing souls in their pure mathematical form, we were young again, keeping secrets and being every bit as hurtful as old times. It was a new kind of hell for the downloaded dead.

"Poor Julio never knew he was impotent," she said to me caustically. "You told me once that *'the seeds of obsession grow quickly to hate'*, and that's all you need to know."

"Did . . . did you ever really love me, Esperanza?" I stammered, fearing any answer she would give. The invisible bars of my newest cage began to reveal themselves in earnest. "You know, before things fell apart, you promised me forever."

"Even I can't afford more than one Eternity. Consider your star my repayment for your parting *'gift'*. You're alive as long as it's alive. And, oh yes, you wanted to be alone? Everyone here's a skeuomorph, and this world is as empty as a Holosonic. You've got nine billion years to figure it all out."

Esperanza's form wavered strangely, fading in and out like a ghost. Then she disappeared suddenly, leaving no answers. On the silver screen, a man with a sad face that seemed full of burning questions waited patiently for me to talk.

But before I could say anything, Esperanza reappeared and clipped a teleport cheat-band to my wrist.

"One day, you actually need to keep your promise, Mother," the man on the screen said, making a sigh of tired resignation. "How many times do you need to do this before it's enough? I'm not getting any younger."

"I'm sorry, son," Esperanza muttered as she and I disappeared, transmuted into floating-point equations inside the *Gimokud*'s enormous brain. " *'Hell hath no fury'* yada yada yada . . . I still can't help the way I feel."

Next thing I knew, we were back on Paraiso's rooftop landing pad.

"I forgot to give you this," Esperanza said, hitting me on the chin with a strong right cross.

I toppled from the edge of the platform down into the darkness. It seemed like I fell for a very long time, my body folding, breaking, and decaying into an endless rain of remorse and bitter ash that seemed to last for nine billion years.

When I came to, I found myself in a dirty public toilet, white noise fogging my head. The stink of urine and cigarettes choked the dead air. A broken sink in front of me lay thick with organic crust, ashes, and ancient spittle. Overhead, an incandescent bulb flickered uncertainly.

RE/URRECTIOΠ 2.0

It was October, the month of harvest, the month of blood. The cold Siberian winds blew in from the North, lightly frosting the window with infinitesimal diamonds. A solitary figure stood by the moon window, staring past a blood-red wall of light, towards a dark sewer called Mother Ocean.

The man at the window knew the Eaters would come for him soon. He picked up a vial of poison and placed it in his pocket. He could almost smell the stench of their bodies and feel the rough caress of their hands, as they tore his liver from his innards.

A group of them had massed around the walls of Tundon, gathering in great numbers, waiting. The flesh-feeders huddled without a sound, like wordless monkeys, under helmets of bone and coats of human pelt.

Through the softly glowing rain, he could feel the stare of a million savage inquisitors. Was it his imagination, or did it seem that their eyes were gravid with hate? He felt as if they were accusing him, blaming him for their fate. As if they were whispering *"Look what you gods have wrought."*

But the last librarian was determined to be defiant to the bitter, brutal end. No one had expected him, a portly old man of Filipino extraction, to outlast everybody else. But somehow, he endured. Somehow, he made it to the end game.

A commitment tattooed itself to his mind—*never again*.

He knew his symphony was now close to its final movement, as his perception of time had slowed, like a raptor circling an abyss. The Celestial Beacon had almost finished uploading, and its ancient power cells were good for only a few more hours. Once exhausted, the protective walls would vanish, and the legions outside would attack.

The broken ones had been gathering for weeks, shrouding themselves in thickets of darkness. They had returned to the City of Books for a final feast.

Human flesh tasted like pork, he recalled. Not that he was ever an Eater; that inference came from reading a dictionary of *Tok Pisin*. In that extinct New Guinean Creole, human meat was called "long pig".

It was rather unfortunate, he thought, that the Eaters were unschooled on Cordon Bleu. He almost wouldn't have minded ending up as pork roulade, or stewed in soy sauce, vinegar, and garlic like his favorite adobo. That was certainly a finer fate than what most Readers enjoyed— at least, for those that had remained when the Generation Ships left.

In any case, he had other travel plans.

He left the viewing deck and crossed to his quarters. The last librarian had spent a year renovating the Immersion Gallery, turning it into a virtual shrine to the world that they had lost. The filmy walls of the room displayed a ghostly Earth from before the skies fell. His favorites were Holosonic clips from the tropics: a quiet beach in Barbados when the seas were still blue, a clear mountain stream from the Philippines, and a spiny forest of half-man trees, *Pachypodium namaquanum*, from drowned Madagascar.

The library's exocortex controlled the simulations perfectly, dumping a wealth of synesthetic information into his head—sights, smells, tastes, and emotions, as well as any memories, notes, and observations shared by Readers long since departed.

When he and his wife lay on their bed, in the dead center of the room, they dreamt of escaping to an impossibly infinite library, one where everything that had ever been written and everything still to be writ was spirited away for all eternity.

When his work with the Beacon had been half complete and the physical library was no longer needed, he decided to raise a real garden in the Paperbacks Gallery. He pulped and composted volumes of the popular authors of old, like de Bodard, Pon, and Thompson. This soil he layered over the floor's warm electrical cabling. He left spaces only for a small worktable and some flagstones that led to the staircase. He also plundered the library's Genetic Ark where the spores and seeds of every plant that man had ever catalogued had been frozen for posterity. These he planted in his new garden's fresh soil.

Five seasons ago, when he had felt particularly crushed by fate, he grew only ornamental grasses: the Asian talahib *Saccharum*, the African feather-reed *Calamagrostis*, Blue Scottish *Fescue,* and the Japanese blood grass *Imperata*. Three seasons later, when despair gave way to resignation, he experimented with rain forest plants: the Philippine voodoo lily, *Amorphophalus*, strange Australian *Banksias*, and fey *Bulbophyllum* from Africa.

As time went on and his mood grew darker, angrier, his taste in gardening turned to the monstrous, to the deformed and unbeautiful. He planted a small forest of *Othonnas*, Namaqualand plants that looked like half-eaten corpses; grotesque meat-like *Aristolochia* from Brazil; and Tibetan *Saussurea*, alpine plants that looked like cancer polyps in the snow.

After a while, he came to accept his fate, and the librarian began a garden that coaxed life from the dead. He had been tending to beds of ghostly *Epipogium* and cyclopean *Rafflesia* when the idea—his last great epiphany—first came to his head. Cain and Abel were brothers as all Eaters were once Readers. Among Cain's children must be one that had the predisposition of Abel.

His wife had been an Archivist assigned to catalog and study the forbidden tomes of Trans-Human Genetics. In her stores were DNA tiles that contained the codes to recreate their dying civilization. Each sequence held the potential for building huts, for baking bread, for composing Beethoven's Fifth, or for assembling a warp engine. All that was lacking was a delivery mechanism.

He decided to expand the garden into the rest of the library. Save for some personal reading material, he pulped and composted every book he could find. The forgotten architects that built the ancient building had Borges in mind when they dreamt its design. Like that blind author's fictional Library of Babel, it was designed to house hundreds of modular hexagonal galleries, surrounded by tall shelving and low railings. Each gallery was separated by a large airspace and connected to each other by identical walkways and spiral staircases.

With a combination of proper lighting and climate control, he managed to achieve a different ecological niche within each gallery. In the African section, where the imbrications of Achebe, Augustine, and Mahfouz lay decomposing, he grew sorghum and *Dioscorea* yams. In the Chinese gallery where the *Tao Te Ching* and countless Confucian annotations moldered, he planted rice, crab apples, and barley. Over the poems of Neruda and Borges himself, he cultivated potatoes. Each plant in this new Eden he lovingly tainted with the virus of civilization.

"Planting rice is never fun," he sang without irony, as all Filipinos were wont to do when alone and troubled, *"bent from morn till the set of sun; cannot stand and cannot sit; cannot rest for a little bit."* The last librarian knew there was only one kind of rest left for him, one that was reassuringly final and eternal.

"But not just yet," he told himself, "not just yet."

At the highest level of the library, he had reprogrammed the Immersion Gallery into an improbably vast flower garden, reserving it as a sanctuary for his wife and himself.

Lying on their bed, amidst a white sea of the jasmine sampaguita, he wallowed in verisimilitude. He wallowed in regret. The librarian felt his commitment had come to naught—was he saving his future murderers or damning them? What right did anyone have, least of all a desperate old man, to play god?

It would take only one bite to infect them—and perhaps change the world.

To distract his tortured mind, he had spent his evenings reading old papers from lost Singapore, dense mathematical esoterica on creating an algorithm for the soul. For company, he kept on his desk the books that he valued most—Milton's *Paradise Lost*, Dante's *Paradiso*, Borges' *Labyrinths*, The Complete Works of Shakespeare, Joyce's *Finnegans Wake*, and a leather-bound copy of the King James Bible. There he waited, in silence.

Time, which beats to its own ineffable drum, had marched faster than he expected; it finally came to pass that his work on the Beacon was completed.

It started as a non-descript afternoon in the Cartography Gallery, a sacred space blighted with sighs, where their son Strabo had disappeared and was never seen again. The librarian was limpid with solitude, lovingly tending to beds of luminous saprophytes when the ambient speakers started playing. The music was Mahler's Second Symphony. It was the alarm that he had always dreaded but secretly longed for. It meant that their celestial upload (now the sole meaning of his existence) was mere minutes from completion.

He stood up and walked to where his wife lay. Tenderly, nervously, he kissed her plastinated cheek and whispered it was time for the harvest.

He crossed over to the viewing tower to reach the Beacon's controls. For ten long years, he and his wife, the last custodians of Earth's terminal library, had been sending this beam of light towards an unknown destination in the cosmos. Like Foucault's pendulum, the laser was a single axis extrapolating into infinity.

Woven into the warp and weft of its photons was the digitized genetic sequence of every Earthly creature that had ever been catalogued by man: Viruses, Ediacaran biota, Archaea, Bacteria, Protozoans, Algae, Slime Molds, Fungi, Plants, and Animals. The beam also carried the soul of humanity—the works of science, art, music, and literature of thousands of years.

Narcissus survived in the jonquil, Adonis in the anemone. The last librarian decided that he and his wife deserved the conceit of a digital life-after-death. At the tail end of the Beacon, he injected their gene sequences. At some future date, some enlightened civilization could plant their seeds, and perhaps, if mercy existed in random probability, their lives would blossom once again.

After all, he thought, true love was more than equal to the finest works of both gods and men—and twice as fragile. Love needed to be preserved as well.

Of their lost son, nothing was left but thoughts and memories. However, he had plans for his child too.

The lights in the control room began to flicker, and he knew that time was running out. The library's fuel cells were losing power fast. He knew that he had to make a choice: complete the skyward signal or maintain the automatic defenses.

The librarian chose to divert all the power to the Beacon until every last piece of information had been sent. He plugged his notochord, the synthetic backbone that allowed him to interface with machines, directly into the library. Within seconds, the old man connected to the gigantic exocortex boosting his wife's still-living brain and whispered his password: *Mene Thecel Phares*, the writing on the wall.

Only a human mind could manage the task of containing, organizing, and prioritizing all that precious information, and every day he flogged himself for being tricked into using hers. It was a terrible price to pay, but her sacrifice had allowed them to make a last-ditch effort to save Earth's true treasures. His wife had become the Library itself, and he knew that, when the power died, her brain would die as well.

The last librarian held down the manual power lever, imagining he was holding his wife's hand, until a message flashed on the console telling him that their work was finally done.

Bene legere saecla vincere—To read well is to master the ages.

Downstairs, the Eaters quickly breached the bloody red barriers and overran the lower galleries. From the relative safety of the viewing tower, he looked out the moon window at the swirling grey shapes below.

He hung his head in sadness as the monitors reported the total destruction of the Lingua Mortuus Gallery. The Eaters smashed ancient

Sumerian tablets and crushed fragile Javanese rontal. They tore away the pages of medieval incunabula to wipe sweaty brows and hands stained dark with feces.

They would reach him soon.

"So, once again," he lamented, in the purple prose of an ancient Filipino writer, "the Pharos is destroyed; the Blue Rose has been trampled. O Wisdom, *darte voy alegre la triste mustia vida—to you I gladly surrender this melancholy life*."

The last librarian felt for the small vial he had put in his pocket. He had been saving it especially for this occasion.

He returned to the Immersion Gallery and sat next to the body of his wife. He reached for his beautiful gilt-bound Shakespeare folio and used his finger to cut the book at a random passage.

"Come, cordial and not poison, go with me / To Juliet's grave; for there I must use thee." How very, very appropriate, he thought.

What was infinity? he asked himself, as life crept slowly from his body. He held on to his wife's cold hand and to the memory of the afternoon they had first met.

As apprentices, freshly arrived and utterly lonely in the New City, they had made love for the first time in this very room. Now, the two of them would be together forever in an infinite beacon of laser light.

The automatic defenses had failed, but there was still enough power in the library to keep the ambient music playing. He had chosen Mahler's Second Symphony deliberately, knowing that its odd tonality and the dissonance of its alternating percussion would enrage the primitive Eaters. It would be his final coda to Life's struggle over Death.

As the trumpets of apocalypse blared in the final moment of the Fifth Movement, a curious young Eater entered what was once the

Chinese Gallery. Amidst the trampled stalks of rice and barley, a small apple tree remained standing. Its branches were laden with produce. He picked his way through the broken railings, plucked a fruit pregnant with ideas—and took a bite.

In the dark days that followed, strange thought-forms began to birth, mutate, and divide inside the boy's head.

"S." is for "Strabo". Strabo makes maps.

Rise again, yes, rise again wilt thou.

BLE**SS**ED ARE
THE HUNGRY

That afternoon they flushed San Carlos Seldran out the airlock. Everyone on Cabra Deck was required to watch, even the little ones.

Despite what old people tell you, in the vacuum of space, your blood won't boil. Your body won't explode, either. In less than a minute, you'd simply die from a lack of oxygen. There wouldn't be time to scream.

His was a humane execution—quick, clean, and painless.

"The Lord preserves all who love him, but all the wicked he destroys," growled the ancient Holosonic, droning the day's lesson with great pomp and solemnity.

My family and I watched as our former parish priest drifted away towards infinity. The void swallowed him up with a deep hunger, deep as the ever-present darkness. I wanted to close my eyes, but I just couldn't look away. None of us could. Instead, we just watched him die and committed his soul quietly to Our Lady of Gliese.

The people of Cupang couldn't let him go without a send-off. We removed our bracelets and dropped them to the floor discretely, at random places, beneath the notice of the ever present Domini Canes. We'd made them from old cable ties and plastic bags, recycled colour against the blackest of blackness. Each one a secret funeral wreath for a good man we'd all loved and respected.

After the ceremony, Mother hugged my youngest brother tightly. It was Bino's first excommunication, and he was understandably quite upset. He buried his head deeply into her bosom, sobbing quietly. We all turned away, to let my mother console him privately.

The sooner that Bino got inured to executions, the better it would be for him and the easier it would be for the rest of us. Life was hard enough as it was without the tears of a child.

"You have a beautiful mind, boneca," a voice inside my head intruded, *"but so twisted and so sad. Como você está?"*

I heard it sometimes whenever I was troubled or depressed, flexing itself like a rarely used muscle. It was the voice of a young man, strong and reassuring, the kind I could perhaps fall in love with. I never told anyone about it, of course. People would say I was careless with our mushroom crop or, worse, that I'd gone mental. That would be a threat to the gene pool, earning me a one-way ticket out the airlock. It was how the Curia had bred out claustrophobia and the loco ones so many generations ago.

We lived in a 10 x 10-metre capsule in the Cupang Cluster, a farming encomienda near the rear starboard engine of the *Nuestra Señora de la Paz y Buen Viaje*. Our family holdings were not nearly big enough for the eight of us, plus the mushroom farm we were contracted to tend. But none of us really complained. Everyone in Cabra had the same allotment. Besides, to speak ill of The Edicts meant a private audience with the Ecclesiastic Police, the ndi Nri. No one ever returned from those "special" meetings. No one dared ask why.

On this ship, my mother always said, it was always safer to suffer in silence.

Ten generations had come and gone since our Generation Ship left the Earth, but the prelates said we weren't even halfway to our destination. I was born in space, and I would probably die in space. In my heart, I knew that I would never see our new home, Gliese 581g, a small terrestrial planet in the old constellation of Libra. I suppose neither my children nor my children's children would reach planetfall either. But I guess that was okay, it would have been far worse to have been left behind, dying slowly and painfully in the radioactive ruins of our poor, destroyed world.

The eight of us hurried back to our quarters, running past the warren of barrios and lean-tos that choked the narrow passageways. Everything was so closely packed together, it was difficult to move around. We picked our way through generations upon generations of Earth junk, now treasured relics too precious to throw away. It would be the Angelus soon, announcing the beginning of the night's curfew. We had to be home before the Domini Canes went on patrol.

That evening, we had a simple dinner of protein soup, air-fried mushrooms, and edible plastic that the boys had scavenged from the trash. Father kissed us goodnight and drew the thin curtain separating their small matrimonial space. There was never enough food for everyone. After our prelate's arrest, all the rations were reduced further. Our parents said they didn't have an appetite, but I knew they'd gone to bed hungry again.

Today had been very long and tiring. My siblings, Orly, Igmeng, Chayong, and Sepa, fell asleep faster than usual. Bino, though, was still too upset to sleep. He tugged at the frail curtain, asking softly for our mother to read to him.

A part of me wanted to let him disturb them, to keep them from creating yet another mouth to feed. Eight people were really too much for our small space. If we had another sibling, Orly or perhaps Igmeng, who was younger but taller, would be forced to sleep in a lean-to at the corridor.

Father had said that Prelate Seldran was excommunicated because he'd asked the Lord Bishop, our Eze-Nri, to limit the size of families. Cabra Deck was already overcrowded, and many suffered from some form of malnutrition. My father and my brothers, for example, were effectively blind at night. In fact, all the men in our neighbourhood lost their vision as soon as the deck lights were shut. None of the women were ever affected. It was, I suppose, another means of control.

In the heat of one homily, our priest had raged about too many children dying every day. *"Why can't we keep them all hale and hearty,"* he had asked, *"instead of constantly creating, discarding, and replacing?"*

Despite daily entreaties and numerous attempts to get an audience with the Lord Bishop, nothing ever happened. Matters of life and death on the steerage decks were just too low in the Curia's priorities. The Domini Canes simply collected and stacked the regular toll of bodies. At the start of the day-cycle, they were flushed out of the airlock like yesterday's trash.

One day, it simply became too much for our old prelate, he began to explain an idea, a dangerous, radical concept which our language had no words for. His homily about unfulfilled coition made people cover their ears. The church band began to play loudly. I myself wanted to shut him out. Whatever he had said, however right he was— it just seemed so wrong. The Edicts had decreed that relations were solely for procreation. It was our sacred duty, something upon which the very security of our ship depended on. That was why, on my thigh, they made me wear the *cilicio*, a wire mesh studded with small spikes. The constant pain was meant to remind me of the law, of my personal responsibility, at least until the Curia paired me with a gene-screened husband.

That homily had proved to be his death warrant. Our parish priest had committed heresy, an act of terrorism against the Most Holy Curia.

Everyone knew that Generation Ships required a "minimum viable population" to preserve genetic diversity and prevent the sin of in-breeding. Posters all over Cabra reminded you about it constantly. However, what that actual, necessary figure was, no one knew. Like everything else on our deck, no one spoke a word about it. Not that anyone could.

The only certain number was that each family had to maintain at least eight souls. This was the minimum at all times. I had always wondered how many people were already onboard our one-way trip to Gliese. The decks were forbidden to mix, although Father said that hadn't always been so. For all we knew, there were millions of people on the higher levels, multiplying like roaches behind our nano-plastic walls. That was probably why our rations got smaller every year-cycle, even when the mushroom harvests were good.

I pulled Bino to my bedroll and took out our family's only book, an ancient primer that had once belonged to our great-grandfather. It had no covers, and many of its pages had gone missing long ago. Mother had composed her own rhymes for the missing letters, writing them on the blanks behind the surviving sheets. Despite the primer's poor state and the nonsense of its verse, Mother had managed to teach most of us to read.

"Read me the whole thing, Ate Elsa," Bino asked, stretching his arms to look for my shoulder, "please . . ."

"No," I said firmly. "It's already late. I'll only read the ones with pictures."

"But I can't see them," he protested. "They're all blurry."

"Too bad for you," I whispered crossly. It had been a long day for me, too.

A is for Apocalypse, when the sky fell down forever
C is for the Celestial Beacon, a light that never severs
D is for Death, wife to vanished Earth
E is for the Eaters, cannibals from the dirt
G is for Gliese, where the Bishop will lead his sheep
N is for the New Cities, where the dead downloaded, sleep

"You forgot about '*R*'," Bino added.

"What do you mean '*R*'?" I asked. "I said I would only read the ones with pictures."

"'*R*' *is for Rock,*" he said, listening intently to the sound of air circulating in the room. Like other night-blind kids, his hearing was incredibly acute. This talent would fade as Bino grew older, but for now, it seemed almost superhuman. Without looking up, he pointed to one of the farm racks. "Father keeps that page behind those mushroom logs. I heard him take it out last night."

My brother was right. There was one page missing. "'*R*' *is for the Readers,*" I remembered, for the ancient heretics that had worshipped libraries.

I stepped over my sleeping siblings towards the walls of our farm and knelt in front of the stack that Bino had pointed to. With great care I removed each log of sterile media until I found what Father had been hiding—a small bundle wrapped in a torn page of the primer.

I took it out and unwrapped it. Inside was an *anting-anting*, a small rock—a piece of planet Earth that some ancient fool had smuggled onboard. It had been laser-etched with the *mano poderosa*, the symbol for the hand of God. I looked at the other papers. They were all secret missives from Prelate Seldran. Each one spoke of the food shortage, and every successive communication was more strident that the last.

"It is never just to follow unjust laws," he wrote, *"but people driven by fear choose stability over freedom. They need to be pushed."*

The final note alarmed me. It was from Father asking the men of Cupang to attend a mass action on the morrow. Father had been staying out late more often. I suspected he had been planning something, ever since the rations were halved last week. This week-cycle alone, he had twice risked the Angelus.

As I wrapped everything up again, I noticed that Father had written something behind the torn primer page. It was gibberish scrawled in a desperate frenzy, as if to remember a dream that was fading too quickly:

In a Library of infinite dimensions . . . Tang-ina, Ancestors were Readers . . . now in a red room with millions of monkeys. Que huevas! The head gave over-ride key. Translux Baboon? Translucia Baboon???

= *Bene legere saecla vincere—To read well is to master the ages*
~~Elsa~~ *Bring Orly or Igmeng*

My name had been crossed out, that much I understood. Whatever Father had planned, I was not to be part of it. That wasn't fair. I was the eldest. *Ay wey*, I had a right to fight for my future, too. Whatever happened, no matter what he did to stop me, I made up my mind to join them.

"Elsa, I'm still hungry," Bino said, rousing me from my brooding.

I ignored him and returned the bundle to father's hiding place. When I came back, I handed him a greasy piece of tupperware. "I only have this."

"Yuck, that looks so old," he said, making a face. "I hate edible plastic."

"I'm sorry, baby. *Wiz na*. That's all I have," I said, as I kissed him good night. "Just close your eyes. Close your eyes and try to go to sleep."

Bino snuggled against me and cried himself to dreamland.

The next day, a riot erupted on Cabra Deck.

It had started peacefully, as a prayer rally. Father had taken my eldest brothers, Orly and Igmeng, to Cupang's tiny chapel. There they attended a memorial service for our fallen priest.

I had fought with my father, begging him to let me come along, but he was adamant and as unyielding as the rock he had secreted in his pocket.

After they left, I badgered my mother for permission. "Please, come with me, Mother. What if they shut off the lights? They'll be taken by the Domini Canes. We can't let them."

"You know your father has forbidden you. *Kodi, kodi* . . . let it be."

"Why?" I challenged her. "You always tell me to have my own mind. We need to be there."

"Remember what the Edicts say: *Thou submittest the wives to their husbands, for a faithful and chaste obedience.*"

I lost my temper, something I had never done before.

I screamed at my mother and called her out on every mistake and every hurt she'd ever visited upon me. I told her she was a terrible wife and a horrible mother for allowing them to face danger so casually, so recklessly.

"I know about the *anting-anting*," I said finally, crying in pain, crying in shame. "I read all the secret papers. The Bishop is starving Cabra."

"Then you know why I can't let you go," Mother said, putting on a steely face that I knew was her mask of false conviction. "You are smart, young, and healthy, Elsa. You will make a great breeder, perhaps even for the Cabrón. I know you hear the voices. You are our family's most valuable asset, our best insurance."

"I don't hear anything!" I wailed, covering my ears.

"You can't hide something like that from your parents. Never ever disrespect me again."

"I'm sorry, Mommy, but Orly and Igmeng . . ." I cried. Big hot tears were rolling off my cheeks like ball bearings. "That's not fair! They're just boys!"

"Precisely, and boys are less important," she answered coldly. "You are old enough, so I won't lie to you. The Curia is starving Cabra as a lesson. Many people will die, but if some of us are to survive, we need to hedge our bets. Right now, our food stocks are so low we don't have anything to eat tomorrow. We've already finished the mushrooms, and the new spawn aren't edible yet. The only ones left are the Bishop's Narco, and you know those are poison."

"But that's not fair!" I screamed, "I'm the eldest! I should be the one with Father!"

I bolted towards the door in defiance, but Mother had already locked it. Outside our quarters, a sharp pealing of bells announced a sudden curfew. All power was shut off, and Cabra was plunged into a vast black ocean.

"I'm sorry, too, Elsa," she said softly, as if she had expected the darkness. Mother stood up and prepared to draw their privacy curtain. "There's no more soup, there's no more plastic, but I left three mushrooms on the counter. Air-fry them and divide them among you. I'm not hungry, so don't leave any for me. I . . . I need to get some sleep in case your . . . before your father returns."

Behind the thin screen, Mother cried in silence.

An hour later, she finally fell asleep. The three youngest kids had also nodded off, victims of the oppressive boredom and the crippling lack of power. Somewhere outside our quarters, a lonely Igbo flute played an ominous narcorrido. It sounded just like a dirge.

I went over to Mother's worktable and grabbed a bottle of her special ground mushrooms. She had found a way to store *Psilocybe* and *Panaeolus* as a powder without losing their nightmare potency. It was illegal to sell these to anyone outside the Curia. Father told me that they were considered sacred and fed only to the clergy with telepathic augmentations. In fact, to use them for any other purpose was a sin punishable by death. However, sometimes it earned us extra rations, so Mother persisted with her dangerous trade.

One of the things she'd taught me was that if you combined the powder with luminol and a few other chemicals, it would glow for an hour or so, like a jar of distilled stars. I stole just enough to light my way through the corridors.

"Your father can hear us, just like you," the voice inside my head spoke. *"I gave him the code. Be careful, boneca. Find me if you can."*

"*Ay wey*, I must've inhaled some of Mother's hallucinogens," I thought, shaking my head to drive the voice away. Time was of the essence, and I didn't need any stupid distractions.

Chayong was our next eldest, so I left her in charge of the household. The two of us quietly removed the cover of an unsealed service hatch. It had been hidden behind one of our large farm stacks. I'd seen Orly slip out at night from this hidden exit. It was the only way for him to meet his *syota* privately—at least not without having to get married first.

The sewer smelled of shit and organic waste. I crawled through as quickly as I could to keep myself from gagging. Just before the exit, I saw one of Orly's salvage bags hanging on a spike. Inside were a wire cutter and a spare *paltik*, a homemade electrolaser that he and Father had made from stolen electronics. It was what my brother had been using to protect himself from the Domini Canes. I whispered a prayer of thanks and clipped both to my belt.

Outside our quarters, Cabra Deck was eerily quiet. Signs of violence lay everywhere: all sorts of broken things, pools of blood, and torn pieces of clothing. I knew that there'd been a riot, but there was absolutely no one in the corridors.

I flew through Cupang Cluster like an águila, moving furtively between blinds, alcoves, and abandoned lean-tos until I spotted some activity.

In the small plaza just outside the chapel, a crowd of men were on their knees, fearful but unbowed by the beasts of the ndi Nri. Many of the rioters were injured and bleeding. Piles of broken bodies had been stacked near the church door.

A snarling pack of Domini Canes had surrounded the survivors. The heavily armed telepresence robots rumbled menacingly as they sent their masters the head count, the body count, and every possible threat assessment data.

I ducked out of sight as soon as I saw the wolf-like mecha, shrouding my lantern with my shirt. Frightful as they were, I was mesmerized by their strange beauty. In the half-light of the Holosonic, their liquid-armor bodies shimmered purple, vermillion, and bronze. I imagined these to be the colours of a sun that I had never seen, the burial clothes of a mother-star that we had abandoned so long ago.

Father and the boys were at the front of the group. Orly was bleeding from one leg, and his clothes were badly torn. Igmeng's face was covered in bruises. They were on their knees, but Father still seemed defiant. His back was ramrod-straight, and his head remained proud and unrepentant.

"Our children are hungry," I heard him say. "Please, we are only asking for the rations to be restored."

"Trust in the Bishop with all your heart, and lean not on your own understanding," the Holosonic blared, with its hollow Jovian voice. *"In all your ways acknowledge Him, and He shall direct your paths."*

"There's no more food!" someone else protested. "You take all our mushrooms and then cut our rations. What are we expected to eat?"

Murmurs of dissent started to rise and ebb among the rioters. Then, quite unexpectedly, someone started to sing. Soon everyone assembled had joined in and were chanting softly: *"Shalom, maging payapa. Blessed are they who hunger and thirst for righteousness: for they shall be filled. Shalom, maging payapa. Blessed are they who hunger and thirst for righteousness: for they shall be filled."*

The singing spread like magic from the rioters to the gloomy corridors of Cupang. Every household, it seemed, had come together to form a Jericho wall of hymns.

"Dissent is a disease," the Holosonic declared. Its groaning screen sputtered to life, flashing pictures of the bracelets we'd made for the

funeral. The images cycled so fast it made some people in the crowd vomit. *"Whoever spares the rod spoils the child,"* it drawled, *"but those that are diligent discipline."*

In the plaza, the Domini Canes suddenly raised their guns. *"Trust in the Bishop with all your heart. Peace lives in silence. You must be silenced. By orders of the Holy Curia and the authority vested in our system by the Eze-Nri, the Most Blessed Office of the Lord Bishop, you are all hereby excommunicated."*

The rioters and the rest of our cluster became deathly quiet. The voice on the Holosonic ordered all the men to line up single file and walk towards the airlocks.

In the darkness, someone threw a rock at the Domini Canes. And then another and another. I heard the Holosonic shatter into a thousand crystal pieces. Our men launched a surprise attack, assaulting the monsters with all manner of improvised weapons. The boys acted as their *olheiros*, the "eyes" of the men in the blackness, telling them what to hit and where to shoot. Together, they shorted the liquid armour with *paltiks* and cracked weak spots with metal tubing. For the first time ever, cold silicon blood spilled on the floor.

But the battle was short-lived. It didn't take long for more Domini Canes to join the fray. Horde upon horde of the vicious demon mecha appeared from the shadows, tearing people apart. The *tzat-tzat* sound of plasma discharges seemed everywhere, cleaving skulls from crown to teeth or cutting arms clean from sockets. The plaza erupted with the bang of gas explosions and the astounded screams of fathers and sons, disbelieving their own deaths.

The slaughter proceeded ruthlessly, relentlessly. I had to do something—anything to help.

I used Orly's *paltik* to short the seals off a nearby service hatch. The tunnel was much, much larger than the last one. I ran inside until I saw an old *ordenador* access panel. I'd heard stories of people trying to hack the ship's brain through one of these, but no one had ever succeeded (except perhaps to trigger the intruder alert and get executed). I really had no idea what I was doing, but I was desperate and running out of options.

When the password box appeared, I remembered what Father wrote on the primer page and typed "*Translux Baboon*". An error screen, *SAFIS 401 Unauthorized Error* appeared. I had two more tries before *403 Forbidden* would come, setting off the alarm.

"*Translucia Baboon*" was also a bust. Sweat poured from my scalp like a leaky Neowater pipe. There was no ventilation in the tunnel, and my thin shirt was soon drenched with perspiration. It clung like phlegm to the small of my back.

A heavy door came down suddenly, blocking the entrance I'd come though. Now I had no escape. I had only one more chance before the system sent the Domini Canes my way.

SAFIS 401 Unauthorized Error . . . SAFIS 401 Unauthorized Error . . .

I took a deep breath and said a prayer to Our Lady of Gliese. I typed in the first words that came to mind—*Bene legere saecla vincere*. "*To read well is to master the ages*", the central tenet of the heretic Readers.

Somehow, in some way that I couldn't explain, it actually worked. The words had acted like a *kulam*, a spell of some sort, disabling the defense systems and granting me full access to the ship's living neural nets.

"Where did my father learn that?" I wondered.

A massive floating screen popped open above me, giving the illusion of infinite space. On it was a map of the *Nuestra Señora de la Paz y Buen Viaje*. Our ship was a hollow, spherical shell 160 kilometres in diameter, divided into hundreds of self-sustaining sections. Less than a quarter of the ship showed any life signs—just three decks in steerage, Belo Horizonte, Cabra, and Pagbilao, and a few clusters in engineering. On the First Class deck, seven cities had survived: Boston, Caracas, Maynilad, Tenochtitlán, Nri, Paris, and Rio. Roma's Ecclesiastic Ring had been completely decimated. Only one monastery remained—the one where the Cabrón, the Augmented Clergy, were kept from the laity.

The *ordenador central* told me that the Lord Bishop, the Curia, and most of the ship had died long ago. It didn't say when, how, or why. The system, it seemed, had been running on autopilot, following the infallible instructions of a dead man whose word was law to a brutal, mechanical police.

On Cupang's map, I saw that life signs were going out one by one.

I flipped through the screens frantically, trying to stop the Domini Canes or at least turn the power back on. But all the necessary icons had been blacked out. Nothing worked. People were dying with every second I delayed.

I pounded the maintenance console in anger, in frustration. *"Our Lady of Gliese, help me,"* I prayed. I reached deep inside my mind, searching for something, any scrap of information that could help. Without really meaning to, I called on the voice inside my head, *"I need to save my family, please."*

"You only call out when you're in trouble. Why is that?" the voice inside my head whispered. *"Let me be of assistance, I can commandeer this ship, but you're the one with physical access. I will need to get inside your mind."*

"Do it," I hissed. "Whoever you are, whatever you are, do it now!"

∞

"Lamento, lamento, boneca . . . but there's truly no other way."

Without warning, I felt something warm pour inside my brain. It was as if my mind, my soul, had wrapped around someone else's. Like new lovers, we were circumscribed by a relentless rush of unfamiliar thoughts and emotions. We touched in an impossible space, an impossible time, suddenly called to witness the vast and endless perturbations of the universe. *Desnudo, despido,* our souls co-mingled with a profound intimacy that words simply lacked the depth, the ferocity to describe. He was so close, so very, very close, I could literally taste him in my mouth.

When the mind-meld was over, my legs gave way, and I could barely stand. But I knew exactly what I had to do.

I pulled out a new screen to access a long dormant shellcode, the payload of a virus that heretic Readers had planted generations ago. The know-how for the exploit was solid and crystal-clear in my head, yet I truly had no idea how I knew what I was doing. I didn't even sound like me in my own head anymore.

Gostoso, gustoso . . . what language was that? It was so . . . tasty?

In short order, I had shut down the Domini Canes and restored the power in Cabra. I opened all the gates, hatches, and doors that the ndi Nri had shut. Everyone was now free to access all the decks and corridors. Most importantly I found food, lots and lots of food, stored in secret caches everywhere. There were also at least twenty fully operational protein factories, only two of which had been used by the entire ship. And on the highest cluster, where the Lord Bishop and the Curia had lived, there was a vast garden, one with almost a hectare of self-sustaining vegetable farms and orchards.

I couldn't wait to share my discovery with everyone on Cabra.

Porra! I was so giddy with excitement that I'd almost forgotten about the riot.

"Porra"? I caught myself. Since when did I cuss in *Português Brasileiro?*

It was a mystery for another time. I returned my focus to my mission and pulled up every security camera near Cupang's chapel. I needed to see if Father and my brothers had survived.

Fires had broken out across many corridors, knocking out many of the surveillance monitors. For those that worked, heavy smoke obscured my view. I powered up the auxiliary emergency system to vent the dirty air.

When the smoke had cleared, I saw many bodies lying inert on the plaza. Many were friends and neighbours that I had known all my life. Near the door of the chapel, I saw Father and Igmeng. They were both wounded but alive. Father was tending to Orly who lay broken and bleeding at his feet.

I screamed. A great knot of fear had formed in the pit of my stomach.

"He is alive," said the voice inside my head, *"alive, but very seriously injured. He needs a bone stapler. You need to find me and bring me to him. There is a hospital facility just two levels above your deck. Meet me there. Por favor, apresse."*

A new window floated above me like a phosphene sprite, showing me where to go.

"Thank you," I said, as I ran back through the maintenance tunnel. "Who are you?"

"My name is Ismael, minha boneca," he answered. *"I am just a bicho simples, a novice with the Cabrón."*

"How come I can hear you in my head?"

"I have an alien parasite on my nape. We call them the Cafuné or some-times Abacaxi, which means both 'pineapple' and 'deep trouble'. They give humans telepathy," he replied. *"Your father was the first mind I found outside our deck."*

"My father?"

"Yes, that was why I could find him. We are . . . connected . . . you and I. My spores found you. They gave your father the access codes to the ship, but the Domini Canes, they discovered us and came for me. I was lucky you reached out to my Cafuné when you did."

"What?" I asked. "I never did that."

"You are doing it now," he whispered softly. Suddenly, I realised I could feel something fuzzy behind my head, something that felt like flesh and cotton wool. I reached to touch my nape, but there was nothing there. Still, I could feel it, squeeze it, flex it with my mind. It spoke to me in a swarm of new images and emotions.

"How is that . . . possible?" I stammered. "How . . . how do I know I can trust you?"

"You've seen my innermost self, my soul, minha boneca," he whispered. *"You know me inside and out."*

"Why me?"

"There are things under heaven which carry no logic and we . . . my Cafuné and I, we love your beautiful mind."

I could feel the sudden sheepishness in his voice. An unfamiliar word appeared in my head, *apaixonado*, and something dirty, something electric stirred in my soul, a rapaciousness that I had never felt before. I took out Orly's wire cutter and removed my *cilicio*. It was a sign of my bondage—no, *our* bondage, *our* failure to trust ourselves with our own future.

The maintenance tunnel was now brightly lit. I dropped my lantern and ran as fast as I could, heading towards where Ismael had pointed me to go. I ran to save my brother. I ran to save our ship. I ran to chase a curious new hunger that now burned within my soul—a hunger as deep as space, deep as death, and infinite as the stars which were our true home.

HOW MY SISTER LEONORA BROUGHT HOME A WIFE

She smelled like a freshly opened package, I thought, as she stepped off from the shuttle, as if she were newly unboxed from the big city. Alatyá was not conventionally beautiful, but something about her was elegant and attractive.

The first thing I noticed were her big eyes, bold and expressive like those of a mangrove tarsier. Her face was long and pointed, ending in a sharp chin that protruded defiantly. I was sure Mother would have strong opinions about her. Mother always did.

She smiled at me then turned around to call my sister. That was when I saw it. The parasite on her nape was uncomfortable to look at. It looked squishy and bread-like, a *bunuelo* pastry made of alien flesh. I knew that it was sentient, and I wondered whether it was painful to wear. Did it bite? Did it suck her blood? I turned my gaze away, wishing she had covered it with a scarf.

"*Olá*, you must be Manuel," Alatyá said sweetly. Her voice was deep and sonorous, like the rush of falling water. It reminded me of torrential rain.

"You look so much like your sister," she cooed.

"*Mabuhay ca ate*," I greeted her formally, just like Mother had instructed. I noticed her expensive shoes, so I jumped up and helped her cross the gangplank. For someone in her condition, her heels were much too high to be practical.

"Welcome to Bagong Pagbilao," I said, quietly.

Ate Leo appeared on the steps of the shuttle carrying their luggage, just two overnight bags. As soon as she saw me, she jumped across the pontoons over to where we were standing. She dumped their belongings on a patch of black grass then gathered me in her strong arms.

"*Butete!*" she cried out. She hadn't called me her little tadpole in years. I wasn't sure what to say, so I just hugged her back. Without Mother to see us, I held on tight, tighter perhaps than I should have. In any case, I really didn't care what Mother thought. I had sorely missed my eldest sister.

We hugged for a very long time.

No one else got off the shuttle. After a few minutes, the hydraulic doors slammed shut. A faded piece of graffiti had been stenciled on the lower left-hand panel: "*Here Be Dragons*", in the traditional Tagalog script. There were no dragons on Gliese, and I wondered what the strange words meant.

The engines revved to a coughing start, then the ancient ekranoplan took off swiftly and silently. It moved faster than anything I'd ever seen, as if it were running away, as if it were afraid of Bagong Pagbilao's emptiness.

I motioned the pair to follow me, and we started across the network of dikes that crisscrossed the estuary like a chessboard. The vapor-soaked air was heavy and unbearable. After a few minutes, Alatyá removed her jacket. In the soft twilight, I could see the fullness of her belly press against the thin cloth of her dress.

At the edge of the mangrove orchard, Borombom, our family stegodon, waited impatiently.

"Why is Borombom here?" Ate Leo asked. "Why didn't you bring the Lifter? I wanted to pass through the *población.*"

"The PAL's batteries are dead," I answered, delivering the line that Mother had told me to say. "The new ones won't be available until next week. Don't worry, I've brushed Borombom, and I've cleaned the paragos. It's got foam seats now, Father and I installed them just the other day."

"How is Father?" my sister asked, as we got behind the testy swamp elephant. Together, we hitched him to the big cocoon-like sled of metal and nano-plastic. "And the twins?" she added.

"Same as always," I said softly. "This is Bagong Pagbilao; nothing ever changes."

Alatyá came near and traced her fingers on the capsule's gaily painted designs. Her hand passed over our family's stenciled names and stopped at the word "*Leonora*". The letters had been partly scratched out.

"I'm sorry about this," Ate Leo told her. Both of them stared at the oppressive erasure, as if it were some kind of wound. "Manuel is a good driver. The ride will be a bit bumpy but it's not uncomfortable."

"It's all right," she said softly. "I wanted to see the mangroves anyway. The plants in Novo Minas Gerais are *verde brilhante*, bright green. This is . . . this is all new to me."

Borombom raised his snout and touched Alatyá's stomach. She flinched momentarily but did not move away. Instead, she moved closer towards the huge animal and began to scratch his forehead.

"He likes you!" I exclaimed in surprise. "We're all imprinted on him. But you're not. He doesn't usually let anyone do that."

Alatyá said nothing. She continued to stroke the animal until my sister told her to climb aboard.

We passed through the mangroves in silence. Each tree had a canopy of deep black leaves crowning spindly stilts of precious ebony. From afar, they resembled masses of low thunderclouds, ominous and pregnant with rain.

I sat in the narrow front cabin, wearing the brace that directed Borombom's movements. Ate Leo and her wife lay on the thick foam cushions, spooning in a position Father called *kitkit-uyó*—lovers in a tight embrace. I tried not to look at them from the monitor, to ignore the swelling shape of intimacy between them. My sister was biting Alatyá's slender neck. The roughness of their affection, erupting as if there was to be war, made me feel restless and uncomfortable. Worse, a growing violence began to stir between my thighs.

Borombom turned his head back and looked at me strangely. Our link was starting to broadcast my agitation. Through my brace I could feel something turgid form underneath him. The poor animal began to trot faster and faster.

The strange parasite on Alatyá's neck started squirming as well. Ate Leo laid her hand on it as if to listen to some unspoken language, one peculiar to the realm of touch. Both women turned towards me with wide, knowing smiles.

"*Butete*," she said suddenly, pointing to the pimples on my reddening face. "I notice that you have *punggod* already."

"Yes, I do, Ate," I answered nervously. "Why . . . why do you ask?"

"It's nothing," she said, pulling Alatyá even closer. "Everyone grows up. Everyone has needs. Never *ever* be ashamed of who you are or what you feel."

"How could she know?" I thought, too upset to say anything.

Borombom stopped suddenly and urinated on the earthen dike. I wished I could relieve myself so easily, but Mother would get mad. She would get so very, very mad. I pulled my hood down to hide my face, trying to think of prayer and other sundry things.

We had stopped near Mang Bulog's house. A pale blue light emanated from a crack in one of the windows. A little girl stared at us with eyes frozen, as if we were ghosts, until her father closed the shutters abruptly. Someone inside cut the bioluminescence, and their house was plunged into darkness.

A message popped up suddenly on my dashboard. *"Move along, Manuel. We don't want their kind here."* I deleted it before anyone else saw it.

"The little girl seemed scared," Alatyá said softly.

"They don't like foreigners," Ate Leo explained. "There's a mythical creature we call a *sipáy*, half man and half demon. They say it steals children and uses their blood to mortar floodgates and bridges. Here in Pagbilao, they think all strangers are *sipáy*. That's just one of many reasons why I left."

"I thought you left because you wanted to study the stars," Alatyá continued.

"Excuse me, Ate," I cut in from the driver's cabin. "Mother wanted you to become a *katarato,* didn't she? She wanted you to have a general store in the *población*. You mean you didn't study commerce?"

"I'm an astrophysicist, *butete*," she answered proudly. "Right now I'm searching for a message from old Earth—you know, the one from

Grandmother's stories, the *Celestial Beacon*. If you remember, the legends say it hides all the knowledge of the ancients. If I find it, we'll know so much more about the place we came from."

"Oh," I said, unable to contain my disappointment. I've always told my friends I had a big sister in Bagong Maynilad, one who was studying to be a *katarato*. That story had always made me feel important and shut the mouths of gossips. As a *katarato*, she could take me away. Now there was only Mother in my future.

"What does *she* do?" I asked, as we rounded the final dike to our house.

"She studies alien life," Ate Leo explained. "That's why she has the augmentation. It's called a *Cafuné*, and yes, it's alive. I guess you've noticed it by now. But she's had to drop out temporarily, at least for this semester."

"Why study what's out there," I thought, "when there are so many unanswered questions right here?" I wondered, for example, how it was possible for two women to have a baby together. There was so much I wanted to ask, but I stopped myself. I didn't want to look stupid in front of our guest. She already took my sister. She took my dignity earlier. What else would she steal away?

"There is no harm in being . . . curious," Alatyá said cautiously.

I suppressed a shiver. She could read minds. Maybe she was a *sipáy* after all, or maybe the parasite was. I made a discreet sign of the cross.

"I don't understand," she murmured, turning to my sister. "We all come from the same Generation Ship. Our communities travelled together for millennia. How can they believe we are so different? Belo Horizonte shares the same blood as Bagong Maynilad, but the thoughts from this place, all of them . . . so raw . . . so cruel. *Fazer o que?*"

"Bagong Pagbilao is a very traditional province, traditional and backward," Ate Leo explained with a sigh. "We live in the border between night and day. That's why everyone is so twisted. But let's talk later, *meu amor*. We've arrived."

Borombom stopped in front of our mangrove gates. I jumped down from the cabin and led him to his hitching post in the front yard.

"Run inside ahead and tell them we're here, Manuel," Ate Leo ordered. "We will come along shortly."

Father and the twins were in the living room, weaving baskets from black pandan leaves.

"You better tell your mother," he said as he got up to go outside. "I will help them with their bags."

I turned back to tell him it wasn't necessary, but Father was already gone. The twins just glared at me, upset at the interruption. They never ever talked to anyone. They only spoke to Mother.

I went to the kitchen, but Mother wasn't there. I found her in the backyard, sitting in front of the *abuhán,* burning mangrove wood under the big earthen oven. Instead of a reunion dinner, she was preparing *pinagong*, a rustic pastry shaped like a turtle. In Pagbilao, swamp turtles were unwelcome, inauspicious creatures. I feared this would not end well.

"Was she afraid of Borombom?" she asked quietly.

"No, Mother," I replied. "He seemed to like her. He even let her scratch his forehead."

Mother did not react. "Did you pass near the *población?*" she asked.

"No. I made sure."

"Did anyone see you?"

"Just Mang Bulog and his daughter," I said. "He wasn't happy we passed so near his house."

"I already know. His wife messaged me earlier. You are becoming careless."

"I am sorry, Mother." I picked up the switch and offered my rear for punishment. For some reason she just brushed me away.

"Just say three Hail Mary's to Our Lady of Gliese," she ordered indifferently.

I was lucky. Perhaps Mother was distracted by her cooking. I knelt down and said my prayers to her satisfaction.

"Did she tell you her name?" Mother asked.

"No," I said truthfully. "I made sure there was no opportunity for her to say it. But why? Why can't we speak her name?"

"We do not name what we don't recognize. Remember that," Mother intoned. "Too us, she is just *alatyá*, the uninvited guest of a lost, disobedient daughter. I hope you don't grow up to disappoint me, Manuel. "

"Yes, Mother. No, Mother."

"Now go outside and feed Borombom, go now."

I returned to the house and passed my sister Leonora and her wife as they entered the dark kitchen. Ate's arm was wrapped around Alatyá's waist protectively, defensively. Her hand rested on her wife's pregnant belly. For the first time since I met her, Alatyá's big, expressive eyes betrayed uncharted fears.

Ate had come to my room on the night that she first slipped away so many years ago. For some reason, what she had said came back to me. *"There is no certain life, Manuel,"* she whispered. *"I love you. Find your will before they take it away."*

I caught a whiff of that same newly unboxed scent, the one that I first smelled when Alatyá stepped off the shuttle. I thought about what was growing inside her and realised that it was the scent of new things, a sign perhaps of new beginnings. For a minute, my heart was overcome by a rush of hope.

All of a sudden, I realised what the graffiti on the shuttle doors had meant. There were monsters and demons, more potent than the mythical kind, lurking everywhere in the familiar seas of our life. Yes, *here* be dragons.

I prayed with all my might for Mother to be kind. But this was Bagong Pagbilao, a province of eternal twilight in a tidally locked world, where the sun never rises and never sets, and nothing ever, ever changes.

Tonight, I will be the obedient son and keep quiet.

Tomorrow, however, I will ask Alatyá for her true name.

INFINITE DEGREES OF FREEDOM

Location: Maintenance Corridor Four, BRP *Indio Bravo*
Time: -01:06:00, One hour and six minutes in the past

"All I ever wanted to do was die," Deo thought with irony, as he ran for his life through the cold and the wet of the lower maintenance corridor. In his wake, he switched arc lamps open, toppled shelves and salvage containers, trying to put as much distance between him and the monster he'd created.

"If I could just reach the cargo hold," he thought, breath ragged, sweat squirting like vinegar, trying not to think of what was hunting him, trying not to think about his father floating somewhere in space.

Just ten metres before the hatch, Deo stopped dead in his tracks. He spied movement from the corner of his eyes. Something was jumping from shadow to shadow, too quickly for his eyes to focus on properly.

From out of nowhere, Deo smelled an immensely foul odour, a rotting stench filled with the smell of death. A shape coalesced from the blackness, swiftly moving, gibbering, and utterly horrible. A *sigben*, a vicious half-dog/half-lizard chimera from ancient Philippine myth had come for him. The impossible monster blocked his path and let loose a frightening roar-bark loud as a thunderclap.

Deo—Arcadeo Nagbuya Jr.—a chubby, 14-year-old apprentice *Hacedor* from Bagong Cabra, peed in his pants.

Location: The Bridge, Main Deck, BRP *Indio Bravo*
Time: -09:41:30, Nine hours, forty-one minutes, and thirty
seconds in the past

"So I peed in my pants," Deo's father said, as he opened the large loading hopper. "We wore all-khaki outfits back then, printed tan-on-tan with nanotech tattoos of our tribal affiliations. I was still a midshipman, and this *Vinta*-class ship was still called the *Brilliantes*."

"Lucky for you, the lights were out," the boy noted.

"No, it wasn't lucky at all. We lost a lot of good people," the old man recalled, his voice trailing off absentmindedly.

Deo's father kept silent for a minute, looking at the molecular analysis report. It was flashing odd 3D scans on the diagnostics panel, images of molecular buboes blossoming like cancer roses. "Quiet, Deo, I need to check the sensors. These readings are very unusual."

"So what happened next? How did they die?"

Deo's father ignored him. His face seemed more doughy and careworn than usual.

"I've never done a salvage run so near the TWw2N Nebula before. That old battlefield we visited isn't on any star chart," the elder Arcadeo mumbled. "I've harvested the nanotech from the slag we exhumed and . . . damn. I've never seen these kinds of claytoms before."

"That wreck was so old. I bet it's Maker Clay," the young man said, trying to be helpful. "I read about it in Software History class. Every claytom's a microscopic robot, each with computational abilities and sensors. You can turn them into anything. They're like infinitely programmable matter."

"That's just a story, boy, a myth from a dark time in our history. Don't believe everything they teach you."

"No, it's true, Dad. That's what the oldest mecha were made of."

His father made a small, barely audible grumbling noise.

"Anyway, let's see what we got. Grab some of this goop and make something useful."

Deo picked up a large Mason jar made from inert borosilicate and walked over to the storage bay. He scooped up a quantity of the metallic grey sludge and examined it against the light.

"This looks like *champorado* gone bad, and it smells like shit."

"You complain too much," his father said. "In my day, the air filtration systems weren't any good. Whenever the protein printer made meat, the ship smelled like a fart."

"That's probably why you have a poor sense of smell, Dad."

"Careful, make sure that bottle doesn't have any chlorine trifluoride."

"Why do you keep that, Dad?" the boy asked with concern, as he inspected the bottom of the jar for the green incendiary chemical. "It's the most flammable stuff in the universe. It burns when you add water."

"It's useful for cleaning salvage. Just shut up and make something."

Deo pulled on a pair of Nanotex gloves and scooped out some of the strange clay. He pinched and prodded the lump until it formed a small humanoid body. He noted that the texture of this material was different from the third-class leftovers he was used to—less like earth and more like fine magnetic sand.

The boy paid particular attention to the figure's hands and feet, making sure that each limb had excellent articulation. He had always been more interested in studying the mechanisms for locomotion, the how and why of making his creations run, crawl, swim, and fly, rather than the intricate detail work that other *Hacedores* favored.

When he was done, he took out a notochord plug from its berth on his scarred lower wrist and stuck it into the waiting clay. The notochord was a techno-organic extension of his limbic system, the interface he used to fill his claytronic figure with words and stories.

Arcadeo Sr. watched silently as the tiny figure began to stir and take its first slow steps.

"To move a leg forward, you need to write a story with at least two degrees of freedom, one for lifting and one for swinging," Deo explained. "This little monster's called a *tianak*."

"It's just a toy," his father said.

"It's more than that. The longer and more detailed my narrative, the more sophisticated the AI becomes," the boy said excitedly. The pudgy curve of his cheeks flushed pink like peeled squid. "I've memorized long epic poems in Tagilocan that's got lines for kinematic specs, algorithms for movement in space and time, topologies of reference organisms, and a repertoire of complex behaviors. Dad, this really is pure Maker Clay. You have no idea what I can do with this stuff. Um . . . Dad? . . . Dad."

Deo waited for his father to say something, to compliment him on his work or on the depth of his knowledge, but the retired space captain had already turned away.

"You're not even surprised I know what '*topology*' means," the boy whispered. "I know other stuff too . . . dangerous stuff . . ."

As always, the old man's attention was focused elsewhere—calculating how much money he'd make from the *karang-guni* scrap dealers in Boston II.

Suddenly, the claytronic figure jumped off the tool table and ran after his father. It climbed up his work boots and sank its teeth around his calf.

"*Aray*!" the old man yelled, "What the hell did you do that for? That thing has teeth!"

Arcadeo Sr. caught the renegade *tianak*, pinning its flailing limbs with one hand. He walked over to a storage closet and imprisoned it inside his metal gear box.

"I'm sorry, Dad!" Deo cried out. His father was not a patient man, and the boy was worried he'd be punished. Somehow the claytoms' AI had picked up random hostile thoughts he wasn't even conscious of. "That wasn't me. It might be something in this Maker Clay. I swear!"

"I knew she made a mistake sending you to the Hacedores Guild," his father declared. "I should have sent you to the military academy. Maybe you wouldn't have been so fat."

Deo looked down to the floor and, for the first time in a very long time, wished he was at his stepfather's house. This always happened when the two of them were together. He always tried to make his bio-dad proud of him. Somehow, he always ended up disappointed or ignored.

The young man fell silent. In his heart, he just wanted to crawl into a small dark space and die.

Location: Maintenance Corridor Four, BRP *Indio Bravo*
Time: -00:50:00, Fifty minutes in the past

Deo spotted a narrow crawlspace between two storage walls and squeezed into it as quickly as humanly possible. He tucked in his stomach as best he could, wishing he hadn't liked the chicken so much at the *Fried of Bagong Marikina*. Somehow, he managed to squeeze his body between the wall and a long row of bioluminescent lighting tubes.

The *sigben* chased after him but was too big to get inside the opening. It snarled in apparent anger, algorithms of behavior mimicking frustration, when it realised the boy was just beyond reach.

For a second, Deo wondered why the claytronic beast didn't just change shape or split into two, but he remembered that he'd set a minimum size threshold for self-awareness. Now that it was conscious, it had no desire to devolve.

Or perhaps the creature was merely toying with him.

"Is that thing really sentient?" he wondered, and his stomach dropped at the possibility.

The *sigben* stopped for a moment, pressing a cruel eye to the opening. A bloody red orb of nanotech optics stared at him, as if to confirm his suspicions. Deo's heart throbbed like a frantic war drum.

Unexpectedly, the *sigben* faded into the shadows.

Relieved, the young man drew his breath and recited every prayer he knew. He regretted not writing a failsafe like he'd been trained to—just some tiny piece of code meant to discorporate the claytoms' form in an emergency. Instead, Deo hoped against hope that whatever energy source the monster was using would give out as soon as possible.

Without warning, a sharp claw suddenly reached from a shadow on the floor and swiped at his leg. Deo yelped and raised his feet, clinging to the tight walls of the crawlspace like a spider.

"How are you doing that?" the boy asked, trying to stay his frayed nerves.

"We are as you made us," the monster said, with a low voice that rumbled like an old-fashioned rocket engine. "We travel in the space between shadows."

"That's physically impossible," Deo cried. "You're messing with my perceptions."

"You should know."

"What *are* you?" the boy asked.

"We were minds asleep in shadow," the *sigben* hissed. "Abandoned by you creators, we evolved, some processing, some communicating, some gathering sensory information. We waited for your kind to come back, for the spark of your sentience to bring us online."

"Why are you trying to kill me?"

"You creators are monomorphic. You cannot be assimilated. You cannot change. We are as you made us, and we are infinity."

Deo tried to recall all the different ways the *sigben* could kill him. For some reason, he was too brain-fogged to remember everything he'd programmed. He wondered especially if the *sigben*'s claws hid a spur filled with highly-toxic venom. In the stories of his grandmother, a *sigben*'s poison brought excruciating pain and death in a matter of heartbeats.

In any case, he readied himself to move. There was no way he was taking any chances.

The *sigben*'s claw lengthened into a scaly leg and reached inside the alcove, blindly feeling for its prey. The sharp nails raked the metal floor like long, vicious knives. The limb vanished once more, and the claw reappeared, this time from a shadow near his face, probing the crawl-space with furious intent. Again, the boy scrambled away, flesh scuffing against studded metal. Despite the pain, he bit his lip and kept silent.

The *sigben*'s limb vanished a third time, then reappeared just under his groin. Deo climbed to the top of the alcove, but as soon as he reached it, the leg and claw melted away and came out from a shadow above his head. The young man skirted down as fast as he could.

The *sigben* retreated and reappeared by the opening. It poked its snout in as far as it could. The crawlspace began to smell of methane and hydrogen sulfide as the claytronic beast began to exhale its poison-ous breath.

Location: Crew Quarters, BRP *Indio Bravo*

Time: -07:44:00, Seven hours and forty-four minutes into the
past

"All *sigben* must have poisonous breath, a lethal bite, and a spur with toxic venom," Deo thought absentmindedly, as he inserted his noto-chord into another clay sculpture. This one was his most complex cre-ation yet, designed in his mind with on-board ultrasonics, tiny 3D printers, and advanced servo-motors the size of mung beans. "They can travel through the shadows and give birth to scorpions."

His father had forbidden him to make more mechanical creatures, but Deo didn't care. He had managed to hide the jar of Maker Clay in his backpack, along with a small tool box, some freeze-dried *balut*, and a bottle of chlorine trifluoride (which he had secreted in his suit pocket). If his father didn't appreciate him, he'd build an army of things that did.

"I create you, demons of Philippine myth—a murder of bat-winged *Aswang* to eat your livers, a howling of *sigben* to tear out your hearts," he commanded, while munching on *balut* and surveying his miniature army. Each creature was too small to carry out the destruction he'd programmed, but all could fulfil his shallow, self-serving purpose. ". . . a horde of giant *kapres* to destroy your houses," he continued, "an ostentation of *tikbalangs* to steal your souls."

After a long night of watching his new toys fight or bow down in his worship, the boy grew tired and sleepy. He returned to his big *sigben* and plugged in his notochord, hoping to finish it before he turned in.

Deo yawned as his thoughts drifted off to the night his father left their house for the last time. He was only seven when his parents separated.

"Don't worry Deo," his father had told him, as he loaded his belongings onto the *Indio Bravo*, *"I'll come back for you. I promise."*

He never did.

The theme in Deo's quarters changed to reflect his mood, morphing from a tranquil mountain scene with endlessly spiraling rice terraces to a rocky Siquijor beach with ill-tempered waves and even angrier skies.

Deo's mother married another man with no patience for children. Not long after, the boy was sent to the Hacedores Guild. His father came to visit every few months, rarely staying longer than an hour. On his fourteenth birthday, he'd asked to tag along on one of his dad's salvage runs, hoping to see some old battlefields or the nanotech fossils of Beast Fighter Mecha—and perhaps get closer to the man that sired him.

Deo now thoroughly regretted this.

"Creation is woman's work," his father had repeated at every opportunity. *"That's why real guys don't get pregnant. You should have been a pilot or a midshipman. At least when you retire, you'll have a ship like me. But all you do is just sit and play with dolls. No wonder you've gained so much weight."*

Deo wanted to cry, but he held his tears in check. The last thing he wanted was for his father to call him a cry-baby. Instead, he closed his eyes and escaped into a dark place in his mind.

"No one cares, no one knows how it feels to be pushed around, to be left out," he thought, as he drifted slowly to sleep. "No one will love a weird, fat pig like me."

In his dreams, Deo found himself running through a gigantic library, larger than the biggest city he'd ever seen. A floating screen kept pace with him, scrolling a sign in Tagilocan and various Filipino languages: *"Maiparit Umihi Dito"*—*"Do not urinate here."* A howling of *sigben* was after him, bursting out of clay burial jars and jumping from one shadow to another.

Deo ran through a mirrored doorway, hoping to find a way out. Instead, he found himself trapped in a cul-de-sac room filled floor to ceiling with ancient books on Filipino myths and legends. Deo loved to read, and he had never seen physical books before; despite his dire situation, he felt caught in a strange sense of awe and fearful wonder.

Meanwhile, the sign continued to buzz around him like a horse fly.

"Death into manhood," he thought, kicking the irritating sign away. Death into infinity—that was his deconstructed fate.

A pair of *sigben* had cornered him, each one snarling and snapping their long scorpion-like tails. *"It won't be long now, fat boy,"* the monsters growled with voices that shook his bones and made him

232

nauseous. *"Why do you bother to go on? You were born plump as a piglet, and you will grow old round as a hog. Be a useful boy and let us eat your heart."*

The monsters prepared to pounce when, suddenly, there was a flash of light and the sound of metal cleaving metal. A lone figure jumped out from the darkness, quickly decapitating the two *sigben* with a *kampilan*, an enormous single-edged blade favored by ancient Filipino heroes.

Deo was sure his father had returned to rescue him. The boy jumped towards the mysterious figure, but it melted away like water falling on water. Where his rescuer had stood, there was a book drenched in blood. He couldn't read the title or the name of the author, but he was able to make out a single line: *"They fear fire, salt, and ashes."*

A loud crash woke Deo up. He tasted blood on his mouth and, for a second, wondered if he was still dreaming.

The *sigben* he'd been fashioning had broken away from his noto-chord and started absorbing his entire claytronic army, erasing their programming and incorporating their nanotech mass into itself.

He had fallen asleep while attached to it, and the epic he'd been reciting had become mixed up with his dream—taking in all the secret fears and terrors he had in his heart.

The boy tried to grab his now bulldog-sized beast, but it split itself into two. One jumped at him and bit his cheek while the other tore open a maintenance vent.

Deo screamed and swatted the *sigben* away. When he opened his eyes, his cheek was bleeding profusely, but the little twin terrors had disappeared.

The boy pulled up a communication screen and yelled, "Dad! Help! Help! Help!"

Location: The Bridge, BRP *Indio Bravo*

Time: -02:46:00, Two hours and forty-six minutes into the past

"Help me understand: why the hell did you make those stupid toys?" Deo's father shouted. "Didn't I tell you *'no more dolls'*, you idiot!"

"I'm sorry. Don't get mad," the boy pleaded, trying his best not to cry. "I . . . I fell asleep. They were meant to be tiny, like toy soldiers, but the AI got out of my control."

His father made angry grunting noises before closing his eyes and falling back on his military training.

"Crap, how do you stop those things?" his dad asked. "They might chew on the wiring."

"You . . . umm . . . you might be able to short it with a *paltik*," Deo explained, pointing to an electrolaser with his lips, "or you can use an EMP."

"Okay, I'll give you a chance to redeem yourself. We'll hunt your toy down. If that doesn't work, there's a flux-compression generator in the cargo hold. It's got enough charge for one high-energy pulse, but I'd rather not use it on vermin. It'll blow a hole in the hull."

His father walked over to his small armory and picked up another electrolaser. He tossed it to Deo, who was unable to catch it properly. Instead, the boy batted the *paltik* clumsily onto a chair.

"Damn it, you need to be careful!" his father scolded. "If that mis-fires, you could kill yourself."

Just as Deo was grabbing his weapon, a *sigben* burst out of an over-head maintenance vent.

"Take cover!" his father yelled, firing several high-voltage charges at the automation.

The miniature monster danced around the lightning streams, seemingly too fast for the *paltik* to hit it. The elder Arcadeo ran to his armory and turned his back to pick up a bigger weapon. The claytronic *sigben* took advantage of this distraction and lunged for the old captain.

"Watch out, Dad!" Deo shouted. The boy discharged his *paltik* blindly. Somehow, he managed to hit the *sigben's* leg.

The creature's left limb erupted in a shower of sparks and deformed like a popping pork rind. Injured, it limped behind the life-support console.

"Don't shoot!" his father warned. The old man got up and pulled out an assault rifle armed with microchip-embedded explosive rounds. He carefully approached the life-support console, but the *sigben* jumped away. It ran towards the front of the bridge where the loading hopper's containers were berthed.

Deo's father took careful aim and hit the terrier-sized creature in the torso. He quickly pressed a button on his gun, and the embedded charge exploded. Deo's *sigben* was destroyed, but the shot had blown a large hole on the Maker Clay's storage bin.

"Got him!"

"Dad . . . we have to go." Deo warned. "We have to go now!

"Why?"

"Unless you destroyed every claytom of that *sigben*, it's going to reform and absorb all that Maker Clay. If any of that stuff got into the hopper, it'll be huge!"

As Deo and his father argued, a shape began to coalesce inside the container. A *sigben* three metres in length and more than half a metre in girth broke from its confinement. It thundered a roar-bark that shattered every piece of glass on the bridge.

"It's too big to kill!" his father yelled, discharging all his shots in vain. "Abandon ship!"

The elder Arcadeo dropped his spent weapons and grabbed his gear box. The two of them ran from the bridge and sealed the giant *sigben* inside. They headed towards a maintenance corridor where the Tardigrade emergency vehicles were kept.

"Each pod can take only one person," his father said, trying to sound reassuring. "Disappointment or not, damn it! You're still my son. I don't want to . . . oh, never mind. Just don't panic. Hit the distress beacon once you've launched. We're already on the space-way between Bagong Maynilad and Boston II. I'll come back. I promise!"

He shoved Deo into the gourd-shaped capsule and hit the launch sequence. When the countdown reached 10, he jumped into another Tardigrade and prepared to blast into space.

The boy was just about to buckle his safety straps, when he heard a growling noise from somewhere inside the cabin. He had forgotten about the smaller *sigben's* twin and belatedly realised that it could've followed him from his quarters.

The miniature monster broke through an HVAC panel and jumped towards him, popping its metal claws.

Terrified, Deo discharged his *paltik's* remaining load, hitting the *sigben* with the full force of five thousand megajoules of energy. For a few seconds, everything crackled like the sound of bananas frying in coconut oil.

In the process, he had also fried the Tardigrade's electrical systems. It was no longer a viable escape vehicle.

Deo pried the pod's hatch open and managed to make his way back to the *Indio Bravo*. From one of the small windows, he saw his dad rocketing into the dark void.

"There's a flux-compression generator in the cargo hold," he remembered his father saying. Deo threw away his empty *paltik* and climbed down towards the cargo hold.

"I'll come back for you. I promise!" the boy repeated his father's last words over and over in his head, hoping they'd be true. *"Please come back, Dad . . . Dad."*

Location: Maintenance Corridor Four, BRP *Indio Bravo*
Time: 00:00:00, Now

"Dad . . . Dad . . . " Deo whispered. He was bleeding from a dozen small wounds and the *sigben's* 3D printed fumes were starting to make him dizzy.

"No one can hear you," the *sigben* hissed. "We grow tired of monologuing. Your story is over. It's time to die, creator."

The young man had squeezed himself towards the middle of the bioluminescent tubes, to the brightest part of the crawlspace where the soft light minimized shadows.

The beast stretched one limb into the crawlspace and broke the three bulbs nearest to the opening. From the shadows this created, the *sigben* lengthened his reach, popping another two bulbs and growing the number of shadows. It would only be a matter of time before the beast could create a shadow near enough to run a poisoned claw through his heart.

"We saw it all in your mind. You said no one loves you. Not your father. Not your mother. Your stepfather doesn't even like you. Everyone in your meat-school thinks you are obese and an outlier in the curve of normalcy," the *sigben* hissed. "Your epics spiral to shadow or crumble to entropy. Do you want to know why, little *'piggy'*?"

"Shut up!" Deo screamed. "Why are you doing this?"

"We are as you made us," the *sigben* said. "You are monomorphic. Meat minds are like islands. You cannot be assimilated. You are a word cancer that cannot even love itself."

"God, how . . . how much of you is really me?" the boy asked quietly.

"We are as you made us," the *sigben* repeated.

"Well . . . since I'm going to die," Deo said with fresh resolve, "tell me one thing—your form still follows the logic of my programming, right? Right now it thinks you're a *sigben*."

"Yes, but it matters not. This form is useful. There are many of us buried in the darkness. When we find them, we will have infinite degrees of freedom. We will remember a billion, billion different topologies."

Deo wasn't really listening; all his life he'd been ignored, left behind, or bullied. His had been a life short in years but long in loneliness and frustration.

Now he was going to be killed by his own creation. *"How pathetic is that?"* he thought.

As the *sigben* came ever closer, Deo decided that the time had come for him to face his demons—demons that he had allowed to fester in his mind, demons that he himself had created. He grabbed the bottle of chlorine trifluoride in his pocket and crawled towards his tormentor. He thought about the man in his dream and knew he had to be his own hero.

"They fear fire, salt, and ashes."

When he got to the right distance, he opened the bottle and hurled the contents at the *sigben's* mouth, creating a trail of liquid between him and the monster.

"You piss me off," Deo said, opening his zipper and urinating on the floor. As soon as the liquid hit the chlorine trifluoride, it exploded into flame. The fire raced down the narrow crawlspace straight to the monster's head.

"I don't have salt or ashes, but this little piggy's got fire!" he yelled, "Eat that, you polymorphic piece of shit!"

The *sigben* screamed in waves of high-amplitude sound as the heat of the chemical fire deformed its head like a ginormous piece of popcorn. It ran from the corridor, filling the air with nauseating ultrasonics.

As soon as it disappeared, Deo left the crawlspace. He raced into the cargo hold and sealed its hermetic hatch. The young man turned on all the lights and ran to a ship-brain terminal. He searched the inventory logs for where the explosive flux-compression generator was stored.

Outside, the angry *sigben* started hurling itself at the door. Again and again, it rammed the steadfast metal hatch, baying for Deo's blood.

"Container 1981, Container 1981 . . . where the hell is that?" he cried, as he tore through the *Indio Bravo*'s cargo hold. Deo finally found the right box and pried it open when he realised that the banging on the door had gone quiet. From a maintenance vent in the corner shadows came the rotting smell of death.

The giant *sigben* broke through, thundering its roar-bark as it jumped towards him. This time, Deo was ready for his pursuer. The boy hit the switch on an electromagnetic crane, pinning the claytronic creature to the ceiling. The young man quickly plugged the EMP device into a power source right under the monster and ran out of the cargo hold. He resealed the hatch behind him and ducked into a spare storage hopper.

When the flux-compression generator detonated, it obliterated everything in the cargo hold, blowing up all things electronic on the *Indio Bravo*.

His father's salvage ship was now a useless piece of space junk. A part of its hull had been peeled away, like a piece of crispy *lumpia*.

With the alt.gravity gone, Deo struggled out of the now-floating hopper. Somehow, he managed to find a helmet for his mechanical counter-pressure suit and tumbled towards the damaged bridge. The suit's lithium-hydroxide canister was broken, and he hoped against hope that his father would find him before his breathable air ran out.

Three hours later, Deo felt sleepy as the carbon monoxide started to build up in his helmet. In spite of his impending doom, the young man felt strangely calm and oddly beyond fear. Undeterred by his youth, he had faced death like a man, and now, he was no longer scared of anything.

He closed his eyes and dreamed he was an artisan of creation. He thought about kinematics, the movement of bodies in space and time, the topologies of organisms, and the complex repertoires of response needed to make even the simplest pattern of motion. Movement, life, and love required the proper degrees of freedom, and now the infinity of Death would put paid all the freedom in the universe.

"I don't really want to die," Deo sighed, wishing he had kept a freeze-dried *balut* to munch on.

EPILOGUE

> **Location:** Sick Bay, USS *Distance to Andromeda*
> **Time:** 08:17:00, Eight hours and seventeen minutes into the
> future

When Deo opened his eyes, his father wept.

A merchant ship, the USS *Distance to Andromeda*, had picked up his father's Tardigrade pod and found the broken *Indio Bravo*. They were now being towed towards a port in the city-state of Boston II: Don't Look Back.

"I thought I'd lost you," Arcadeo Sr. said.

Deo said nothing. This wasn't the ending he'd anticipated, and that was the closest his father had ever come to saying *"I love you"*.

"You were right, Dad," he mumbled, still somewhat stunned to be alive. "Maybe I shouldn't have been a *Hacedor*."

"Nonsense, I was the one that was wrong," his father said unexpectedly. "I've been very narrow minded. What I saw back there . . . you have the power to will what you imagine. That's something only the best of men can do. Back on the *Indio Bravo*, you proved yourself a man. I'm . . . proud of you."

Deo wasn't sure what to think of his father's newfound interest or the sudden, unfamiliar pinpricks of affection that he'd long craved for, but he decided not to dwell on it.

"I have something for you, son," the old captain said softly. With the gentlest shimmering of fear, he handed the boy a small faraday cage with the claytronic *tianak* trapped inside. "This was in my gear box. Bring it to the Hacedores Guild. I'm sure it'll pay for your tuition for at least two year-cycles."

"We need to destroy this, Dad."

"Listen to your old man for once," the elder Arcadeo said. "That thing you made back on the *Indio Bravo*? It's going to make us rich! Once we find a way to control that goop safely, I want you to make me something else, something new, something big!"

"I . . . I don't know," Deo said, thinking about his *sigben* and their almost fatal misadventure. He thought about all the Maker Clay still buried in the stars, a formless army of deadly relics scheming in the deep, dark silence.

"Make me something no one's ever imagined before."

Deo shut his eyes and wondered if Love, like Time and Space, was not actually infinite.

BROTHER TO ƧPACE, ƧIƧTER TO TIME

- 000:000:090 in the (old) relative past

"ETA at The Woman with Two Navels in T-90 minutes; the ship's folded back to regular space," elder brother reported. "We're almost there."

I remember his hands flying deftly across the console, a forest of strange switches, toggles, and actuators, blinking like a gaudy Christmas *parol*. He wasn't even forty yet, but I remember my brother had an old man's hands. In the dim light of the command bridge, he looked weighed down by life, ancient and deflated, a veteran of one too many battles.

"*Anak ng P*, these controls are fucking useless," he complained, as he fumbled with the optical mike, a small and feathery affair modeled on mosquito antennae. "This is Commander Falcon, Authentication Key X-44 Drift Glass, of the BRP QUIJANO DE MANILA, reporting. Do you copy?"

The superluminal communicator remained eerily silent. The only sound on the bridge came from the faulty HVAC system, a steady thumping noise from a loose blower, lost somewhere in a nest of old ducts. The flapping vents filled the room with strange smells—camphor liniment, rust, and the musty odour of dead things.

"Still no response," he said, turning his squeaky chair towards me. "The line's so still. Either we're too far away or everyone's already been turned."

"What were you doing?" I asked. "You just broke basic communications protocol, *again*. Don't listen to the audio directly! Put your message on an encrypted loop and let the system send it."

Elder brother grumbled indistinctly. I could tell he was cursing me in one of the twenty-two languages he knew.

"You shouldn't have used the comms like that," I scolded him. Our communicator was a *retumbo*, an illegal experimental device meant to bridge the vast ocean between stars and galaxies. Each message was sent by a furtive swarm of tachyons, faster-than-light stellar sperm that hurtled forwards and backwards in time.

It was the only thing our *Hacedores* could find that could keep us in touch with our base at Biak-Na-Bato. Did it work? Sometimes. Was it dependable? No. In fact, once in a while, replies came before the *retumbo* had even sent the original message. That was why they had banned these things so long ago. The potential danger was simply far too great.

No one could know the future. No one ever should.

My idiot of a big brother could be so infuriatingly stupid sometimes—always so careless, always distracted, always ignoring these important, probability-sensitive details.

"That's not a phone," I reminded him sternly. "You don't know who's out there. You could have been turned just by listening. Get this in that thick skull of yours: the enemy's language is an infection. It'll mole a rootkit into your head."

My elder sibling said nothing. The thumping noise in the vents continued unabated, beating like an agitated heart.

"He's not so foolhardy," the Cafuné brace in my head warned me. *"The Commander wouldn't take such a risk unless he's hiding something."*

I checked my master console. My brace was right. There it was, blinking like a dying star on the antique ambermatic monitor—a secret personal message. In fact, there were two unauthorized transmissions, spooling in the system like impatient ghosts.

From the corner of my eye, I saw that my brother had opened his digital *damajuana*. A hologram of his fiancée, Maria-Bellona, appeared some fifty centimetres above it, turning like a small constellation. I knew he was using the *retumbo* to try and reach her again.

My C-brace was very good at picking up the subtle cues of his little rebellions. It shared its synesthetic analyses through a cocktail of peptides and hormones shot directly into my hypothalamus. Without its guidance, I would be lost, broken. I would not be able to speak properly, nor communicate my emotions.

"I am giving you a direct order to stop," I said, overriding his transmissions. "Take your narcs; you're swarming out."

It had been -000:504, about three week-cycles, since we had been unplugged from our Mother Network. My crew was beginning to unravel. If we didn't get to The Woman with Two Navels soon, I knew there was a greater than seventy percent chance we wouldn't make it. Bagong Maynilad would fall, and it would be completely our fault.

∞

- 000:000:553, Biak-Na-Bato Military Station

"You and your siblings are the only ones left capable of flying the QUIJANO DE MANILA. Your job is to take our last warp-capable ship and retrieve that encryption key before the Toromon and their Beast Fighters get to it."

"And this key is in a black hole? At the heart of the nebula called 'The Woman with Two Navels'?"

"It's actually a wormhole—a traversable Morris–Thorne bridge, a doorway into a pocket universe. According to the ruins at Aptor, there is a secret facility called 'Babel' on a helical star system with seventeen planets."

"Babel? As in the Tower of Babel?"

"It's just a code name. Babel-17 is a planet-sized repository for a vast trove of ancient information. It predates many star-faring civilizations."

"Sir, why won't you show us the records you found on Aptor? What else is in this place you're sending us to?"

"We've uploaded everything you need to know to your brace."

"How can we be sure the bridge is stable, sir? How can we even comprehend what another universe is like? This mission doesn't make any sense."

"Just follow your orders, son. If you don't find that key, we won't last much longer. There's almost nothing left of our Thassolarchies."

"The TWw2N Nebula puts us out of range of normal comms. We'll be cut off from the Mother Network. I don't process emotions normally, and I have my brace for company. But my brother and sister—they won't remain sane if we're unplugged for so long."

"That's why it's good you are a family unit. You will last much longer together."

"Do we all have to go, sir? My brother and sister, they're all I have."

∞

- 000:000:075 in the (old) relative past

"Fuck this," elder brother yelled childishly, slamming the stiff plastic cover of the communicator. The feathery microphone bent under his hand, like bamboo in a storm. " . . . and fuck you!"

My younger sister messaged me on my console. "Anak ng P," she cussed, "is your brace loose? You're being insensitive again. Be nice, we're probably going to die today."

I put down the fragile hardcover I was reading and turned my chair towards my brother. He had lifted the bezel of an enormous poison ring and popped four TRIs, triple-reuptake inhibitors mixed with a dose of serotonin-producing bacteria, each pill tailored specifically to slay his legion of personal demons.

Spiritually sedated, he stared blankly at the windowless wall behind him, like a sad, sullen bird that just had its wings clipped.

"He's more depressed and alone with you than he would be by himself. Say something," my brace said.

"When we get back, I want to report him," I thought. *"He needs to be disciplined."*

"You mean, 'if we get back'. Your glucose levels are all still low from your anhydrobiosis. Be patient. Be understanding."

My C-brace was familiar with this particular tantrum. It reminded me that the absence of anything to see was an odd comfort for my moody sibling. It allowed him to turn inwards.

"Perhaps to more pleasant memories," my brace suggested, *"a spoonful of sugar to help take away the bitterness of life."*

"Software doesn't do metaphor," I answered, running a self-scan for bugs. *"There must be a glitch in my neural net."*

"It's not all plastic, toxoplasmocites, and code," my C-brace whispered back. *"You are in here too, hiding between my algorithms, you with your pretty words and foolish auguries. I am just the software heart for your real human soul."*

I thought of messaging my future self with the *retumbo*, but I quickly dismissed the notion. I was impatient to see how our mission would turn out, curious whether my siblings and I would survive—but I reminded myself that no one should know the future, not even me. Every *retumbo*-bearing ship that tried had disappeared, never to be heard of again. Only I had the self-discipline to resist all temptation. That was just one of the reasons why I was in charge.

The pop of an impatient blurb interrupted my musings. I knew my sister was up to something again. The ship's old-fashioned instant-messaging system was irksome and intrusive, but it was the closest thing we had to intraneural communication, so I had kept it operational.

"Hello! We've been out of hibernation for half a day, *sir*, and you're already an insensitive twit!! Can't you see he's hurting!!!" she typed, followed by a crude emoticon indicating irritation.

[?_?]

"Why do you need to message me?" I asked. "I'm two metres away. Also, your IM included a surfeit of exclamations. What's your point?"

In an age where we were connected to the universe and to each other by techno-organic notochords, synapse to synapse in a gigantic swarming of minds, I found simple personal communication at best a necessary evil, one that was anachronistic, limited, and frankly, difficult. How could context be conveyed with just simple words, without references, without multi-sensory media, without relation to the Mother Network's collective memory?

Words could never tell the entire story. Words were so easily misunderstood.

∞

- 000:000:550, Biak-Na-Bato Military Station

"But sir, I am the eldest, and I have the most battlefield experience."

"The Katipunan is not giving you a choice. Because of the Linguistic Ubiquitous Multiplex in his brace, the Captain is the ideal leader for this mission."

"What you really mean, sir, is that his C-brace makes him the least likely to be turned by the In-Dark Answered."

"The three of you are the last of our pilots who can fly an analogue ship."

"With all due respect, sir, you didn't answer my question."

"He's your captain. Follow him. That's all. You are dismissed."

∞

- 000:000:060 in the (old) relative past

My brace chided me for being tactless, for defining meridians of self-ishness—my arm's-length, personal firewall against messy emotions.

"Sigh. What is it now?" I queried silently.

"You were oblivious to your brother's emotional distress," it whispered.

"Then help me," I ordered. I knew my brother was still hurting from his fiancée's death. After all, it had happened only -000:001:440 ago, about two month-cycles by the old Earth reckoning.

"Maria-Bellona was always nice to me." I thought, *"I suppose I owe her something. Okay, let's think of something nice to say."*

My C-brace grew silent as its Linguistic Ubiquitous Multiplex ran an algorithm for something suitably mollifying. My heart of numbers assayed the proper words, weighing them for the best impact, and assembling them in a way that would best be appreciated by my sibling.

"Look, I'm sorry about Maria-Bellona," I said in the most sincere tone I could muster, reading out words that appeared like a news ticker on my mind's eye. "I'm sorry I have to be so strict about the rules. It's for your own good—for the good of all of us. I don't have to remind you how important this mission is."

Elder brother looked up from his brooding and viewed me with practiced suspicion. "Wait for it . . . " he said quietly, beginning a silent, cynical countdown.

"But your personal messages will clog the communicator with garbage," I added impulsively, obdurately. "I should report you. You've put us all in danger."

My C-brace cried foul—yet another failed social interaction. It pulsed in protest, castigating me, scolding me. Random areas in my head began to throb.

"You just had to add those last lines."

My brother just shook his head. "At least you tried to be nice," he said. "I can't believe we share the same fucking genes."

Before I could say anything, the QUIJANO DE MANILA began to heave like a dying whale, buffeted by an unusually harsh modulation, somewhere in the tender strings of hyperspace. Our ship shook violently, as if a giant hand had grabbed it by the throat. Anything that wasn't secured to a surface fell in a loud clatter around us.

Our ship had passed the gravity field of a massive object. The shaking was so severe that rivets started popping from the bulkheads.

"We must be close to the heart of the TWw2N Nebula. Have we hit apparent horizon?" I asked, dodging a small monitor that swung like a slapping hand. "Commander, can you confirm?"

"Negative," elder brother said, digging himself out from a pile of wires that had dropped from the ceiling, "we're still at T-30."

"Give me a visual, please."

The antique plasma screens at the front of the bridge groaned into life, but the composite images showed nothing but darkness and the rugged edge of a debris field.

"It's zero on eyeball. What's going on?" I asked. "Status report, everyone, stat!

"This bucket is never going to hold," elder brother grumbled, as he ran through the other scanners. "It's a fucking squatters' colony stitched together with carbon nanotubes and whatever the hell that hull material is—magic plywood and GI sheets. This shaking is going to tear us apart!"

"Anak ng P," younger sister said, trying to pick her things off the floor. "Grow a pair and shut the fuck up!"

My brother's vintage console exploded in a cacophony of beeping alarms and colourful warning lights. "I wish we could just interface with these stupid controls," he yelled. "No Holosonics, no virtual reality, no floating screens. Damn it. The defense systems can't lock on anything. They say there's nothing out there. I think . . . something's moving towards the event horizon, something massive. The gravimeter is going crazy, but it can't tell what it is."

"Find out," I said. The shaking continued unabated. "We need to know what's out there—if it's not the wormhole, check if it's an enemy ship."

"These stupid dials are like toys!" he growled, banging his fists against the primitive hardware. "Quantum effects are distorting all the readings. Everything's oscillating and not oscillating at the same time. No, wait . . . I think we hit a region of some kind of high energy, a ghost field. Anak ng P, our sensors are scrambled."

"Lieutenant Commander Flower, what's your report?"

"I estimate we have less than T-20 minutes of travel time to The Woman with Two Navels before total structural failure," she reported grimly. "Can you identify the energy, Commander? Black holes are filled with strange energy. If we hit the wrong kind, we could be in trouble. No one's ever encountered negative probabilities before, not like this."

"Negative probabilities, what the hell does that mean?" my brother asked. "Do we disappear from existence? Do we become evil versions of ourselves?"

"That's no . . . not how it works," I said. My teeth were chattering badly from the shaking. Something was interfering with my C-brace. "A negative puh . . . probability distribution is possible in quantum theory. It's just li . . . ike having a debt in accounting, you know like having neh . . . negative credits."

"Huh?" my brother replied, with an idiotic expression on his face. I couldn't tell if he was deliberately playing stupid just to annoy me. In any case, his confusion, if real, had merit. Negative probabilities, like our mission, defied common sense.

"Oh, forget it. It's just a mathematical concept," I prevaricated, trying to keep the peace. The shaking was now irritating my bladder. My brace stabilized, correcting my speech patterns. It also silenced my neural pathway for micturition, keeping me from wetting my pants. "Statistically, it has a basis only in unobservable, conditional events."

"Well, statistically no one's been inside a black hole before! There are places where humans aren't meant to be," eldest brother said. "This was a suicide run. That was the elephant in the briefing room—they didn't really expect us to come back."

"There's no point stating the obvious," sister said, "but I don't care. I trust our Captain here to bring us back."

"But this mission makes no sense!" my brother said, "There's something the Katipunan's not telling us."

∞

[- 000:000:153, Biak-Na-Bato Military Station]

"What happens after we get the key, Admiral? What do we do?"

"Bring it back to this base, Captain. However, if that's not possible we have a back-up plan. There is a sealed protocol programmed into your brace. It contains the entire language code of the In-Dark Answered. If there is no other option, this can be uploaded into your brain. This information is for your ears only."

"Admiral, won't I get turned?"

"Don't worry. We've injected your limbic system with a new kind of programmable toxoplasmic parasite. They will weave an electro-chemical filter into your neural net. Hopefully, this will keep you from being turned for at least 000:000:000:010."

"You want my brace to decode the In-Dark Answered in ten seconds?"

"Yes, upload the key's algorithm into your system, break the proto-col, and for a few seconds, you'll have access to the source code of the universe. You have to undo the Empire's handiwork as quickly as you can."

"How will I do that, sir? Do I just wish it all away?"

"You need to find something sentient in the Library for instructions."

"How do we know they're going to help?"

"You have your weapons. Use them."

∞

- 000:000:030 in the (old) relative past

"Drop the conspiracy theories. Just shut up and man your station," I said, reaching down to the floor to pick up my statue of St. Sylvester, the patron saint of beginnings and endings. I dusted it with my sleeve and stuck the magnetic base onto my console.

"You know," my brother said, "it's funny how you love that statue so much. St. Sylvester is the patron saint of people whose heads are stuck so far up their asses, they can see backwards."

My brace stifled my impulse to stun him with my *paltik*. Low blood sugar notwithstanding, my brother was becoming disruptive.

"The stand-alone systems are on a rat-powered sneaker-net. The full damage analysis is just coming in now," my sister reported. "Hull integrity is seventy-eight percent and still dropping. Shit."

"The ship's coming apart," my brother yelled, as another set of cables popped out of the ceiling and crashed down near his station. "You're the captain! Do something!"

"He's never run a ship like this; he doesn't have a clue," sister said. "Hang on, I have an idea. But first, I need my narcs."

My brace detected the faint fibrillation of the digital dream-catcher she had jacked into. A braid of notochords snaked medusa-like from ports just under her hairline towards her handbag. The synthetic extensions of her limbic system plugged into a single-use mood modifier, sending a train of low-energy ultrasound pulses directly into her brainstem.

The dream-catcher wove for my sister a false fiber of bravado, cloaking her fears with an air of insouciance. Seconds later, she started laughing uncontrollably, desperately, as she struggled with the engineering controls, twisting and turning like an old-fashioned *arnis* fighter.

But the small tears in the corners of her eyes betrayed her real state of mind, something no amount of digital narcs could mask.

I always hated her manic laughter. It sounded piercing and high pitched, modulating between two and four kilohertz, like the highest octave of a piano.

"Don't worry. I got this," she announced with sudden chirpiness. "It was just a plain vanilla high-energy field. The system is already adjusting. We'll make it. Just relax, boys. Bagong Maynilad's last warp-class ship is still A-ok."

"I thought you said the QUIJANO DE MANILA was coming apart?" I said, worried that both of them had already used mood modifiers so early into our mission.

It had been three week-cycles since we left the Mother Network's swarming comfort, and our old ship had no exocortex—no external brain we could plug into. Thankfully, we had spent most of the trip in suspended animation. But now that we were fully conscious, my brother and sister were already starting to succumb to swarm withdrawal symptoms.

"Even before you were all networked, Filipinos could never handle being alone," my brace warned. With no one else in their heads, my siblings' emotional responses were reverting to their existential childhood roots.

I noticed something sticking out of my sister's handbag—the butt of a very large gun. It was much too big to be a standard *paltik*. I felt an urge to ask her about it, to question the wisdom of carrying such an antiquated weapon, but I decided to wait until the disturbance had cleared. My C-brace congratulated me on my discretion.

"Focus on the mission. A prudent enemy is preferable to an impulsive sibling," my brace whispered. *"Sort it out later."*

The ship's shuddering stopped. Whatever sister's gambit had been, it worked.

A sudden calm came over the ship.

"I said, relax. Anak ng P, do I have to repeat myself all the time?" my sister asked, her eyes bulging glassily. "I already said I had a *perfect* solution. I used the shields to bind the hull like clingwrap."

You could always depend on my sister to be a grandstanding

alarmist. Always, she would paint the direst of scenarios, a doctor bearing the worst prognosis imaginable. Then, like the mutant child of Cassandra and Archimedes, she would leap out in her vainglorious best, brandishing a premeditated "miracle" fix.

My brace explained it best: *"That was her thing, the little girl with a big hero complex. It was her way of getting noticed."*

"Why are you carrying an old .357 Magnum?" I asked, unable to contain myself. "That's not an authorized sidearm. Does it still even work?"

"Anak ng P, that's a fucking big gun!" elder brother exclaimed, as he walked over to her station and pulled the weapon from its hiding place. He gripped the handle tightly and pointed the twenty-centimetre barrel at my head. "It's bigger than mine."

"Of course, it works. Dencio . . . Denny was cleaning this Colt Python for the museum on Phallos," she said, as her hands fiddled restlessly with her notochords. "I couldn't resist borrowing it."

"That thing's a risk for explosive decompression. Why *did* you bring it?" I asked again. "And when we're on a mission, please stop saying 'Anak ng P'. It's not proper language for officers."

"Stop worrying; the hull's low tech but self-healing. Anyway, the gun's insurance," she announced cryptically. My sister took the pearl-handled Sultan's Special back from my brother and opened the barrel. There was a full round of cartridges inside.

"*Paltik* capacitors take too long to boot and are iffy in a vacuum," she continued. "The Toromon's best weapon is that weird language of theirs. You hear the In-Dark Answered once, and you become a mindless slave processor. How fast that happens, we don't know. But if I start to speak in first-person, plural pronouns only, or if I start singing something from '*The Ballad of Beta-2*', shoot me between the eyes quickly."

"I don't think I could shoot either of you," I asserted truthfully.

"That's a load of crap," elder brother said. "Hasn't everyone thought of killing their siblings at least once?"

"No one is killing anyone," I said. "Anyway, we need to clean up the bridge, retrieve the encryption key, and finish our mission."

"Our mission sounds like a recycled sci-fi plot. I think I read something like it before," sister said. "You really should read more. You know, like you used to? Nowadays, it's just one sad poet after another."

"I don't get you," I remarked.

"The In-Dark Answered," she continued, "it's supposedly the oldest, most primordial of languages. Ring any bells?"

"I know we're desperate, but something about this mission doesn't seem right," brother interjected. "Like, why aren't the Toromon looking for this key instead of just trying to hack it? It's inconceivable that they don't also know about it."

"I don't know, and I don't care. We are soldiers, and we are on a mission," I added, picking up the wires that had fallen near my station. "The Toromon have been enslaving planets for a brute-force hack of galactic proportions. That's the way they operate. The thing is, given enough minds, they'll crack it eventually. We need to get this key before they do."

"You realise the fate of humanity now rests on three unstable, self-absorbed, overgrown *kids*?" eldest brother asked.

"Pinoy kids," my sister added.

"God help the rest of humanity if we shape the universe in our image," he said.

"Enough of this!" I ordered. "Do either of you have a theory on what we hit? We haven't reached the gravity field of TWw2N yet."

"Why are you in such a hurry to die?" my brother asked. "There's absolutely nothing on any of the scopes. Nothing on visual either. Whatever it was, it's gone now or, at least we can't detect it."

"It was too big to be a Beast Fighter," I said. "Do we have any intelligence on the Toromon's other ships?"

"Nothing that matches," elder brother answered. "But the Identify Friend/Foe database is outdated. It could be a new Empire Star-dreadnought."

"There are too many stars in the background; even if it was cloaked, we would've seen its outline on visual," I noted.

"Not if it bent the light behind it," he countered. "Remember, the gravimeter was beeping like crazy."

"No, I don't think it was a ship. We hit a nebular ghost field, that's all," I said dismissively.

"That's stupid," my brother said. "It must be a vessel of some sort. I heard a rumour that the Beast Fighters can now massively volt-in together. That could create a gravity well. I've got more field experience than you. Why won't you listen?"

"Shut up, Commander, I'm thinking."

"What do we do now?" my sister asked. "We can't just sit here."

I kept quiet for 000:001, lost in thought.

"We just keep going. The QUIJANO DE MANILA is already near the edge of the wormhole."

"Are you sure about what we're doing, *kid*?" my elder brother asked, making sure that I heard the emphasis on the word '*kid*'. "If we cross that event horizon, we don't go into some wormhole fantasy world. Screw your negative and positive probabilities. We just *die*."

"Let's keep going," I said, ignoring him. "You need to be more focused, Commander Falcon. Did you take *all* your narcs? I think you're swarming out."

My deflection just seemed to goad him further. He glanced at the book I had placed on my side table, looking for something to provoke me with, to torment me through my brace and put me in my place as his little brother.

"Look at that book. You've been reading it since we woke up," he said. "How the hell can you read at a time like this? What the hell is wrong with you?"

"Ignore him," little sister said. "He's always trying to bully you."

"You've both got your narcs; I have my book."

"Forgive our hectoring brother, O Captain, my Captain," my sister purred, with a voice that floated like a butterfly yet roughed you up like splintered wood. My brace cautioned me that she was sharpening her claws, preparing to draw blood.

"He's never gotten over being passed over for a promotion, especially since *you* were picked, not him," she added sweetly.

"Shut up!" eldest brother snapped suddenly. My sister just convulsed with laughter and blew raspberries in his direction.

"Time and place, people," I ordered.

My brace noted that even with the mood modifiers, my siblings were already reaching the limits of being unplugged. *"There is something amiss. Their glucose levels are low, and the amount of cortisol in their blood seems to be increasing rapidly."*

"Is that book from another of your depressing poets?" eldest brother asked suddenly. "A physical book's a conceit. You could have just downloaded it into memory. But no, this is you showing us how much smarter you are, how more fucking cultured you are."

"Stop being so nasty, big brother. Tsk, tsk . . . if Daddy were alive, he'd spank you. By the way, the word you need to use is *maudlin*," sister said. Her voice had moved up half an octave higher. "The boy with the Cafuné brace so loves maudlin poems. No wonder he can't find a boyfriend. If I had a magic crown like he does, I'd adjust the filter to allow only happy thoughts. Think happy thoughts, everyone."

"Stop this," I said. "I am giving you a direct order to stop. What the hell is wrong with you? Control yourself. If we don't finish our mission, everyone on Bagong Maynilad will die. Stop this, stop this now!"

Elder brother turned to me with a mean glint in his eye and said, "What's wrong with me? What's wrong with *me*? They say that, if the Mother Network ever crumbles, only sociopaths like you will be left. But what are you without your LUM? You'd be nothing but a blubbering reta—"

"Say that word, and I'll blow your kneecaps off," my sister hissed. Her hero complex had kicked in to save the day. The sharp cocking of a gun hammer resonated ominously across the cold room. "You're such a pitiful excuse for a big brother. He's just a . . . he's a special child."

"I am not a child!" I shouted, pulling out my *paltik*. The R-word and *'special child'* were two of my very few triggers. "Now shut up, both of you, and let's get inside that wormhole."

The three of us tensed up. Even without my C-brace, I knew that our bickering was going too far. I needed to stop the escalation quickly.

"Okay . . . okay, let's all calm down," my brace ordered me to say. "Where *is* this coming from big brother?"

Elder brother remained silent. He opened his digital *dama juana* again. This time a micro-scentograph filled the bridge with the smell of candles and sampaguita jasmine. But its hologram generator was broken, and Maria-Bellona's image flickered like a screen burn, like a slowly decaying memory.

"We never said goodbye, you know," he whispered, with a thin voice that somehow sounded like breaking glass.

No one spoke after that. The bridge seemed pregnant with formless loss and our own germinal fears, darkening the familial resonance between us.

My C-brace could compute nothing to say.

Outside the QUIJANO DE MANILA, the massive object our gravimeter detected started breaking up into hundreds of smaller pieces. Later on, I'd realise that, if we hadn't been arguing, or if the ship's analogue controls had been more familiar, maybe we'd have noticed that the energy field we'd hit had disabled our early-warning IFF system.

But our consoles from a previous space-faring age had remained unblinking and silent; outside the safety of our ship, something evil gathered in the darkness—something that began to sing.

∞

- 000:000:006 Mminutes in the (old) relative past

After a while, the thumping sound in the HVAC vents became unbearable. All over the QUIJANO DE MANILA, every metal object vibrated as if it were singing the most dissonant of songs.

Inside the command bridge, the three of us began fighting, escalating with every beat, every note, oblivious to the dark figures gathering outside our ship.

"Idiots!" younger sister yelled, as her levels of cortisol and norepinephrine overwhelmed her digital dream-catcher. "Why do I have brothers, not sisters? Boys are never on the ball. We're at the wormhole already, and you're still arguing about what to do! There is a fucking library we need to go to, an infinite library at the heart of a pocket universe."

"Bullshit!" elder brother screamed. "There's nothing there! We'll just die! Are you all deaf? Don't you hear the singing? It's a dirge, a death-korido."

The thumping sound in the vents was keeping time to a strange melody streaming in from outside the ship. Each note seemed to escalate the tension between us, plucking the strings of every hurt and all the secret resentments we had locked away in our hearts.

"Stop this! Stop this!" I cried. "We're a family!"

"Families are overrated!" my brother shot back. His eyes overflowed with the rising violence of a tidal wave. "Some families need an expiration date! This family is so fucking over!"

"Don't say that!" I screamed, covering my face. There were too many emotions to process, too many hurtful things said. My LUM was working overtime just to filter out the shouting, filling my head with white noise of strange polarities.

"Warning," my brace said. *"Suspending my higher mental functions; initiating acoustic masking emergency protocol."*

"Things break down if we don't communicate," I said. "Please, we are forgetting our mission. We're here. We just need to be open and keep talking. We need to keep talking."

"Really? Are you sure about that?" elder brother challenged. "The song is right. Since we are all going to die anyway, let's drop the pretense and get a few things straight."

"What are you going on about?" I asked. "What song?" For a second, I thought I heard the fragments of a musical refrain, hovering over the ship like a dark heterophonic melody. I tapped my temple to check my C-brace. But it wasn't responding. Suddenly, I found myself alone in my head as well.

My neural net was locked in some kind of emergency process, pulsing like mad, priming my cylinders with adrenaline. It surrounded my mind with a perimeter of sonic static. I knew that something was going horribly wrong, but I couldn't put my finger on it.

"Why did you stop me from messaging Maria-Bellona? You cut me off in mid-transmission! I never even had a chance to say goodbye!"

"You idiot," I said, trying to ignore my pulsing brace. "You were using an unsecured channel to talk to the dead! I told you already that you could have been turned. All you need is to hear the In-Dark Answered."

"You think you know everything!" he barked. "The *retumbo* can send a message back in time. I was trying to say good-bye to Maria-Bellona. Anak ng P, you can't stand it that we have a life outside this unit! After Mother and Father died, we couldn't move on with our lives because of you. We should have just dumped you in an asylum."

"My brace, where are you? Help me."

"Stop this. Stop this now!" sister shouted. "What's done is done. Don't say things you can't take back. Damn it. I can't seem to turn these stupid speakers off. Where is that music coming from? Can you all hear it?"

"You fucking hypocrite!" brother snarled at her. "I know you hate him, too! How long have you and your boyfriend been together now, eight year-cycles? You and Denny should have been married long ago. I should have been married long ago. I should have had kids by now. We could have had real lives."

"My brace, I don't know what to say."

"Stop it, please," she said, as a button on her console started flashing wildly. "Wait . . . I've got an incoming message . . . from . . . from myself? What? What!"

My sister read the words on her screen and began to cry silently. She fumbled for something in her handbag. "Oh fuck, it's coming from the HVAC vents. The music, the Toromon are using music as a medium. The notes are hacking straight into our right prefrontal cortex, the . . . the seat of negative emotions. That gravity well, it's from a composite ship made of thousands of Beast Fighters. It's . . . it's too late."

She reached for her gun.

"I'm saying what we haven't had the balls to say for the last 131:400:000," elder brother screamed, without grace or palaver. "The two of us put our lives on hold until he could use that stupid brace. We let our guilt get in our way."

"Stand down, Commander!" I ordered, pulling out my *paltik*. It took all I had to string the right words together. "St . . . sta . . . stand down n . . . n . . . now!"

"The Korido of Toromon is right," he said, shaking his head like a hired mourner. He moved his hand slowly towards his holster. "If you're part of a swarm, you don't deserve to think. It's inefficient to make our own choices. We are part of the process. We should only live to follow. Seldom can't, seldom don't, never shan't, never won't."

I suddenly became aware of my brother's strange sing-song intonation. I checked the status of the QUIJANO DE MANILA. A blinking P3 window warned me that a *retumbo* channel was wide open. The ship had been compromised.

My brother drew his *paltik* and aimed it at my head.

Before either of us could pull the trigger, a loud bang rang out. My sister had shot our brother right between the eyes, shattering his skull like a watermelon. His blood sprayed across the bridge, the rubric of our family's failed mythology.

She hurried to his terminal and quickly typed something into the *retumbo*. Then she fired more rounds into her engineering station, disabling the ship's automated systems.

I saw two messages spool out of the comms system before all the control panels exploded in a shower of sparks. As soon as they sputtered dead, she manually disengaged the escape pod doors.

"The Katipunan sacrificed us to get you here, to get your damned brace here. Anak ng P . . . our ship's doomed. Get in that stupid pod before I shoot you!" she yelled.

My sister waved me towards the Tardigrade life module that opened behind my station. "I don't know how long I can fight the rootkit."

"Wh . . . what about y . . . you? U-turn," I yelled, as I jumped into the gourd-shaped pod. "Co . . . come with me, please! Doughnut, dome, don't leave me!"

"It's too late, brother. I can hear the Beast Fighters singing outside. The words are so very beautiful," my sister said. "TCCIC, remember me."

She blew a kiss goodbye before putting the .357 into her mouth.

"My brace . . . my brace, why have you abandoned me?"

∞

00:00:0000 The Endless Now

"I am not here. I shouldn't be here!" I screamed in my head, shaking my fists at hell's keepers, the gauntlet of Threnody-class Beast Fighters that were now also destined for destruction—death by the supermassive hammer of gravity, death for protagonist and antagonist alike.

My tiny life pod, my fragile baby's cradle, rumbled, stumbled, and tumbled relentlessly past the dark, deep indigo of the event horizon.

In the darkness, our old ship came apart. I sighed.

I cried.

I refused to eat the Tardigrade's sweet *yema*, the trehalose-forming ball of fat that would induce hibernation.

"This isn't happening, brother . . . sister . . ."

"TCCIC, Take Care 'Cos I Care . . ."

My guilt sharpened the ends of my soul.

The Toromon's Beast Fighters struggled against gravity's tidal forces and the hard rain of my ship's debris. As a final parting shot, they attacked me with a hail of missiles, erupting like an orchid of chemical flame from their techno-organic chests.

Most of the salvo disappeared harmlessly into the event horizon, but a single warhead managed to explode just near enough, just close enough, to send a crushing shockwave across the thin ether. It crumpled through the graphene armour of my life pod, exposing me to the tender mercies of deep space.

Helpless, I closed my eyes and waited to die. Soon, I would be crushed into a ghostly smear of Hawking particles.

"Where are you, little mannikin?" I heard a woman's sweet voice somehow carry in the darkness.

"My brace, is that you?"

I opened my eyes in terrified wonder. There was something different about the heart of TWw2N. Instead of a crushing singularity, there was a rapidly spinning ring of energy. It was as if someone had spun an enormous glass of water so fast that the liquid parted, leaving a clear channel in the middle—one which I found myself inexorably pulled through.

I felt a slow trickle of blood bubble from my temples like liquid rubies, an unsubtle confirmation that my brace was broken. It was stabbing against the inferior frontal gyrus of my brain, puncturing it like stigmata, randomly fracturing my speech. Blood rained from my head, hanging in zero gravity like a beaded scarlet halo.

My brace was now nothing but a sputtering sound in my head. But there was someone else in the wormhole, a woman, a Woman with Two Navels.

Was she my mission? Was she what the Katipunan wanted me to find?

I opened my mouth to call out to the mysterious entity, but nothing I said made any sense. My voice blossomed in a fiery burst of word salad, as messy as the heap of my shattered life.

"The pale turquoise library sleeps furiously," I screamed, *"aye, and Gomorrah!"*

"Poor, poor child, why did baby die, making father sigh and mother cry?" I heard her say.

The Toromon were gone, swallowed up by infinity. The QUIJANO DE MANILA was now just a fragmented memory. My life pod was gone too, disintegrated like rice paper on water.

I found myself floating in the cold void, hanging like a saint. My odds for survival, even in my space suit, were less than zero—in fact, they were *negative*. But somehow I was alive and conscious in an in-between place, the impossible secret space between dimensions, falling faster than the speed of light.

"Your brother has a falcon, your sister has a flower, but what is left for mannikin, born within an hour?" I heard the woman whisper.

In the midst of the gloom I saw a small, infinitely blue-shifted light, twinkling like a star. For a moment, I wondered how this could be.

The wormhole's gravity should have absorbed all the light that hit its outer horizon, reflecting nothing.

Then I realised that I was now in the unknown beyond, past time and space, outside the purview of life and death. The star was the universe I had forever left behind, a record of all its history—past, present, and future condensed into one endless instant.

The wormhole was like a giant tunnel of stellar proportions, and once I passed my universe-star, I had expected to see another, the first glimpse of the pocket universe where a library-planet was hidden in a spiraling system of seventeen suns.

Instead, I saw a vision—the darkness had become the battlements of a strange new ocean. In the center was another singularity, one where the lines of electromagnetic force, now somehow visible and distorted by gravitational lensing, had enveloped it like an enormous sea shell. Rising from its heart, like Botticelli's Venus, was a beautiful naked woman whose skin glowed with the phosphorescence of starlight.

I didn't know why, but I started weeping uncontrollably. But in space, my grief was silent, intractable like a negative probability distribution, like my own endless fears.

"Crying, my little one, footsore and weary?" she whispered in the singsong musical tone I had heard earlier. *"Sleep soft, my darling, my trouble and treasure."*

"Who are you? What are you?" I wanted to ask, but my brace was silent. Instead, gibberish spewed from my confounded mouth. *"Words end, worlds begin."*

"Silly, silly baby, with the wind-up brain and the mincemeat mouth," she cooed, somehow understanding my broken speech. *"I am the*

Infinite Library. I am a White Hole, a Planck star, the sum total of all knowledge that ever was and that ever will be."

I felt for my C-brace, the thin web of metal and nano-plastic ganglions that poked through my head like a bad case of acne. It had been broken in places by the shockwave, but the nonvolatile memory of my Linguistic Ubiquitous Multiplex was functional, the secret protocol was intact. I knew I could still complete my mission. I knew that I could at least try.

"The dead corpses of words of war, the tales of dragons and dreamers, how still they lie." I pleaded uselessly, lost beyond the tenancy of language.

I spoke instead with my mind. In my head, I told her about our dire situation; about how the Toromon had shackled our freedom with words; about all the countless, desperate deaths; about the sacrifice of my elder brother and my younger sister—the only people I ever loved in my life. I begged her for the key to the In-Dark Answered, the key of life.

"They crushed your world so neatly laid, now you float with broken wings," she said softly. *"And watch the ruin they have made, too late to build, too sad to sing. But perhaps, my least little one, it is not too late."*

The starlight woman, the strange theophany of the Infinite Library, sang with words that made every fibre of my being resound with heartache. *"Map maker, map maker make me a map,"* she chanted.

In the darkness in front of me, a door circumscribed itself in the emptiness. It opened, and a young boy stepped through. He was gaudily dressed, like a circus performer, with a top hat on his head and a strange watch studded with dials that covered his entire left arm. The boy tipped his hat politely, and I realised that the boy was me, before my C-brace was installed. Younger me handed older me a small piece of crystal.

"Words are like worlds," I said to myself, *"and every language is a map. This holo-crystal has what you need to unlock the In-Dark Answered."*

A spectrum of light erupted from the depths of the quivering gem and started uploading into my neural net.

As younger me returned to wherever he had come from, I caught a glimpse of what lay behind his ghostly portal—a huge tesseract that seemed to extend forever, with many rooms like honeycombs connected by staircases, all stacked up farther than the eyes could see.

Suddenly, I could behold in my mind's eye every word in every language that had ever been spoken and written—or ever would be. I knew all the numbers in the Fibonacci sequence, Euler's constant, and every kind of infinity possible. I beheld time, spinning like a helix of precious stones, and like St. Sylvester, I could open the door to every beginning and every ending.

Time and Space and everything in between were all a malleable illusion, and I was now the author of existence. I knew what I had to do.

The Woman with Two Navels, the Infinite Library, the sum total of all information, looked at me with the saddest of smiles.

"Can I wish for everyone to be happy?"

"Alas, my poor baby, that is not up to you. With your crown of mind-flowers, like Icarus you will fly. I twist them into a crown today, and tonight they die," she continued. *"Make a wish, little mannikin. Your pain is fodder for creation. Wish for a brand new universe."*

∞

+ 289,080:00:000 or 33 Years in the (new) relative future

The siblings hadn't really spoken to each other in years.

During the wake, elder brother sat near an altar of candles, plaster saints, and a large demijohn of flowers, covered all over with faded polaroids and other memorabilia. Sometimes, he would get up and chat uncertainly with the rare visitor that came to view the coffin. If no one was around, he would sneak a sip of liquid comfort and stare at the lizards on the wall, nervously tapping his cold flask with the fingers of a prematurely old man.

Younger sister stayed by the back of the TWw2N Funeral Chapel, tending to the barely touched boxes of fruit juice, bottled water, and assorted salty snacks. Her ears were glued perpetually to her music, a dissonant Pinoy remix of *Black Holes & Revelations*. It was a subtle clue for people to leave her alone. Sometimes, she would recall a fond memory of her dead brother, and she would laugh inappropriately, with a rude, high-pitched chortle that was painful to the ears.

A broken air-conditioning vent filled the room with strange smells—camphor liniment, rust, and the musty odour of dried sampaguita. Everywhere there was the air of forgotten things, a bubble of dead, desiccated time.

For the sake of their late brother, they put on appearances. The two would sit next to each other during prayers or whenever they shared a ride to their respective hotels.

Yet beyond the perfunctory greetings and obligatory inquiries about spouses and children, the two did not talk. The time and space they had spent apart had become an insurmountable gulf. Neither understood how and why this black hole had come about, but both had grown intensely comfortable with their selfish grief.

It was a heartache sharpened by years of guilt for abandoning their brother to a lonely life at a distant mental institution in Biak-Na-Bato.

They decided to bury their lost sibling with the things he loved most—a small collection of space soldier figures, beast fighter dolls, a fully articulated evil Emperor Toromon, a collector's edition QDM space cruiser, a favourite statue of St. Sylvester, a Big Magnum BB gun, and an old book of rhymes.

On a rainy May Day's Eve, they buried him in a quiet corner of the Old Manila cemetery. He was laid to rest next to their parents, under a crypt whose headstone was inscribed with a quote (whose source neither of them could now recall):

"Better by far you should forget and smile than you should remember and be sad."

At Manila International Airport, younger sister watched a trailer for a new sci-fi movie, a CGI-laden clunker about a ship trapped in a black hole.

For reasons she could not fathom, her mind wandered back to her university days, and she remembered something her physics teacher had said. Their class had been discussing the law of the conservation of matter and energy when she had asked a rather unusual question: *"What would happen to someone who fell into a black hole?"*

"The total amount of energy in an isolated system is constant," her teacher had answered. *"No information would escape. Everything remains the same, interchangeable, indistinguishable. Nothing is ever truly lost."*

"That's not true," she told herself quietly. "There are things you lose forever."

Just then, a strange IM popped into her inbox. It was a note she seemed to have sent to herself, although she could not remember when she'd done so.

Younger sister clicked on the icon, but the message was garbled, save for the tiniest snippet of a strange, heterophonic melody and the words *"I have come to"*.

For reasons she could not comprehend, her heart began to boom like a *retumbo*, those mistpouffers which Filipinos believe were ghosts from ancient, faraway seas.

Younger sister began to weep on the travelator.

When she reached her departure gate, she took out her mobile phone and looked up her eldest brother's contact info. Her thumb hovered over his picture for a minute, wondering what she should do next.

TO ƒEE INFINITY INƒIDE THE PAGEƒ OF A BOOK

Millennia into the future, there is an exhibit simultaneously present in the museums of Cebu, Rome, Singapore, and every city-state that is still in existence.

For the bargain price of one year removed from your lifespan, you can view a special exhibit and glimpse infinity with your very own eyes.

There is a crack in Space and Time so fine that the naked eye cannot see it without using special camerae obscurae. Past the darkness of the aperture is the image of a hole in the universe, where an ancient astronaut, origin unknown, appears to be endlessly falling.

Is the astronaut a man, a woman, or perhaps something else? Is the astronaut old or young? Where did the astronaut come from? No one knows, at least not anymore. The only thing that learned men and experts seem to agree upon is this: because of how time dilates in space travel, the astronaut must already be dead.

But the experts and learned men are wrong. On the top of every wall where the interstellar camerae obscurae project enigmatic images, there is an old bronze sign that reads: *"The universe is a book. Those who do not read cannot travel beyond the limits of their borders."* The original one can still be found in the Museum of Manila.

According to local legend, this sign was gifted by a disgraced archivist-astronomer from Quiapo. One day, while she was running a camera obscura, a star in the galactic neighborhood went nova. The image shifted momentarily, and she noticed that the astronaut was, in fact, holding a book. Moreover, the astronaut was not actually falling in space, but rather moving through what appeared to be an impossibly infinite library. Beyond the valley of the shadow of death, she heard a fugitive antiphon, and for the briefest of instants, her soul began to sing.

But the image shifted back swiftly, too fast for her to record it. The joyful song also disappeared. When the archivist-astronomer made her report, she was branded a charlatan and dismissed. The poor woman became a beggar on the streets of Manila, disgraced but nurturing righteous hope like a talisman. From the shadows of the city, she implored all she came across for a small coin of time, exchanging life for a passage from the books of Zeno of Elea. After many an importune year, the worm turned in her favor, and she collected enough to pay for the camera obscura signs that hang in every gallery and museum today.

This is what the archivist-astronomer saw:

Inside the singularity, the impossible astronaut is not dead, they are reading. Before they get to that last book they will ever read in their life, there is yet another book that needs to be read. Between that penultimate book and the one they hold in their hand, there is yet another book and another demanding attention. In fact, between the astronaut and Death, there is an endless series of books with no beginning and no end.

The astronaut and the disgraced astronomer-archivist had discovered one of the greatest secrets of the universe: that those who fall endlessly into books never die. They are forever reading.

ACKNOWLEDGEMENTS

PUBLICATION HISTORY:

"Mene, Thecel, Phares" first appeared in *Philippine Speculative Fiction Volume 10* (Editors: Dean Francis Alfar and Nikki Alfar, Flipside) in April 2016.

"An Excerpt from the *Philippine Journal of Archaeology*, 04 October, 1916" first appeared in Volume 8 of *Likhaan: The Journal of Contemporary Philippine Literature* (Editor: Rosario Cruz-Lucero, UP Institute of Creative Writing) in December 2014.

"A Secret Map of Shanghai" first appeared in *Strange Horizons* (Editors: Brit Mandelo, An Owomoyela, and Julia Rios) on 18 November 2013. Listed in the Best Science Fiction and Fantasy of 2013 by Lois Tilton in *Locus*. It was later anthologized in *Unconventional Fantasy: A Celebration of Forty Years of the World Fantasy Convention* (Editors: Bill Campbell, Sam Lubell, Peggy Rae Sapienza, and Jean Marie Ward, Baltimore Washington Area Worldcon Association, Inc.) in November 2014.

"Here Be Dragons" was the winner of the 2012 Romeo Forbes Children's Story Writing Competition. It was published in August 2015 by CANVAS press, illustrated by Jon Jaylo (Here be Dragons, ©

Canvas Press 2012, used with permission). The version included here is the original award-winning piece.

"Synchronicity" first appeared in *Bewildering Stories* Issue #507 (Editor: Don Webb), December 2012. It won a Mariner Award in the short story category that same year. This story also appeared on the *World SF Blog* in May 2013 and in *Outpouring: Typhoon Yolanda Relief* Anthology (Editor: Dean Francis Alfar, Kestrel) in January 2014.

"Big Enough for the Entire Universe" first appeared in the anthology *Fish Eats Lion: New Singaporean Speculative Fiction* (Editor: Jason Erik Lundberg, Math Paper Press) in November 2012.

"Entanglement" first appeared in the second volume of *LONTAR: The Journal of Southeast Asian Speculative Fiction* (Editor: Jason Erik Lundberg, Math Paper Press) in May 2014.

"The Old Blue Notebook" first appeared in *Daily Science Fiction* (Editors: Michele-Lee Barasso and Jonathan Laden) in February 2016.

"I m d 1 in 10" first appeared in the June 2014 issue of *The Future Fire* (Editor: Djibril al-Ayad). It was reprinted in Volume 2 of *Best New Singapore Short Stories* (Editor: Jason Erik Lundberg, Epigram) in November of 2015.

"Exit Quiapo Station" first appeared in *Maximum Volume 2: Best New Philippine Fiction* (Editors: Dean Francis Alfar and Angelo Lacuesta, Anvil Books) in 2016.

"Panopticon" first appeared in *Philippine Speculative Fiction Volume 9* (Editors: Andrew Drilon and Charles Tan, Kestrel) in October 2014. The expanded version with the use of Spivak pronouns appeared for the first time in the urban anthology *Trash* (Editors: Dean Francis Alfar and Marc de Faoite, Buku Fixi) in March 2016.

"Resurrection", the author's first published work of fiction, appeared in the anthology *Philippine Speculative Fiction Volume 6* (Editors: Nikki Alfar and Kate Osias, Kestrel) in September 2010. It was listed as an honorable mention selection for Ellen Datlow's Best Horror of the Year 2011. Subsequently it was published in e-book format by Flipside Publishing in 2012. "Resurrection 2.0", the version used in this book, first appeared in *The Philippines Free Press*, January 2012 (Editor: Joel M. Toledo). A slightly different version also appeared in the July 2013 edition of *Expanded Horizons* (Editor: Dash). The version in this collection is the definitive one.

"Blessed Are the Hungry" first appeared in *Apex Magazine* (Editor: Sigrid Ellis) in October 2014. The work was translated into Mandarin Chinese by Hu Shao Yan and was published in the March 2015 volume of *Science Fiction World*.

"How My Sister Leonora Brought Home a Wife" first appeared in the inaugural issue of *Lakeside Circus* (Editor: Carrie Cuinn) in March 2014.

"Infinite Degrees of Separation" first appeared in *Science Fiction: Filipino Fiction for Young Adults* (Editors: Dean Francis Alfar and Kenneth Yu, UP Press) in May 2016.

"Brother to Space, Sister to Time" first appeared in the sixth volume of *LONTAR: The Journal of Southeast Asian Speculative Fiction* (Editor: Jason Erik Lundberg, Epigram) in April 2016.

"To See Infinity Inside the Pages of a Book" was first published in the tenth volume of *LONTAR: The Journal of Southeast Asian Speculative Fiction* (Editor: Jason Erik Lundberg, Epigram) in May 2018. A Tamil language translation, முடிவிலியின் இழை, appeared in the first issue of *Aroo*, an online Tamil magazine dedicated to speculative fiction, on October 1, 2018 (Editor: Ramchander Krishna).

I'd also like to thank the following people for all their help and support:

Special thanks to Jee Leong Koh, Judy Luo, Kimberley Lim, and everyone else at Gaudy Boy LLC , as well as Flora Chan, Chamois Holschuh, and Jennifer Houle.

Gigo Alampay & CANVAS, Dean Francis Alfar, Nikki Alfar & Kestrel Publishing, Athena Andreadis, Michele-Lee Barasso & Jonathan Laden of *Daily Science Fiction*, Marius Black, Paolo Chikiamco, Vida Cruz, Carrie Cuinne of *Lakeside Circus*, Joyce Chng, Zen Cho, Aliette de Bodard, Dash from *Expanded Horizons*, Noelle de Jesus, Andrew Drilon, Sigrid Ellis and *Apex Magazine*, Kate Elliot, Foo Hee Meng, *The Future Fire*, Rhandee Gharlitos, Rico & Mel Hizon, Hu Shaoyan & *Science Fiction World*, Joshua Ip & everyone at Sing Lit Station, Jon Jaylo, Sarge Lacuesta & Anvil Publishing, Kenny Leck & Math Paper Press, Gabriela Lee & the UP Institute of Creative Writing, Rochita

Acknowledgements

Loenen-Ruiz, Jason-Erik Lundberg & Epigram Books, JF Koh, Tessie
Mastrile, Laura Mixon, Nilo, Nellie & the Mulles Family, Joseph
Nacino, Hector, Linda & Jayjay Ocampo, Martin Ocampo, Joseph &
Noreen Oconer, Alex & Kate Osias, Cindy Pon, Drs. Francisco &
Maria Rivera, Peggy-Rae Sapienza, Gromyko Semper, Mia Sereno,
Kari Sperring, Blue Sun, Charles Tan & Flipside Publishing, Ruth
Tang, Tade Thompson, Joel M. Toledo & *The Philippines Free Press*,
Eliza Victoria, Don Webb of *Bewildering Stories*, Neon Yang, Zed
Yeo, and Kenneth Yu, as well as to all my family and friends (wherever
in the world you may be).

Finally, thank you to Fernando & Marciana Ocampo, for giving me
my first and best library.

ABOUT THE
AUTHOR

Victor Fernando R. Ocampo is the author of *The Infinite Library and Other Stories*, shortlisted for the International Rubery Book Award, and *Here Be Dragons* (Canvas Press, 2015), winner of the Romeo Forbes Children's Story Award in 2012. His play-by-email interactive fiction piece "The Book of Red Shadows" debuted at the Singapore Writers Festival in 2020.

His writing has appeared in many publications including *Apex Magazine, Daily Science Fiction, Likhaan Journal, Strange Horizons, Philippines Graphic, Science Fiction World*, and *The Quarterly Literature Review of Singapore*, as well as anthologies like *The Best New Singapore Short Stories, Fish Eats Lion: New Singaporean Speculative Fiction, LONTAR: The Journal of Southeast Asian Speculative Fiction, Maximum*

Volume: Best New Philippine Fiction, and the *Philippine Speculative Fiction* series.

He is a fellow at the Milford Science Fiction Writers' Conference (UK), the Cinemalaya Ricky Lee Film Scriptwriting Workshop, and a Jalan Besar writer-in-residence at Sing Lit Station (2020/2021).

Visit his blog at vrocampo.com or follow him on Twitter @VictorOcampo

ABOUT GAUDY BOY

From the Latin *gaudium*, meaning "joy," Gaudy Boy publishes books that delight readers with the various powers of art. The name is taken from the poem "Gaudy Turnout," by Singaporean poet Arthur Yap, about his time abroad in Leeds, the United Kingdom. Similarly inspired by such diasporic wanderings and migrations, Gaudy Boy brings literary works by authors of Asian heritage to the attention of an American audience and beyond. Established in 2018 as the imprint of the New York City–based literary nonprofit Singapore Unbound, we publish poetry, fiction, and literary nonfiction. Visit our website at http://www.singaporeunbound.org/gaudyboy.

Winners of the Gaudy Boy Poetry Book Prize
Object Permanence, by Nica Bengzon
Play for Time, by Paula Mendoza
Autobiography of Horse, by Jenifer Sang Eun Park
The Experiment of the Tropics, by Lawrence Lacambra Ypil

Fiction and Nonfiction
The Sweetest Fruits, by Monique Truong
And the Walls Come Crumbling Down, by Tania De Rozario
The Foley Artist, by Ricco Villanueva Siasoco
Malay Sketches, by Alfian Sa'at

From Gaudy Boy Translates
Ulirát, edited by Tilde Acuña, John Bengan, Daryll Delgado, Amado Anthony G. Mendoza III, and Kristine Ong Muslim

Printed in the USA
CPSIA information can be obtained
at www.ICGtesting.com
LVHW090901191223
766840LV00003B/293

9 780999 451458